Czech
Folktales

T0307072

Czech
Folktales

Introduction by Rajendra Chitnis

General Editor: Jake Jackson

**FLAME TREE
PUBLISHING**

This is a FLAME TREE Book

FLAME TREE PUBLISHING
6 Melbray Mews
Fulham, London SW6 3NS
United Kingdom
www.flametreepublishing.com

First published 2024
Copyright © 2024 Flame Tree Publishing Ltd

24 26 28 27 25
1 3 5 7 9 8 6 4 2

ISBN: 978-1-80417-781-5

The cover image is © copyright 2024 Flame Tree Publishing Ltd,
based on artwork courtesy of Shutterstock.com/M.Loraine.

All inside images courtesy of Shutterstock.com and the following:
Lukas Kurka, ann_etc and Mahmoud Ahmed Shabana.

The text in this book is selected and edited from the following original sources:
Czech Folktales by Josef Baudis, 1917 (George Allen
& Unwin Ltd., London), *Czechoslovak Fairy Tales* by
Parker Fillmore, 1919 (Harcourt, Brace and Company, New York) and
The Shoemaker's Apron: Czechoslovak Folk and Fairy Tales by
Parker Fillmore, 1920 (Harcourt, Brace and Company, New York).

Printed and bound in China

Contents

Series Foreword

STRETCHING BACK to the oral traditions of thousands of years ago, tales of heroes and disaster, creation and conquest have been told by many different civilizations in many different ways. Their impact sits deep within our culture even though the detail in the tales themselves are a loose mix of historical record, transformed narrative and the distortions of hundreds of storytellers.

Today the language of mythology lives with us: our mood is jovial, our countenance is saturnine, we are narcissistic and our modern life is hermetically sealed from others. The nuances of myths and legends form part of our daily routines and help us navigate the world around us, with its half truths and biased reported facts.

The nature of a myth is that its story is already known by most of those who hear it, or read it. Every generation brings a new emphasis, but the fundamentals remain the same: a desire to understand and describe the events and relationships of the world. Many of the great stories are archetypes that help us find our own place, equipping us with tools for self-understanding, both individually and as part of a broader culture.

For Western societies it is Greek mythology that speaks to us most clearly. It greatly influenced the mythological heritage of the ancient Roman civilization and is the lens through which we still see the Celts, the Norse and many of the other great peoples and religions. The Greeks themselves learned much from their neighbours, the Egyptians, an older culture that became weak with age and incestuous leadership.

It is important to understand that what we perceive now as mythology had its own origins in perceptions of the divine and the rituals of the sacred. The earliest civilizations, in the crucible of the Middle East, in the Sumer of the third millennium BC, are the source to which many of the mythic archetypes can be traced. As humankind collected together in cities for the first time, developed writing and industrial scale agriculture, started to irrigate the rivers and attempted to control rather than be at the mercy of its environment, humanity began to write down its tentative explanations of natural events, of floods and plagues, of disease.

Early stories tell of Gods (or god-like animals in the case of tribal societies such as African, Native American or Aboriginal cultures) who are crafty and use their wits to survive, and it is reasonable to suggest that these were the first rulers of the gathering peoples of the earth, later elevated to god-like status with the distance of time. Such tales became more political as cities vied with each other for supremacy, creating new Gods, new hierarchies for their pantheons. The older Gods took on primordial roles and became the preserve of creation and destruction, leaving the new gods to deal with more current, everyday affairs. Empires rose and fell, with Babylon assuming the mantle from Sumeria in the 1800s BC, then in turn to be swept away by the Assyrians of the 1200s BC; then the Assyrians and the Egyptians were subjugated by the Greeks, the Greeks by the Romans and so on, leading to the spread and assimilation of common themes, ideas and stories throughout the world.

The survival of history is dependent on the telling of good tales, but each one must have the 'feeling' of truth, otherwise it will be ignored. Around the firesides, or embedded in a book or a computer, the myths and legends of the past are still the living materials of retold myth, not restricted to an exploration of origins. Now we have devices and global communications that give us unparalleled access to a diversity of traditions. We can find out about Native American, Indian, Chinese and tribal African mythology in a way that was denied to our ancestors, we can find connections, match the archaeology, religion and the mythologies of the world to build a comprehensive image of the human experience that is endlessly fascinating.

The stories in this book provide an introduction to the themes and concerns of the myths and legends of their respective cultures, with a short introduction to provide a linguistic, geographic and political context. This is where the myths have arrived today, but undoubtedly over the next millennia, they will transform again whilst retaining their essential truths and signs.

Jake Jackson
General Editor

Introduction to
Czech Folktales

IKE OTHER Central and East European nations, the Czechs have long been popularly associated with folk culture. International awareness of a distinctive Czech culture grew in the late nineteenth and early twentieth centuries through the music of Bedřich Smetana, Antonín Dvořák and Leoš Janáček, all of whom use Bohemian, Moravian and Slavonic folk themes and motifs in their work. In 1889, an English clergyman and schoolmaster of Bohemian descent, Albert Wratislaw, published a volume of Slavonic folktales translated from a Czech source, and since then most English-speaking readers' first and possibly only encounter with Czech literature has been through adaptations of folktales in anthologies for children.

The Czechs themselves have undoubtedly encouraged this association. As elsewhere in Europe, folk culture played a central part in the formation of modern Czech national identity in the nineteenth century. The Czechs remain attached to a folkish, pre-modern self-image, which manifests itself in an insatiable appetite for screen adaptations of fairy tales, especially at Christmas, and in the ubiquity of types and tropes from folk literature in everything from high literature to the art-house animated films, children's cartoons, graphic novels and puppet theatre for which the Czechs are renowned. We may worry that continuing to privilege a nation's folk culture over its modern high culture infantilizes it, preventing it from attaining the cultural status of others. The stories contained in this volume are, however, not mere childish anachronisms, but reflect a still-living cultural inheritance, the history and nature of which are outlined here.

Who Are the Czechs?

The Czechs trace their ancestry back to Slav tribes that settled in Central Europe from the late sixth century and eventually established the medieval state of Bohemia, first as a duchy in the ninth and tenth centuries, then as a kingdom from 1198. The modern-day Czech Republic, bordered by Austria, Germany, Poland and Slovakia, quite closely matches the core territory of this kingdom: the larger, western part, including Prague, is called Bohemia, the eastern part, including Brno, is called Moravia, with a small part of Silesia to the north on the Polish border. In the 1620s, the Bohemian crownlands were formally absorbed into the Austrian (Habsburg) Empire. Independent Czechoslovakia emerged from collapsing Austro-Hungary in 1918 and joined most of historical Bohemia with neighbouring Slovakia. Czechoslovakia broke up into the independent Czech and Slovak republics in 1993.

While nowadays it seems straightforward to define a Czech as someone from the Czech Republic, for most of their history the Czechs lived alongside others in a multi-lingual, multi-cultural state, most notably with Germans, Jews, Poles and Romani, and later Slovaks and Hungarians. In this longer context, as asserted in 1314 in the earliest Czech-language chronicle of Bohemian history, a Czech is not just someone born in Bohemia, but someone who speaks Czech. Czech folktales are therefore those identified as belonging to a Czech-language oral tradition, told by Czech speakers to other Czech speakers in a variety of contexts for many centuries.

Czechs and Slovaks

The present volume also includes some stories of Slovak origin. Czech and Slovak are linguistically very close and until the 1840s Slovak was generally considered a dialect of Czech. In the early nineteenth century, moreover, the idea of a common Slav identity to counter the German identity dominant in Central Europe initially co-existed with and even outweighed notions of individual identities among Austria's different Slav peoples. The inclusion under a Czech label of Slovak folktales, alongside folktales from historical regions of the Bohemian crownlands, reflects that the original recorders of these stories did not regard them as belonging to a different national culture in the same way as German, Jewish or Romani equivalents. The translations incorporated in this volume were, moreover, first published in three anthologies in 1917 (Josef Baudiš's *Czech Folk Tales*) and in 1919 and 1920 (Parker Fillmore's two volumes of Czechoslovak fairy tales) at the time of the creation of Czechoslovakia, when advocates of the new state regularly emphasized the close affinities between Czechs and Slovaks, and indeed sought to establish a new Czechoslovak identity.

The Czech Oral Tradition

The folktales we read are relatively modern literary adaptations of stories that existed perhaps for centuries as part of an oral tradition. In Bohemia, as throughout medieval and early modern Europe, that tradition lived invisibly alongside written literature, revealing its existence only through inclusions, references or stylistic imitations in chronicles, sermons, lives of saints, plays and other texts. The limited archaeological findings about the lives, customs and beliefs of the Czechs in the early centuries after their arrival have to compete even now with a much richer collection of legends about their forefather, Boemus (or Čech), who brought his people to the hill named Říp; his apparent heir, Crocco (or Krok); and Krok's daughter, the seer Lubossa (Libussa in German or Libuše in Czech), who told the people where to build Prague and where to find their king. Some elements of these legends appear in the Legend of Christianus, deemed by many scholars to date from the 990s, which describes the coming of Christianity to Bohemia through St Ludmila and her grandson, St Wenceslas (Duke Václav), the 'good king' of the English carol. Their first more substantial source, however, is the twelfth-century Latin chronicle of the history of Bohemia by the monk, Cosmas of Prague. Although Cosmas undoubtedly embellishes these stories to entertain and imbue them with contemporary meaning, it is assumed that he is drawing on a long-standing oral heritage.

This anthology begins with a version of the oldest attested Czech folktale, 'The Twelve Months', a Latin fragment of which (about picking strawberries in February) appeared in 1366 in *Exemplarius auctorum*, a volume of diverting but instructive stories for the use of monks when preaching, compiled by Master Klaret (Bartholomew of Chlumec), a canon of St Vitus's Cathedral in Prague. The version here was composed from a Slovak model by the major Czech nineteenth-century writer and collector of folktales, Božena Němcová. In 1976, the folklorist Karel Dvořák published a volume of 'the oldest Czech fairytales', which attempted to reconstruct the Czech folktale as it was at the end of the fourteenth century. It contained Czech translations from Latin of over one hundred stories, originally recorded for use in sermons, the earliest taken from Cosmas's chronicle. In the eighteenth and nineteenth centuries, local stories, superstitions, sayings and songs also regularly permeated chronicles and memoirs about particular localities, typically written by local stewards of estates, so-called *Písmáks*, a term originally designating lay interpreters of the Scriptures.

Folktales Become Literature

By the late eighteenth century, however, the relationship between oral and written literature was changing. From the 1780s onwards, we see the printing of popular Czech-language chapbooks (books of popular stories, ballads and so on) containing written versions of folktales. At a similar time, the German Enlightenment philosopher Johann Gottfried von Herder's assertion that a nation's identity was found in its language and oral culture encouraged the brothers Jacob and Wilhelm Grimm in the early nineteenth century to collect and publish versions of traditional German folktales. This in turn provided a model for intellectuals in Bohemia seeking to revive a Czech national identity that they believed had been suppressed and all but eradicated during nearly two centuries of Habsburg German rule. An important inspiration was the discovery in 1817 and 1818 of manuscripts containing Czech-language epic and lyric poems and fragments of legends that suggested the existence of a written Czech literature earlier than the end of the thirteenth century. Although later exposed as contemporary forgeries, they galvanized the search for a 'lost' Czech literary heritage. An anthology of Czech folk songs appeared in 1819, followed in 1838 by the first collection of Czech folktales by Jakub Malý.

The stories in the present volume are taken from collections published in subsequent decades, at the high point of this activity. The largest number come from collections published between the 1840s and 1860s by arguably the two most famous Czech writers of this period, Karel Jaromír Erben (who collected mainly from south, east and central Bohemia) and Němcová (including stories she collected in Slovakia in the early 1850s). Many folktales were collected in peripheral historical regions, often in more remote, rural border areas perceived to retain a closer connection to an older way of life, and these are represented here through examples from the isolated, mountainous region of Moravian Wallachia, on the Slovak border in the far east of the contemporary Czech Republic, published by Beneš Method Kulda in 1874 and by Václav Tille in 1901, and from the historical north Bohemian region of Kładsko, since 1919 part of Polish Silesia, published by Josef Štefan Kubín in 1908–10. Among his 'Czechoslovak' fairy tales, Fillmore also includes examples published in the early 1880s by the most prominent Slovak collector, Pavol Dobšinský.

These collections were not initially intended only or mainly for children, but, as well as entertaining a wide popular audience, sought to deepen that audience's identification with its Czech origins. As the Czech-language reading public grew in the second half of the nineteenth century, however, many other kinds of popular literature became available, and folktales increasingly become children's literature, for amusement and moral education, as Kulda suggests in his 1874 collection, which includes the stories 'Boots, Cloak and Ring', 'Silly Jura', 'Sleepy John' and 'The Bird with the Golden Gizzard' contained here.

What Makes Czech Folktales Czech?

Baudiš claims in the introduction to his 1917 anthology that 'the present collection is intended to exemplify the spirit of the Czech race'. The view that folktales reveal a nation's character emerged in the late eighteenth century alongside the seemingly contradictory notion that folktales contain echoes of the ancient pagan myths of a universal humanity. For over a century, however, studies of folklore have cast doubt on the notion of an easily defined 'national' quality to folktales.

First, for folklore scholars, folktales are an oral phenomenon, marked by their variability and mutability as they are passed down through generations and told and retold by different tellers, from different backgrounds and with different manners and talents, to different audiences in different circumstances. As transnational indexes of folktale plots, themes and motifs reveal, this fluidity extends to their ability to cross linguistic and cultural borders, and it is extremely difficult to identify where a particular story or figure originated. Moreover, as Tille, the father of modern Czech folklore studies, noticed in 1909, oral stories collected may already reveal the interference of earlier printed versions, including versions from other languages, a fact that he attributed not only to chapbooks but also to the longer history of book-printing and literacy in Bohemia interacting with the oral tradition. In any event, it is only when folktales are written down and reading displaces listening as the main way of circulating stories that, over time, a preferred, fixed 'national' version of a story told in various ways in many places is established. At best, then, the stories in his volume express an idea of Czechness conceived by authors in the nineteenth century and perpetuated by subsequent generations.

The Localization of Stories

As Baudiš acknowledges, local character emerges not so much in the content of the stories, which may substantially overlap with stories told in other languages, but 'in the manner of their telling'. The eminent Czech folklorist, Oldřich Sirovátka, argues that the plots and basic motifs of stories do not differ hugely between, say, Czech, German, Hungarian and Russian, but 'the bare bones of the story acclimatize to the region and become an expression of the place' by using local names for people and places, and making references to local customs and traditions or features of the landscape.

This 'expression of place' is, however, typically more regional than national. As we have seen, Czech stories were collected from specific regions at a time in the nineteenth century when local identity remained more embedded in rural people than the modern notion of Czech national identity developing in urban settings. We consequently find more similarity between stories told in Czech in the far west of Bohemia and in German in eastern Bavaria, than between west Bohemian Czech-language stories and those told in Czech in eastern Moravia, which bear more resemblance to those told over the hill in Slovak. In this anthology, for example, Kulda's story 'Silly Jura' (pronounced 'Yura') points to its east Moravian origin through its use of the local variant of 'George' (Jiří). This character type, perhaps best known in English folklore as Jack in 'Jack and the Beanstalk', appears in Bohemia by contrast as 'hloupý Honza' (foolish Johnny, showing the connection to the German 'Hans'), in Silesia as 'hlópé Janek' (closer to Polish) and in Slovakia as 'hlupy Vojtek'. In Dobšinský's story, 'Batcha and the Dragon', Batcha is not in fact the name of the shepherd, but the Slovak word for a head shepherd (bača, taken from the Romanian bacì), also used in similarly rugged eastern Moravia, where sheep are also widely kept.

Between Slav and German:
the Exotic and the Everyday

As we have seen, in the nineteenth century patriotic intellectuals anticipated and welcomed continuity between Slavonic folk cultures. For Sirovátka, the interpenetration between Czech, Slovak and Polish stories is facilitated by linguistic similarities, especially in border areas where dialects are much closer than the standard languages. He notes, however, that several nouns in Czech denoting certain demonic figures are taken from German and co-exist with Czech equivalents, indicating not only transfer between German and Czech (and vice versa), but also the presence of bilingual storytellers and audiences able to incorporate words from the other language into their story. Overall, in fact, studies of folk narratives trace gradual changes in style and features from east to west, with Czech much closer to Central European, German models, seen to reflect more modern developments, than to Slavonic models from eastern and south-eastern Europe. This modernity manifests itself in many of the stories in this volume in a certain relativization of the drama and power of the magical, supernatural and heroic through an emphasis on the ordinary world of peasants and artisans. While some stories transport the audience and main characters to an alternative, magical reality in strange, faraway lands, in others, discrete elements of that alternative reality appear to live alongside the characters in their daily lives.

This merging of the magical and the everyday is reflected in the language of Czech folktales. Whereas Russian and Slovak folktales retain a more archaic, defamiliarizing language, Czech tends towards a more contemporaneous, even colloquial register. We also notice a distinct change in the way that folktales begin and end from Russian through Slovak to Czech. Jiří Polívka has shown how the variety and richness of these rhetorical frames declines from the elaborate introductions and conclusions of Russian folktales, which ostentatiously mark the border between the mundane world of the audience or reader and the fabulous world encountered in the tale, to the much briefer, simpler and more formulaic examples found in most stories in this volume. Alongside numerous variations on 'Once upon a time, there lived...', the beginning of Dobšinský's Slovak story, 'The Flaming Horse', gives us some sense of the contrast: 'There was once a land that was dreary and dark as the grave, for the sun of heaven never shone upon it.' Indeed, the depiction in this story of a horse with a burning sun on its forehead and a seer, alongside creatures like the voracious griffins in 'Vít'azko' (from Němcová's Slovak tales), the monstrous serpents, flying dragon and terrifying wizard in 'Batcha and the Dragon' or the horrible witch in Dobšinský's 'The Golden Duck', all Slovak stories, gives us a glimpse of a more dramatic, eastern folktale landscape. To emphasize the witch's distinctive, exotic nature, the translator even prefers to keep an anglicized form of the Slovak/Czech word for witch, Yezibaba (*ježibaba*), literally 'an old woman who makes one's hair stand on end', whose best-known incarnation is the Russian Baba Yaga.

Czech Humour

In bringing high-flown tales down to earth, Czech folktales have contributed greatly to what is often characterized as 'typically Czech' humour, understood as the pragmatic, playful subversion of authority and a broadly cheery acceptance of life's imperfections and disappointments, and epitomized by the internationally best-known figure from Czech literature, Jaroslav Hašek's the Good Soldier Švejk, himself very much a refugee from folk literature. Baudiš writes: 'in every case the story-teller, instead of assuming the attitude of the morality preacher or of indulging in theatrical invective against the wickedness of the times, rests content with a good-humoured gibe at the folly of the world, at the frailty of his fellow-men, and, it may be, at his own'. Baudiš is far from alone in associating this humour with the historical narrative of Czech misfortune and victimhood developed in the nineteenth century and advanced at the time of Baudiš's anthology in support of their calls for Czech and Slovak independence from Austria. Commentators identify the same humour in subsequent periods of oppression, especially during the Communist period (1948–89). Baudiš, however, undoubtedly underplays the longstanding didactic tendency in Czech culture; many of these stories may easily be read as moral or cautionary tales, as well as assertions of their nineteenth-century authors' broader visions of society and national life.

Devils

The more typically Czech stories in this volume show that supernatural figures, who range in Slavonic folklore from terrifying embodiments of evil to the merely troublesome or indeed the positively helpful, in Czech folktales tend towards the milder end of the spectrum. We see this in the benevolent personification of Death in several stories, and especially in the devil figures. Although shown explicitly to be agents of Lucifer, sent into the world to capture souls for him, they are more comical than chilling, merry, mischievous, often incompetent or easily thwarted, even vulnerable and inviting our sympathy, as in 'Gentle Dora'. This representation of devils recurs in Czech family films and is also found in Czech traditions marking the Feast of St Nicholas, when – like Krampus and St Nicholas in Bavaria – a devil, typically covered in soot and jangling chains, accompanies St Nicholas and an angel as they visit children to see who has been good over the year.

Water Goblins

Another such figure from the stories who deserves attention is the water goblin or water sprite; the different connotations of 'goblin' and 'sprite' reflect that his characterization also falls on a spectrum from evil and malevolent to playful and even helpful. Known in Czech as *hastrman* (from German) or, since the nineteenth century, *vodník*, the figure is rendered by both translators in this volume through neologisms – 'waternick' for Baudiš, 'nickerman' for Fillmore – presumably because they could find no adequate word in English. The 'nick' replicates the Czech suffix '-ník' while perhaps evoking Old Nick, the Devil, and the German 'nix', a water spirit from Germanic folklore. Fillmore's 'nickerman' may also allude to the Celtic 'wicker man'. The absence of an English equivalent reflects the view, reasserted most recently by Pavel Šidák in an exhaustive study of the figure, that the water goblin, as he is characterized in stories like those in this volume, seems to have his origins in the ubiquitous lakes, ponds and marshes of Bohemia. Comparable water spirits in German or Polish folklore appear most prevalently in stories from areas that border Bohemia, possibly as imports.

Like other demonic figures, the water goblin is thought to have its origins in pre-Christian, animistic belief systems as a water spirit, who subsequently blends with the Christian notion of devils and is immensely widespread in Bohemian folklore; well into the nineteenth century, every body of water there still seemed to have one. As we see in the stories here, the water goblin lures people to his underwater abode, where he drowns them and keeps their souls in teapots or trapped under pots. He has a man's body, but it is green and with gills, and while he sometimes appears naked, he is often portrayed as a dandy, wearing a green coat with water dripping from the tails, a red hat, red trousers and yellow shoes, though he occasionally has webbed feet or hooves to indicate his demonic nature. He has the capacity to change into other people, animals or objects, and is striking among demonic figures for being a family man, with a wife and children.

As Šidák documents, since his modern entry into written Czech literature in the 1820s through folktales, the water goblin has never ceased to inspire Czech writers, artists and film-makers. His most canonical incarnation is in Erben's 1853 narrative poem 'The Water Goblin', which appeared in a cycle of stylized verse folktales, Kytice (A Bouquet of Czech Folktales), available in competing English translations by Susan Reynolds and by Marcela Sulak, and inspired

Dvořák's 1896 tone poem. Here, Erben combines the use of the figure to warn children not to go into dangerous bodies of water with his implicit seductive aspect as an embodiment of irresistible male sexuality, enticing an adolescent girl to a terrible fate. More recently, in a 2001 novel by the popular Czech writer, Miloš Urban, the water goblin becomes a radical defender of the natural environment from destructive human activity.

The Different Styles of the Folktales

Of the authors represented here, three – chronologically Erben, Němcová and Kulda – are sufficient to demonstrate the contrasting approaches taken by collectors in the nineteenth century to reproducing oral stories. Ethnographers regret that writers then did not record stories verbatim from experienced storytellers, including notes on the audience and context, but instead very often elaborated on summaries of stories reported to them, for example in letters from friends. As Fillmore indicates in the foreword to his *Czechoslovak Tales*, where he refers to the 'bald narrative of "The Bird with the Golden Gizzard", which Kulda reports with phonographic exactness', Kulda is held to have striven most to capture the stories as they were told to him, paying attention to the style of the folk narrator, but as a result his collections were judged by critics to lack the aesthetic charm of others.

Erben, as later Dobšinský in Slovak, occupies the status accorded to the Grimm brothers, the practical and philosophical models for his approach. Sirovátka writes that Erben, whose stories here include 'Longshanks, Girth and Keen', 'The Three Golden Hairs', 'Grandfather's Eyes' and 'Zlatovlaska the Golden-Haired', used different variants of a story to create what he considered an ideal version, and similarly sought to create an idealized folk narrative style. Sirovátka describes Erben's style as 'objective and measured'; he notes his brevity, his use of short, dense sentences, rhyme, folk sayings and non-standard forms, not all of which are replicated in the translations. Erben's interpretations of the stories consistently reflect his interest in uncovering the prehistoric, pagan myths that he believed underlay them.

By contrast, Němcová, whose stories here also include 'Prince Bayaya', 'Katcha and the Devil', 'The Wood Maiden', 'The Golden Spinning Wheel', 'The Story That Never Ends' and 'Clever Manka', is more forward-looking, and most creative in her exploitation of folktale material, which typically serves as a basis for the development of her own literary style and the expression of her own views about society and love. This is not to say that Němcová was necessarily unfaithful to the folk heritage she gathers; rather, as Felix Vodička notes, where Erben seeks what is fixed and constant in the folktale, Němcová embraces the scope for improvisation inherent in the oral tradition. While Erben's stories (in contrast to the verse cycle Kytice) are dominated by male characters, Němcová, as throughout her writing, focuses much more on female characters who often, through pluck, ingenuity and generosity of heart, emancipate themselves from oppressive situations. Her male characters are often ideals of a strong, kind, noble masculinity; a reflection of Němcová's broader utopian view that love saves. Her stories also frequently feature social inequality, where the wealthy are cruel, selfish and inactive and typically suffer punishment, while the poor are good and, through determination and action, triumph. Erben provided the Czechs with the best remembered record of their folk heritage; Němcová showed Czech writers and other creative artists how to renew that heritage and give it life.

Rajendra Chitnis (Introduction) is associate professor of Czech and Slovak at the University of Oxford, where he teaches Czech and Slovak literature from the fourteenth century to the present. He writes mainly on twentieth-century and contemporary Czech, Russian and Slovak literature. He is the author of *Literature in Post-Communist Russia and Eastern Europe* (2005) and *Vladislav Vančura: The Heart of the Czech Avant-garde* (2007) and lead editor of *Translating the Literatures of Small European Nations* (2020).

Adventure,
Adversity & Trials

THIS COLLECTION of tales is intended to exemplify the spirit of the Czech people. It may perhaps be said that folktales are part of a common stock belonging to all European people, but though this is perfectly true, it is also no less certain that the spirit of the nation manifests itself in the manner of their telling.

Two things are common to all of the stories in this section: their moral tendency and sense of humour. It is not morality in the sense of retribution for evil, or of filial devotion, or the sentimental insistence upon 'everyone living happily ever after' and above all upon Jack marrying his Molly. It is that higher sort of morality which was the mainspring of Protestantism. The Czech nation was the first to adopt the Protestant faith.

A Gullible World

THERE WAS ONCE A POOR farm laborer, so poor that all he owned in the world was a hen. He told his wife to take this hen to market and sell it.

"How much shall I ask for it?" the woman wanted to know.

"Ask as much as they'll pay, of course," the laborer said.

So the woman took the hen by the feet and set out. Near the village she met a farmer.

"Good day," the farmer said. "Where are you going with that hen?"

"I'm going to market to sell it for as much as they'll pay me."

The farmer weighed the hen in his hand, pursed his lips, thought a moment, and said:

"You better sell it to me. I'll pay you three pennies for it."

"Three pennies? Are you sure that's as much as you'll pay?"

"Yes," the farmer said, "three pennies is as much as I'll pay."

So the laborer's wife sold the hen for three pennies. She went on to the village and there she bought a pretty little paper bag with one of the pennies and a piece of ribbon with another penny. She put the third penny into the bag, tied the bag with the ribbon, slipped the ribbon on a stick, put the stick over her shoulder, and then, feeling that she had done a very good day's work, she tramped home to her husband.

When the laborer heard how stupidly his wife had acted, he flew into a great rage and at first threatened to give her a sound beating.

"Was there ever such a foolish woman in the world?" he shouted angrily.

The poor woman, who by this time was snuffling and weeping, whimpered out:

"I don't see why you find so much fault with me! I'm sure I'm not the only gullible person in the world."

"Well," the laborer said, "I don't know. Perhaps there are people in the world as gullible as you. I tell you what I'll do: I'll go out and see if I can find them. If I do, I won't beat you."

So the laborer went out into the world to see if he could find any one as gullible as his wife. He traveled several days until he reached a countryside where he was unknown. Here he came to a fine castle at the window of which stood the lady of the castle looking out.

"Now then, my lady," the laborer said to himself, "we'll see how gullible you are."

He stood in the middle of the road, looked intently up at the sky, and then reaching out his arms as if he were trying to catch hold of something he began jumping up and down.

The lady of the castle watched him for a few moments and then dispatched one of her servants to ask him what he was doing. The servant hurried out and questioned him and this is the story the clever rascal made up:

"I'm trying to jump back into heaven. You see I live up there. I was wrestling up there with one of my comrades and he pitched me out and now I can't find the hole I fell through."

With his eyes popping out of his head, the servant hurried back to his mistress and repeated the laborer's story word for word.

The lady of the castle instantly sent for the laborer.

"You say you were in heaven?" she asked him.

"Yes, my lady, that's where I live and I'm going back at once."

"I have a dear son in heaven," the lady said. "Do you know him?"

"Of course I know him. The last time I saw him he was sitting far back in the chimney corner looking very sad and lonely."

"What! My son sitting far back in the chimney corner! Poor boy, he must be in need of money! My good man, will you take him something from me? I'd like to send him three hundred golden ducats and material for six fine shirts. And tell him not to be lonely as I'll come to him soon."

The laborer was delighted at the success of his yarn and he told the lady of the castle he'd gladly take with him the ducats and the fine shirting and he asked her to give them to him at once as he had to get back to heaven without delay.

The foolish woman wrapped up the shirting and counted out the money and the laborer hurried off.

Once out of sight of the castle he sat down by the roadside, stuffed the fine shirting into the legs of his trousers, and hid the ducats in his pockets. Then he stretched himself out to rest.

Meantime the lord of the castle got home and his wife at once told him the whole story and asked him if he didn't think she was fortunate to find a man who had consented to deliver to their son in heaven three hundred golden ducats and material for six fine shirts.

"What!" cried the husband. "Oh, what a gullible creature you are! Who ever heard of a man falling out of heaven! And if he were to fall, how could he climb back? The rogue has swindled you! Which way did he go?"

And without waiting to hear the poor lady's lamentations, the nobleman mounted his horse and galloped off in the direction the laborer had taken.

The laborer, who was still resting by the wayside, saw him coming and guessed who he was.

"Now, my lord, we'll try you," he said to himself.

He took off his broad-trimmed hat and put it on the ground beside him over a clod of earth.

"My good fellow," said the nobleman, "I am looking for a man with a bundle over his shoulder. Have you seen him pass this way?"

The laborer scratched his head and pretended to think.

"Yes, master," he said, "seems to me I did see a man with a bundle. He was running over there towards the woods and looking back all the time. He was a stranger to these parts. I remember now thinking to myself that he looked like one of those rogues that come from big cities to swindle honest country folk. Yes, master, that's the way he went, over there."

The laborer seemed such an honest simple fellow that at once the nobleman told him how the stranger had swindled his wife.

"Oh, the rogue!" the laborer cried. "To think of his swindling such a fine lady, too! Master, I wish I could help you. I'd take that horse of yours and go after him myself if I could. But I can't. I'm carrying a bird of great value to a gentleman who lives in the next town. I have the bird here under my hat and I daren't leave it."

The nobleman thought that as the laborer had seen the swindler he might be able to catch him. So he said:

"My good man, if I sat here and guarded your hat, would you be willing to mount my horse and follow that rascal?"

"Indeed I would, my lord, in a minute, for I can't bear to think of that rogue swindling such a fine lady as your wife. But I must beg you to be very careful of this bird. Don't put your hand under my hat or it might escape and then I should have to bear the loss of it."

The nobleman promised to be most careful of the bird and, dismounting, he handed his bridle to the laborer. That one mounted the nobleman's horse and galloped off.

It is needless to say the nobleman never saw either man or horse again. He waited and waited. At last when he could wait no longer he decided that he would have to take the bird home with him and let the laborer follow. So he lifted the edge of the hat very carefully, slipped in his hand, and clutched – the dry clod of earth!

Deeply chagrined he went home and had to bear the smiles of his people as they whispered among themselves that my lord as well as my lady had been swindled.

The laborer as he neared his cottage called out to his wife:

"It's all right, wife! You won't get that beating! I find that the world is full of people even more gullible than you!"

The Blacksmith's Stool

A LONG TIME AGO, when Lord Jesus and the blessed St. Peter walked about together on earth, it happened one evening that they stopped at a blacksmith's cottage and asked for a night's lodging.

"You are welcome," the blacksmith said. "I am a poor man but whatever I have I will gladly share with you."

He threw down his hammer and led his guests into the kitchen. There he entertained them with a good supper and after they had eaten he said to them:

"I see that you are tired from your day's journey. There is my bed. Lie down on it and sleep until morning."

"And where will you sleep?" St. Peter asked.

"I? Don't think of me," the blacksmith said. "I'll go out to the barn and sleep on the straw."

The next morning he gave his guests a fine breakfast, and then sent them on their way with good wishes for their journey.

As they were leaving, St. Peter plucked Lord Jesus by the sleeve and whispered:

"Master, aren't you going to reward this man? He is poor but yet has treated us most hospitably."

Lord Jesus answered Peter:

"The reward of this world is an empty reward. I was thinking to prepare him a place in heaven. However, I will grant him something now."

Then he turned to the blacksmith and said:

"Ask what you will. Make three wishes and they will be fulfilled."

The blacksmith was overjoyed. For his first wish he said:

"I should like to live for a hundred years and always be as strong and healthy as I am this moment."

Lord Jesus said:

"Very well, that will be granted you. What is your second wish?"

The blacksmith thought for a moment. Then he said:

"I wish that I may prosper in this world and always have as much as I need. May work in my shop always be as plentiful as it is today."

"This, too, will be granted you," Lord Jesus said. "Now for your third wish."

Our blacksmith thought and thought, unable at first to decide on a third wish. At last he said:

"Grant that whoever sits on the stool where you sat last night at supper may be unable to get up until I release him."

St. Peter laughed at this, but Lord Jesus nodded and said:

"This wish, too, will be fulfilled."

So they parted, Lord Jesus and blessed St. Peter going on their way, and the blacksmith returning home to his forge.

Things came to pass as Lord Jesus had promised they should. Work in plenty flowed into the blacksmith's shop. The years went by but they made no impression on the blacksmith. He was as young as ever and as vigorous. His friends grew old and one by one died. His children grew up, married, and had children of their own. These in turn grew up. The years brought youth and maturity and old age to them all. The blacksmith alone remained unchanged.

A hundred years is a long time but at last even it runs out.

One night as the blacksmith was putting away his tools, there came a knock at the door. The blacksmith stopped his singing to call out:

"Who's there?"

"It is I, Death," a voice answered. "Open the door, blacksmith. Your time has come."

The blacksmith threw open the door.

"Welcome," he said to the woman standing there. "I'll be ready in a moment when I put away my tools." He smiled a little to himself. "Won't you sit down on this stool, dear lady, and rest you for a moment? You must be weary going to and fro over the earth."

Death, suspecting nothing, seated herself on the stool.

The blacksmith burst into a loud laugh.

"Now I have you, my lady! Stay where you are until I release you!"

Death tried to stand up but could not. She squirmed this way and that. She rattled her hollow bones. She gnashed her teeth. But do what she would she could not arise from the stool.

Chuckling and singing, the blacksmith left her there and went about his business.

But soon he found that chaining up Death had unexpected results. To begin with, he wanted at once to celebrate his escape with a feast. He had a hog which had been fattening for some time. He would slaughter this hog and chop it up into fine spicy sausages which his neighbors and friends would help him eat. The hams he would hang in the chimney to smoke.

But when he tried to slaughter the animal, the blow of his axe had no effect. He struck the hog on the head and, to be sure, it rolled over on the ground. But when he stopped to cut the throat, the creature jumped up and with a grunt went scampering off. Before the blacksmith could recover from his surprise, the hog had disappeared.

Next he tried to kill a goose. He had a fat one which he had been stuffing for the village fair.

"Since those sausages have escaped me," he said. "I'll have to be satisfied with roast goose."

But when he tried to cut the goose's throat, the knife drew no blood. In his surprise he loosened his hold and the goose slipped from his hands and went cackling off after the hog.

"What's come over things today?" the blacksmith asked himself. "It seems I'm not to have sausage or roast goose. I suppose I'll have to be satisfied with a pair of pigeons."

He went out to the pigeon-house and caught two pigeons. He put them on the chopping-block and with one mighty blow of his ax cut off both their heads.

"There!" he cried in triumph. "I've got you!"

But even as he spoke the little severed heads returned to their bodies, the heads and bodies grew together as if nothing had happened, and cooing happily the two pigeons flew away.

Then at last the truth flashed upon the blacksmith's mind. So long as he kept Death fastened to that stool, nothing could die! Of course not! So no more spicy sausages, no more smoked hams, no more roast goose – not even a broiled pigeon! The prospect was not a pleasing one, for the blacksmith loved good things to eat. But what could he do? Release Death? Never that! He would be her first victim! Well then, if he could have no fresh meat, he would have to be content to live on peas and porridge and wheaten cakes.

This actually was what he had to do and what every one else had to do when their old provisions were exhausted.

Summer passed and winter followed. Then spring came bringing new and unforeseen miseries. With the first breath of warm weather all the pests and insects of the summer before revived, for not one of them had been killed by the winter cold. And the eggs they had laid all hatched out until the earth and the air and the water swarmed with living creatures. Birds and rats and grasshoppers, insects and bugs and vermin of every kind, covered the fields and ate up every green thing. The meadows looked as if a fire had swept them clean. The orchards were stripped bare of every leaf and blossom.

Such hordes of fish and frogs and water creatures filled the lakes and the rivers that the water was polluted and it was impossible for man to drink it.

Water and land alike were swarming with living creatures not one of which could be killed. Even the air was thick with clouds of mosquitoes and gnats and flies.

Men and women walked about looking like tormented ghosts. They had no desire to live on but they had to live on for they could not die.

The blacksmith came at last to a realization of all the misery which his foolish wish was bringing upon the world.

"I see now," he said, "that God Almighty did well when He sent Death to the world. She has her work to do and I am wrong to hold her prisoner."

So he released Death from the stool and made no outcry when she put her bony fingers to his throat.

The Shoemaker's Apron

I

THERE WAS ONCE a shoemaker who made so little at his trade that his wife suffered and his children went hungry. In desperation he offered to sell his soul to a devil.

"How much do you want for your soul?" the devil asked him.

"I want work enough to give me a good livelihood," the shoemaker said, "so that my wife won't suffer nor my children starve."

The devil agreed to this and the shoemaker put his mark on the contract. After that trade improved and soon the little shoemaker was happy and prosperous.

Now one night it happened that Christ and the blessed St. Peter, who were walking about on earth, stopped at the little shoemaker's cottage and asked for a night's lodging. The shoemaker received them most hospitably. He had his wife cook them a fine supper and after supper he gave them his own bed to sleep on while he and his wife went to the garret and slept on straw.

In the morning he had his wife prepare them a good breakfast and after breakfast he took them on their way for a mile or two.

As he was leaving them, St. Peter whispered to Christ:

"Master, this poor man has given us of his best. Don't you think you ought to reward him?"

Christ nodded and, turning to the little shoemaker, he said:

"For your kindness to us this day I will reward you. Make three wishes and they will be granted."

The shoemaker thanked Christ and said:

"Well then, these are my wishes: first, may whoever sits down on my cobbler's stool be unable to get up until I permit him; second, may whoever looks into the window of my cottage have to stand there until I let him go; and third, may whoever shakes the pear-tree in my garden stick to the tree until I set him free."

"Your wishes will be granted," Christ promised. Then he and St. Peter went on their way and the shoemaker returned to his cottage.

The years went by and at last one afternoon the devil stood before the shoemaker and said:

"Ho, shoemaker, your time has come! Are you ready?"

"Just let me have a bite of supper first," the shoemaker said. "In the meantime you sit down here on my stool and rest yourself."

The devil who had been walking up and down the earth since sunrise was tired and so was glad enough to sit down.

After supper the little shoemaker said:

"Now then, I'm ready. Come on."

The devil tried to stand up but of course he couldn't. He pulled this way and that. He stretched, he rolled from side to side until his bones ached, but all to no avail. He could not get up from the stool.

"Brother!" he cried in terror, "help me off this cursed stool and I'll give you seven more years – I swear I will!"

At that promise the shoemaker allowed the devil to stand up, and the devil scurried off as fast as he could.

He was true to his word. He didn't come back for seven years. When he did come he was too clever to risk sitting down again on the cobbler's stool. He didn't even venture inside the cottage door. Instead, he stood at the window and called out:

"Ho, shoemaker, here I am again! Your time has come! Are you ready?"

"I'll be ready in a moment," the shoemaker said, "Just let me put a last stitch in these shoes."

When the shoemaker had finished sewing the shoes, he put aside his work, bade his wife good-bye, and said to the devil:

"Now then, I'm ready. Let us go."

But the devil when he tried to move away from the window found that he was held fast. It was as if his feet had been soldered to the earth. In great fright he cried out:

"Oh, my dear little shoemaker, help me! I can't move!"

"What's this trick you're playing on me?" the shoemaker said. "Now I'm ready to go and you aren't! What do you mean by making a fool of me this way?"

"Just help me to get free," the devil cried, "and I'll do anything in the world for you! I'll give you seven more years! I swear I will!"

"Very well," the shoemaker said, "then I'll help you this time. But never again! Now remember: I won't let you make a fool of me a third time!"

So the shoemaker freed the devil from the window and the devil without another word scurried off.

At the end of another seven years he appeared again. But this time he was too clever to look in the window. He didn't even come near the cottage. Instead he stood off in the garden under the pear-tree and called out:

"Ho, there, shoemaker! Your time has come and I am here to get you! Are you ready?"

"I'll be ready in a moment," the shoemaker said. "Just wait until I put away my tools. If you feel like it, shake yourself down a nice ripe pear."

The devil shook the pear-tree and of course when he tried to stop he couldn't. He shook until all the pears had fallen. He kept on and presently he had shaken off all the leaves.

When the shoemaker came out and saw the tree stripped and bare and the devil still shaking it, he pretended to fall into a fearful rage.

"Hi, there, you! What do you mean shaking down all my pears! Stop it! Do you hear me? Stop it!"

"But I can't stop it!" the poor devil cried.

"We'll see about that!" the shoemaker said.

He ran back into the cottage and got a long leather strap. Then he began beating the devil unmercifully over his head and shoulders.

The devil made such an outcry that all the village heard him and came running to see what was the matter.

"Help! Help!" the devil cried. "Make the shoemaker stop beating me!"

But all the people thought the shoemaker was doing just right to punish the black fellow for shaking down all his pears and they urged the shoemaker to beat him harder.

"My poor head! My poor shoulders!" the devil moaned. "If ever I get loose from this cursed pear-tree I'll never come back here! I swear I won't!"

The shoemaker, when he heard this, laughed in his sleeve and let the devil go.

The devil was true to his word. He never again returned. So the shoemaker lived, untroubled, to a ripe old age.

Just before he died he asked that his cobbler's apron be buried with him and his sons carried out his wish.

As soon as he died the little shoemaker trudged up to heaven and knocked timidly at the golden gate. St. Peter opened the gate a little crack and peeped out. When he saw the shoemaker he shook his head and said:

"Little shoemaker, heaven is no place for you. While you were alive you sold your soul to the ruler of the other place and now you must go there."

With that St. Peter shut the golden gate and locked it.

The little shoemaker sighed and said to himself:

"Well, I suppose I must go where St. Peter says."

So he put on a bold front and tramped down to hell. When the devil who knew him saw him coming, he shouted out to his fellow devils:

"Brothers, on guard! Here comes that terrible little shoemaker! Lock every gate! Don't let him in or he'll drive us all out of hell!"

The devils in great fright scurried about and locked and barred all the gates, and the little shoemaker when he arrived could not get in.

He knocked and knocked but no one would answer.

"They don't seem to want me here," he said to himself. "I suppose I'll have to try heaven again."

So he trudged back to St. Peter and explained to him that hell was locked up tight.

"No matter," St. Peter said. "As I told you before heaven is no place for you."

The little shoemaker, tired and dejected, went back to hell but again the devils, when they saw him coming, locked every gate and kept him out.

In desperation the little shoemaker returned to heaven and pounded loudly on the golden gate. Thinking from the noise that some very important saint had arrived, St. Peter flung open the gate. Quick as a flash the little shoemaker threw his leather apron inside, then hopped in himself under St. Peter's elbow and squatted down on the apron.

In great excitement St. Peter tried to turn him out of heaven, but the little shoemaker shouted:

"You can't touch me! You can't touch me! I'm sitting on my own property! Let me alone!"

He raised such a hubbub that all the angels and the blessed saints came running to see what was happening. Presently Lord Jesus himself came and the little shoemaker explained to him how he just had to stay in heaven as the devils wouldn't let him into hell.

"Now, Master," St. Peter said, "what am I to do? You know yourself we can't keep this fellow in heaven."

But Lord Jesus, looking with pity on the poor little shoemaker, said to St. Peter:

"Just let him stay where he is. He won't bother any one sitting here near the gate."

Boots, Cloak and Ring

ONCE THERE WAS A BLACKSMITH, and he had only one son, John by name. They sent him to school, but fortune changed and his parents fell into poverty, so they were forced to take their son home again. John had already passed through the higher standard, but he could not support his parents. So one day he said:

"Father and mother! What can I do at home? There is no business here, so I can't be a clerk, and I am too old now to learn a trade. So I will go out into the world and find myself a job, and, whenever I can, I will send you some money. And when I get a good job, you must sell your cottage and come and live with me."

His father and mother wept, because he wanted to leave them, but they knew that he was right, for there was no chance for him if he stayed at home. So they let him go. They gave him their blessing before he went out into the world. John wept till his heart nearly broke at parting with his aged parents.

He walked on till noon. At noon he sat down beneath a lime-tree beside a well, and had his meal and a drink. Then, strengthened and refreshed, he walked on till nightfall. The country was quite unknown to him, so he had to spend the night in the forest. The next day he went on again till he came into a wild mountain country. There he stopped and thought over what he should do next. He stood awhile, and then he went on again. He reached a pleasant valley, and there he found three brothers. They were quarrelling and on the point of coming to blows. John asked them what the matter was. The eldest answered:

"Our father has died, and he bequeathed to us these boots, this cloak, and this hat. And each of us would like to own the boots."

"Why?" asked John.

"Because they have the property that whoever puts them on can cover ten miles in the moment he wishes it. The cloak has the property that its owner can fly as far and as high as he likes. And the property of the hat is that it makes its wearer invisible."

John said: "You are brothers, and you ought not to quarrel. You must love one another. So that you won't quarrel any more, I will decide the matter for you. Give me those things."

They gave him the boots, the cloak, and the hat. He put the hat on, and they couldn't see him any more; he wrapped himself in the cloak, took the boots, and flew away.

He flew some distance before he alighted upon a log and put the boots on. As he sat on the log, it turned over, and he saw a big hole under it. He went down the hole and came to some stairs, and went down them to the bottom without any difficulty. There he found a big room without any human being in it. The table was laid for one person. He thought: "I am hungry. Shall I eat this meal?" Finally he decided to risk it; he took off his hat and began to eat.

When he had finished, an old crone entered the room, and asked: "Did you like your meal?"

"Oh, it was very nice indeed," answered John; "and, by the way, could you give me lodging for the night?"

"I will, if you can stand it; for at midnight twenty-four ghosts will come, and they will try to make you play cards with them and dance with them. But you must sit still and not so much as look at them."

So the first night came. John was sitting eating his meal. When he had finished, he remained at table. After eleven o'clock two dozen ghosts entered the room and asked him to play cards with them. He refused, so they began preparations for playing skittles, and again asked him to join them, but he would not. Then a delightful music began to play, and they asked him to dance with them. No, he wouldn't; he did not so much as look at them. They kept on dragging him about, tearing and biting him, till he began to think it was all over with him. But just then it struck twelve, and the ghosts vanished.

In the morning the old crone came back and waked him, for he was still asleep on the ground. She asked him: "How did you sleep?"

"Very well," said John.

"Did you, now?" answered the old woman. "Well, next night will be still worse, if you can stand it. Two score of ghosts will come, and they'll urge you to play cards and skittles with them and to dance with them. But you must sit quiet; don't so much as look at them."

He stayed there that day, and had a good time. Then the second night came. After eleven o'clock twoscore ghosts rushed in. They urged him to play cards and skittles with them and to dance with them. But John wouldn't. He sat still, without so much as looking at them. So they began to torture him again, and dragged him about even worse than before. But when it struck twelve they left him on the ground and disappeared.

In the morning the old crone came. She washed him with some lotion till he recovered. She asked him: "How did you sleep?"

"Splendidly," said he.

"Did you, now?" said she. "It was a bad lodging for you, but the third night will be even worse, if you can stand it. Three score of ghosts will come, and will urge you to play cards and skittles and to dance with them. But you must sit still and not so much as look at them."

All that day he had a good time again. The third night came, and after eleven o'clock three score of ghosts rushed in. They gathered round him, and urged, prayed, and besought him to play and dance with him. When he refused, they seized him and began knocking him against the ground, tearing and biting him, so that he lost his senses and did not see them go away.

In the morning the old crone came and anointed him with a precious salve till he recovered. The old woman said: "You wouldn't have had such a bad time if you had not stolen the boots, the cloak, and the hat. The ghosts would simply have pressed you; they would have had no power over you. As you followed my advice and did not play with them, you have delivered an enchanted town and a beautiful princess. She will come to you at once. Now you are rich, return the stolen goods."

Then there came a girl in a white robe. It was the beautiful princess, and she thanked him for delivering her and the whole town. He went to the window, and outside he saw streets full of people and soldiers and a great bustle going on. The princess said:

"My father is a king, and you will marry me and succeed him. But my father dwells far from here, and we will go to him. Do you take this ring here."

So they went off. When the wedding was to take place, John wanted his parents to be present, so he asked the princess: "May I go to see my parents? I would like them to be at our wedding."

The princess answered: "They live a great way from us, but you will be able to get to them. The ring I gave you has the property that, when you turn it on your finger and wish to go a hundred miles, you will cover that distance in a moment. On your way you will come to a king who has a beautiful daughter. But you must not think of her nor of me, for then you will lose the ring, and you will not be able to go any farther."

John started. He turned the ring, and in a moment he was a hundred miles off, and found himself with a king who had several sons. They entertained him splendidly. Then he came to another king who had an only daughter, and she was very vulgar. The king insisted that John should marry her. John thought: "What are you thinking of, my man? My bright one is so beautiful that there is not her equal in the wide world, while your daughter is only a vulgar creature." At the moment he thought of his bride the ring slipped from his finger and disappeared.

John left them then. He was very sad, and considered what he should do. "My bride is far away now," he thought. "I cannot find my way either to her or to my parents."

As he was walking along in this sad mood, he thought of his cloak, and it came into his mind that, if he could reach the Sun's abode the same day, he could ask where his bride's castle was. As soon as he thought of this he was at the Sun's house. The Sun was not in; only his housekeeper was at home. He asked her for a lodging, and said that he would like to ask the Sun whether he knew the castle where his bride dwelt. She gave him the lodging. When the Sun returned home in the evening, John asked him whether he had any knowledge of the castle in which his wife dwelt. The Sun answered: "I don't know. I never shone there. But go and ask the Moon."

The next day, as soon as he woke, he flew off on his cloak to the Moon's castle. When he got there, the Moon was not in, and John asked the housekeeper for a night's lodging. He said he would like to ask the Moon's advice.

The housekeeper said: "You must wait till the Moon comes home, but you will be very cold, for my mistress is an extremely cold person."

"I will crouch in a corner and wait till the mistress comes; in any case, my cloak is warm enough."

When the morning drew near, the Moon returned home, and John asked her whether she knew where his bride's castle was.

The Moon said: "I never shone there. But go to the Wind. He is a fellow who penetrates everywhere, and so he is likely to know where that castle is."

So John went to the Wind's house. The Wind was not in, but Melusine, his wife, was alone at home. John asked her to let him stay there for the night. She tried to dissuade him.

"It is impossible, good sir. My lord is used to blow terribly. It will be exceedingly cold."

He answered: "I will cover myself up and crouch somewhere. I can endure cold, and, anyhow, my cloak is warm enough." So he stayed there for the night.

After midnight the Wind came home and asked: "Who is here with you, wife? I smell a man."

"Who should be here?" she said. "Your nose is still full of the human smell."

But the Wind persisted: "There is somebody here! Tell me!"

So she confessed. "Don't be angry, dear husband! There is a man staying here for the night, and he wants to ask you whether you will be kind enough to take him to his bride's castle."

The Wind answered: "It is very far from here, and I must ask the Lord how strongly I am to blow, if we are to get there. I was there yesterday;

they are going to celebrate a wedding there, and they have been drying some shirts ready for it, and I have been helping them."

The Wind went to ask the Lord; and when he came back, he said to John: "I can blow strongly enough, but I don't know whether you will be able to keep step with me."

John answered: "I have got good boots, and I am sure I can."

So he wrapped himself in his cloak, covered his head with his hat, and put his boots on, and he went ahead so quickly that the Wind could hardly keep step with him. As they drew near to the castle, the Wind said: "Here it is," and disappeared in a whirl.

The other bridegroom had already arrived, and was at the wedding feast. John passed through the castle, and came to the table at which they were dining. Nobody could see him. He remained standing near the bride, and whenever she lifted the food to her mouth, he ate it before it could reach her mouth, so that the spoon reached her mouth empty.

After the banquet she said: "My plates were well filled, and yet it is as though I had been eating nothing at all. Who is it that has eaten my food? My glass was full too. I have not drunk, and yet it is empty. Who has drunk my wine?"

Then she went to the kitchen, and John followed close at her heels. When she was alone he revealed himself. He took his hat off, and she knew him. She was greatly rejoiced at this, and ran to the room and said:

"Gentlemen, I would like to ask you a question. I had a golden key and I lost it. So I had a silver key made for me, and, now that it is made, I have found the golden key. Would you be so kind as to advise me which of them I ought to keep?"

The bridegroom stepped forward and said: "Keep the golden key."

Off she went. She dressed John in beautiful garments, and then presented him to the guests, saying: "This is my golden key. He delivered me from torment, and I was to marry him. He went to see his parents, but he could not reach them. Now he has come back to me just as I was going to marry another man, the silver key of my story, though I had given up all hope of his return. Yet he has come back, and I shall keep him, the golden key, for the silver key has himself decided so."

The wedding was celebrated the next day, and John took charge of the old king's kingdom. Then they both went to visit his old parents, and brought them back with them to the palace. On their way back they called on the three brothers, and John gave them back the boots, the cloak, and the hat. And if they haven't died since, they are still alive enjoying their kingdom.

Silly Jura

ONCE THERE WERE TWO BROTHERS. They were lazy fellows, and thieves into the bargain. They were expected to give a feast. They said to one another: "We haven't got anything. Wherever shall we find food for the feast?"

So the first said: "I'll go to our neighbour's. He has some fine apples, and I'll pluck some of them."

The second said: "I'll go to the shepherd's. He has some fine rams. I'll steal a ram from him."

These two brothers hated the third, and so they abused him: "Silly Jura! You won't get anything yourself, but you'll be ready enough to eat what we get."

So Jura said: "I'll go to the burgomaster's and get some nuts."

In the evening they went their ways. When he had finished plucking the nuts, Jura went into the charnel-house at the back of the church and began to crack the nuts there. The watchmen heard the cracking in the charnel-house, and they thought the place was haunted. As there was no priest in the village (he lived in the next village), they went to the burgomaster and asked him to go with them to the charnel-house, saying that the place was haunted.

The burgomaster said: "I am so ill that I can't stand on my feet; no doctor can help me."

But the watchmen insisted, and so the burgomaster told his servant to take him on his back and carry him to the place. The servant carried him along, and the watchmen called at the churchwarden's to ask for some holy water.

When they came near to the charnel-house, Jura thought it was his brother bringing the ram, so he called out: "Are you bringing him?"

The servant was frightened, and let the burgomaster fall and ran away. The burgomaster was terrified too. He jumped up and ran after the servant. He cleared a wooden fence with one leap in his flight, and it wasn't long till he reached home. His family wondered to see him cured so quickly without the help of a doctor.

Next day the burgomaster proclaimed that he would give a pound to the man who had stolen his nuts the day before, if he would only come to see him. So Jura went to him, and the burgomaster said: "I ought to punish you for stealing, but since you have cured my illness which nobody was able to cure, I'll give you the pound I promised, but you mustn't steal any more." So Jura promised not to steal any more, and went home.

The brothers grew very fond of him now that he had money. They borrowed the money from him and bought themselves new clothes, and said: "We'll go to see the world and to get wives for ourselves. As for you, Silly Jura, you must stay at home; you'd never get a good wife for yourself."

So off they went. But Jura went too. He went to the forest and he was utterly dazzled. He had often heard that there was an enchanted castle in that forest. When he came to the place where the ruins of the castle were, night overtook him, and so he could see nothing except what looked like a light in a cellar. So he went into the cellar to make his night's lodging there. There was nobody in the cellar but a cat. The cat greeted him: "Welcome, dear Jura! How did you come here?"

Jura was frightened when he heard the cat speak, and was going to run away. But the cat told him not to go; there was no need to be frightened. He must come back, and no harm would be done to him. If he wanted to eat, he could go into the storeroom and take what he wanted. She would take him for her servant.

So he stayed there a year and had a good time. He never saw a cook, but he always found meals ready prepared in the storeroom. He had nothing to do but get firewood, and at the end of the year he was told to make a great pile of it. Then the cat said: "You must light the pile to-day, and throw me into the fire. You must not help me out, however I entreat you, but you must let me be consumed."

Jura answered: "I can't do that. I have had a good time with you. Why should I repay you in such an evil way?"

The cat said: "If you don't do as I have said, you will be very unhappy. If you do it, you will be happy."

So Jura kindled the pile, and, when it was well alight, he picked up the cat and threw her into the fire. She wanted to escape from the fire, but he wouldn't let her go. At last he was so weary that he was forced to lie down, and soon he fell asleep. When he awoke, he opened his eyes, and behold! there was no ruin; he heard delightful music and saw a beautiful palace with crowds of servants. He was wondering at all this, when a splendidly dressed lady came up to him and asked him if he did not know her.

Jura said: "How should I know your ladyship? I never saw you before in my life."

The lady said: "I am that cat. Witches had put me under enchantment in the shape of a cat. Now we will go after your brothers who hated you so much and see how they are getting on."

She ordered her people to dress him in fine clothes, a fine carriage was prepared, and they drove off. As they were approaching the village, the lady said to her bridegroom: "Put your old clothes on." Then she called an old, ragged beggarwoman and sent him with her. She herself remained outside of the village.

When the brothers saw Jura coming with the ragged beggarwoman, they shouted: "He is bringing home an old ragged bride, and he's in rags too." The other brothers were married too, and they were pretty badly off, so they turned him out and wouldn't have him at home.

So Jura went out of the village; he changed his clothes and drove back with the lady to his brothers' cottage. When the carriage stopped before the cottage, the brothers said: "What a fine carriage! Who is that noble lord and the beautiful lady who have come to our cottage?" They did not recognize their brother.

So she said: "Look here. You were always hard on your brother, always sneering at him, and now you are badly off enough, while he is getting on splendidly. If you mend your ways, you will get on too."

Afterwards she gave them some money and went away with Jura.

The Twin Brothers

O NCE THERE WAS A PRINCESS, and she was under a curse and enchantment, so that she had to spend her life in the shape of a fish. One day a woman happened to be working in the meadow by the river, and she saw a flock of birds flying above the river and talking to the fish. The woman wondered what it was that was there, so she went to the waterside and looked in. All she saw was a fish swimming about. So she said: "I should like to eat you, fish. I feel sure you would do me good."

Now, when she said that, the fish answered: "You could save me. You will have twin sons, although you have never had any children before."

The woman said that, if she could help her in that, there was nothing the fish could ask that she would not do to deliver her.

The fish answered: "Catch me and take me to your field. There you must bury me and plant a rose-tree over me. When the roses first come into bloom you will bear twin sons. After three years, dig in the place where you buried me and you will find two swords, and these you must keep. Your mare will have two foals and your bitch will have two pups, and each of your twins will have a sword, a horse, and a dog. Those swords will have the virtue that they will help your sons to victory over everybody. I shall be delivered as soon as my body has rotted."

When the twin sons grew up they were very clever, and so they said: "We must try our luck in the world. We are bold enough. One of us will go to the East and one to the West. Each of us must look at his sword every morning to see if the other needs his help. For the sword will begin to rust as soon as one of us is in peril."

So they cast lots which way they should go, and each of them took his sword, his horse, and his dog, and away they went.

The first rode through deep forests, and he met a fierce dragon and a lion; so he attacked the dragon, which had nine heads. The lion stayed quiet while the knight attacked the dragon, and at last he succeeded in cutting one of the dragon's heads off. He felt tired then, and the lion took his place; then the knight cut two more heads off the dragon. And so it went on till he had all the heads cut off. Then he cut out the tongues from all the nine heads and kept them, and so went forward on his adventurous journey.

Now, it chanced that there were some woodcutters in these forests, and one of them collected all the dragon's heads, having come across them by chance. That dragon used to come to the town and devour one person every visit. This time the lot had fallen upon the princess, and so she was to be devoured by the dragon. So the town was all hung with black cloth. The woodcutter knew all about this, so he went with the heads to the town to sue for the princess, for it had been proclaimed that whoever killed the dragon should be her husband. When the princess saw that such a low-born man was to be her husband she was taken aback, and tried by all the means in her power to delay the wedding.

The knight happened to come to the town just then, and he saw a good inn, so he rode up to it. The innkeeper came at once to ask what he could do for him. Now, there were other guests there, and it was a busy place. The guests were all talking of the one matter: when the princess was going to marry the man who had killed the dragon. The wedding ought to have been long ago, but the bride and her parents kept putting it off. The knight listened to all this talk, and then he asked:

"Are you sure that it was that woodcutter who killed the dragon?"

They answered that it certainly was, for the heads were preserved in the palace.

The knight said nothing, but when he thought the proper time had come he rode to the palace. The princess saw him from the window, and she wondered who it might be. He was ushered in, and he went straight to the princess and told her everything. He asked her whether he might attend the wedding.

She answered: "I am not at all pleased with my marriage. I would much rather marry you, sir."

He asked her why.

"If he killed the dragon he must be a great man."

"He is such a low-born man," said she, "that it is not likely that he killed the dragon."

"I should like to see him," said he.

So they brought the woodcutter before him, and the knight asked to see the heads. So they brought the heads. He looked at the heads and said:

"There are no tongues in these heads. Where are the tongues?"

Then he turned to the woodcutter: "Did you really kill the cruel dragon?" he said.

The woodcutter persisted in his story.

"And how did you cut the heads off?"

"With my hatchet."

"Why, you couldn't do it with your hatchet. You are a liar."

The woodcutter was taken aback and did not know what to say. He was frightened already, but he said: "It happened that the dragon didn't have any tongues."

The knight produced the tongues and said: "Here are the tongues, and it was I who killed the cruel dragon."

The princess took hold of him and embraced and kissed him, and she was ready to marry him on the spot. As for the woodcutter, he was kicked out in disgrace, and they put him into jail for some time too. So the princess married the knight and they lived happily together.

One day, looking out of the window, he saw in the distance, among the mountains, a black castle. He asked his wife what castle it was and to whom it belonged.

"That is an enchanted castle, and nobody who goes into it ever returns."

But he could not rest, and he was eager to explore the castle. So one morning he ordered his horse to be saddled, and, accompanied by his dog, he rode to the castle. When they reached it they found the gate open. As he went in he saw men and animals all turned to stone. In the hall an old hag was sitting by the fire. When she saw him she pretended to tremble.

"Dear lord," said she, "bind your dog. He might bite me."

He said: "Do not be afraid. He will do you no harm."

He bent down to pat the dog, and at that moment the hag took her wand and struck him with it. He was turned to stone, and his horse and dog too.

The princess waited for her lord, but he did not return. She mourned for him, and the citizens, who loved their lord, were grieved at his loss.

Now, the other brother looked at his sword, and the sword began to rust; so he was sure that his brother was in trouble. He felt that he must help him, so he rode off in that direction and came to the town. The town was hung with black flags. As he rode through the streets the citizens saw him, and they thought he was their lord, for he had a horse and a dog just like their lord's horse and dog. When the princess saw him, she embraced him and said: "Where have you been so long, my dear husband?"

He said that he had lost his way in the forest and that he had fallen among robbers, and, since he had no choice, he had to pretend to be a robber too, and to promise to stay with them and to show them good hiding-places. The robbers, so he said, admitted him to be of their company, and he had not been able to escape before this.

Everybody was delighted, and the lord's brother was careful enough not to say that he was only the brother. But, whenever they went to bed, he put his sword between himself and the lady. The princess was troubled at this, and she tried to find different explanations for the conduct of her supposed husband. One morning, as he was looking out of the window, he saw that same castle, and he asked what castle it was.

She answered: "I have told you already that it is an enchanted castle, and that nobody who goes there ever returns."

So he thought: "It is surely there that my brother is."

He ordered his horse to be saddled and, without saying a word to anybody, he rode off to the castle. As soon as he entered the castle he saw his brother and his dog turned to stone. He saw, too, all the petrified knights and their horses, and the hag sitting and keeping up the fire.

He said: "You old hag, unless you bring my brother to life again I'll hew you in pieces with this sword of mine."

The hag knew that the sword had magical virtues, and so she said:

"Pray, sir, do not be angry with me. Take that box there and rub the ointment beneath his nose and he will come to life again."

"Curse you, you evil old hag; do it yourself, and instantly."

And he went and caught hold of her wand and struck her with it, and at once she was turned into stone. He had not meant to do that, for he did not know that the wand had such power. He took the box and rubbed the ointment beneath his brother's nose, and the brother came to life again. Then he anointed all the others who had been turned to stone, and they all came to life again. As for the hag, he left her there just as she was.

Then the brothers rode off to the princess. When she saw them, she did not know which of them was her husband, they were so like one another.

So she said: "What am I to do now? Which of you is my lord?"

They came before her and bade her choose the right one. But still she hesitated. So her husband went up to her and took her by the hand and said: "I am the right one and that is my brother."

He told her everything, and she was glad that her real husband had come again. So they lived happily together, and, as for the other brother, he went to seek his fortune elsewhere.

The Waternick

ONCE UPON A TIME there were two children, a boy and a girl. They only had a mother, who was a widow. One day their mother sent them to get some wood for the fire. Off they

went. The girl was just learning to knit, so she put a ball of wool in her pocket. They went on as far as they knew the way. Then suddenly they began to wonder whether they could find their way home.

The girl said: "I will bind the end of the thread to a tree, and so we shall be able to find our way back."

So they went on till the thread had all run out. Then they turned back, but they found that wild creatures had broken the thread. What were they to do? They wandered on till night fell, and then they saw that they would have to spend the night in the forest. They came to a pond, and they found that they could not go any farther. So they walked round the pond till the Waternick got hold of them. He took them with him, and there they were.

When he got home with them, his wife was waiting for him. Round the stove there were some shelves for vessels that they used for catching poor souls in. The Waternick and his wife were delighted with the children; they decided that they would employ them as servants, so Mrs. Waternick took charge of them. The children spent some years in this way and learned about everything under the water.

One day the Waternick went away to catch some human souls, and he gave orders to Mrs. Waternick not to leave the children alone. But the old hag fell asleep, and the children walked some distance from the hut, till they thought she would scold them, and so they returned home. But they meant to go farther the next day, if only the old hag went to sleep again. As soon as they were sure that she was asleep they ran out of the hut and went as far as they could.

The old hag woke up and cried out: "Where are you, children?"

She jumped to her feet and ran after them. They were within a few steps of getting safe away, when, alas! she overtook them. She took them back and forced them to work, and they had to stay at home besides.

When the Waternick came home, she told him all about it, and the Waternick said: "Never mind, I'll set them to work, and they won't have time to think about making their way home."

So in the morning he took them to the forest and gave them a wooden hatchet and a wooden saw and bade them, fell the trees.

"When they are all cut down, you shall go back again."

So the Waternick left them, and the children began the work at once. They took the saw and tried to cut down a tree. But the saw soon broke and they were done for. So they took the hatchet, and the hatchet split in two after one stroke. They began to cry.

"Things look bad for us," they said.

Since they saw that they could not help themselves, they stayed where they were, and presently they fell asleep. I don't know how long they had been sleeping. But it was already time to go back.

The Waternick came and asked: "Have you finished?"

They said that the hatchet and saw were only made of wood, and that both were broken. He took them home.

Next day the Waternick went about his work, while Mrs. Waternick was busy outside the hut. The children looked at the cups on the shelves. The cups were tilted up. So the girl lifted one of them. And she heard the words: "God speed you!" She lifted another, and the same greeting came again. So she kept on lifting the cups till she had lifted all of them. Human souls had been imprisoned under those cups. Now the hag came into the room and she saw that all the cups had been lifted. She began to curse, and she said that the children would certainly get a good thrashing when the old man came home.

The children often felt lonely; they thought of their mother and wondered if she were still alive, and what they could do to get away. So they decided that the next day, when the hag was sleeping, they would try how far they could get.

"If only we could get as far as home, it would be all right then."

In the morning the girl had to comb Mrs. Waternick's hair and dress her in her smart dress. When she had finished, Mrs. Waternick had a sleep. Now the children took to their heels; they were as quick as ravens, trying to get away before Mrs. Waternick should wake. Being swift of foot, they reached the shore. They leapt out and ran straight on again. Of course they heard the hag screeching behind them, but they were on dry land, so they thought: "We needn't care for anything now."

The hag soon stopped her pursuit. The children were tired, so they lay down under a tree in the forest and fell asleep. As they were sleeping, somebody woke them up. It was the forester. They told him that they were afraid of falling into the Waternick's hands again. But the forester told them not to be afraid, and asked how they came there. The children told him everything just as it had happened.

Now, the forester remembered that he had heard of a widow who had lost her children. So he thought that these must be the children. He said nothing, but he told his wife to get them some food, and asked the children to sit down and eat. The children thought the food was very nice, so he asked them what they were accustomed to eat. They said they were accustomed to eat flowers. So they ate plenty.

The forester decided to do all he could to get the children home. At last it was discovered where their mother lived, and so the children came back to her, and they lived with her until they died.

The Man Who Met Misery

ONCE UPON A TIME there lived a rich man, so rich that you might almost say he oozed gold. He had a son, and from his boyhood the lad was a real spendthrift, for he knew nothing about hard times. Yet he had often been told that there was Misery in the world. So when he was grown up, he thought: "Well, I'm sick of staying at home, so I'll go out into the world to see if I can meet Misery."

He told this to his father, and his father said at once: "Yes, you can go. If you stay at home, you'll soon turn into a lazy old woman. You'll get experience in the world, and that can't do you any harm."

So our Francis – that was his name, though really it doesn't matter very much what his name was – took everything he wanted and started off on his travels. So long as he had enough money, he was all right, he couldn't meet with Misery. But when his money was all spent – that's when everybody feels the pinch – he began to hang his head and his travels lost a good deal of their charm. But he told people his name and his father's name, and for a time they helped him. But at last he came into a country that was quite strange to him. There was a vast desert, through which he walked for a long time, and he began to feel hungry and thirsty, but there was no water – no, not so much as would moisten his tongue.

Now, as he went on his way, he saw a flight of stairs going down into a hole, and, without hesitating, down he went.

He came into a cellar, and there he saw a man lying on a table. It was an awfully big man, of the kind that used to be called ogres, and he was snoring like a circular saw.

Francis looked about him, and he saw all sorts of human bones lying about. He thought: "That's a nice mess. I expect the fellow's a man-eater, and he'll swallow me down like a currant. I'm done for now."

He would have liked to go away, but he was afraid to move. But he had a dagger, so he drew it from its sheath without making any noise, and tried to steal up to the ogre quietly. The ogre's head was lying on the table, so he pierced both his eyes with the dagger. The ogre sprang up, cursing horribly. He groped about him and found that he was totally blind.

Francis cleared the stairs in two jumps and off he ran, trying to get as far from the ogre as he could. But the ogre knew the place well and kept close on his heels.

"To think that a shrimp like that could make me suffer so!" he thought; and yet he found that, run as he would, he couldn't catch the lad. So he cried out: "Wait a bit, you worm! Since you're such a champion and have managed to tackle me, I'll give you something to remember me by."

As he said this, he flung a ring at the lad, and the jewel in it shone like flame. The lad heard the ring tinkle as he ran by, so he picked it up and put it on his finger. But as soon as the ring was on his finger, the giant called out: "Where are you, ring?" And the ring answered: "Here I am," and the ogre ran after the sound. Francis jumped on one side, but the ogre called out again, "Where are you?" and the ring answered: "Here!"

So it went on for some time, until Francis was so tired that his only thought was: "Well, if he kills me, he kills me." He tried to pull the ring off, but it clung tight, really cutting into the flesh, and the ogre was still following close on his heels. At last – there was no other choice, for the ring kept on calling out "Here I am" – Francis stretched out that finger, and the ogre broke it off with one grip. Off ran Francis, glad enough to get off with his life.

When he reached home, they asked him: "Did you meet Misery?"

"Indeed I did. I know what it is now. It gave me a nice run for it. It's an awful thing, and there's no joking with it."

Nine at a Blow

ONCE UPON A TIME there was a tailor, and, whenever he hadn't a job, he used to spend his time mending stockings. One day after dinner the table was covered with flies. The tailor struck at them with a stocking and killed nine of them at a blow.

As he hadn't any job in hand, he started out to see the world, and his belt had written on it "Nine at a blow." On his way he met a boy, who asked him to buy a finch from him. He bought it, put it in his knapsack, and went on his way. Then he came to a farm where the farmer's wife was making cheese. He asked her for something to eat, so she gave him some sour milk and a piece of Yorkshire cheese. The tailor drank the milk and put the cheese in his knapsack and went on his way. At last he reached a town. It was a hot day, so he lay down and fell asleep. Now, a giant happened to pass that way, and he saw written in golden letters: "Nine at a blow."

So he waked the tailor and asked him: "Have you really killed nine at a blow?"

The tailor answered that he had, and the giant said: "Let's have a trial which of us is the stronger. I'll cast a stone, and it will be an hour before it comes down."

The tailor said: "I'll cast a stone that won't come down at all."

So the giant cast a stone, and it was a full hour before it came down again. Instead of casting a stone, the tailor let the finch go, and, of course, it didn't come back again.

So the giant said: "Let's have another try. I'll crush a stone to powder."

The tailor said: "I'll squeeze water from a stone."

So the giant took a pebble and crushed it to powder. The tailor took the cheese and squeezed it till the water oozed out of it.

The giant gave in, and acknowledged that the tailor was the stronger of the two. So they went on together till they came to a cherry-tree growing near a meadow, and the cherries were ripe. They wanted to pick some of the cherries for themselves. So the tailor climbed the tree, but the giant simply bent down the top of the tree and began to pluck the cherries. When he had finished he let go, and the tailor was flung onto a heap of dry grass piled up in the meadow. So the tailor said: "If it hadn't been for my skill in flying, I should have broken my neck," and he promised to teach the giant how to fly.

So they went on their way again, and they came to a town. The town was all in mourning. They asked the reason, and they were told that a dragon had taken up his headquarters in the church and was killing the people. The king would give a thousand pounds to whoever could kill the dragon. So they told the king that they would kill the dragon.

They ordered a big hammer and a big pair of tongs to be made for them. When they were made, the giant took the tongs and he gave the hammer to the tailor to carry. But the tailor said: "Wouldn't it shame you if people should see us, each carrying such a trifle? Take both the things yourself."

When they came near the church door, the giant gave the hammer to the tailor, who stuck fast to it. Then the dragon came dashing out, and flung the tailor behind him, but the giant split him in twain. But the tailor protested:

"A nice mess you've made of it. I meant to take the dragon alive. We should have got more money for him so." Then he said: "Now I will teach you how to fly."

So they climbed up the church steeple, and the tailor said: "When I say 'One, two, three,' you must jump." And the giant jumped and broke his neck.

The tailor told the king that the dragon had killed the giant, so he pocketed the thousand pounds for himself.

A Clever Lass

ONCE UPON A TIME there was a shepherd. He used to pasture his sheep upon a hill, and one day he saw something glittering on the opposite hill. So he went there to see what it was. It was a golden mortar. He took it up and said to his daughter: "I will give this mortar to our king."

But she said: "Don't do that. If you give him the mortar, you won't have the pestle, and he is sure to ask for it, and then you will get into trouble."

But the shepherd thought that she was only a silly girl. He took the mortar, and, when he came before the king, he said: "Begging your pardon, Mr. King, I want to give you this mortar."

The king answered him roughly: "If you give me the mortar, I must have the pestle as well. Unless the pestle is here within three days, your life will be forfeit."

The shepherd began to lament: "My daughter was right when she said that when you had got the mortar you would want the pestle too. I wouldn't listen to her, so it serves me right."

"Have you such a clever daughter as that?" asked the king.

"Indeed I have," said the shepherd.

"Then tell your daughter that I will marry her, if she comes neither walking nor riding, clothed nor unclothed, neither by day nor by night, neither at noon nor in the morning. And I won't ask for the pestle either."

The shepherd went home and said: "You can get me out of this, if you go to Mr. King neither clothed nor unclothed," and the rest of it.

But the daughter wasn't a bit frightened. She came with the fall of dusk (and that was neither at noon nor in the morning); she dressed herself in fishing-nets; she took a goat, and she partly rode on the goat and partly she walked.

And when the king saw that she had only a fishing-net on, that she came with the approach of dusk, and that she was partly walking, partly riding on the goat, he was bound to marry her. But he said to her: "You will be my wife so long as you don't give advice to anybody; but if you do, you must part with me."

Well, she didn't give advice to anybody until one day there was a market in the town, and a farmer's mare had a foal at the market. The foal ran away to another farmer, who was there with a gelding, and the farmer said: "This foal belongs to me."

They went to law about it, and at last the matter came before the king. And the king, considering that every animal ought to run to its mother, decided that a gelding had had a foal.

The farmer who owned the mare went down the stairs, saying over and over again: "The gelding has foaled! the gelding has foaled!"

The queen heard him, and she said: "Man, you are talking nonsense."

So he told her that he had been at the market, that his mare had foaled, but the foal ran to another farmer who was there with a gelding. "And now," he said, "it has been decided that the gelding has foaled." So he thought there could be no mistake; at any rate, he couldn't help it.

When the queen heard this story she said: "To-morrow, my lord the king will go out for a stroll. Take a fishing-net, and begin fishing on the road in front of him. The king will ask you: 'Why are you fishing on a dry road?' And you must answer: 'Why not? it's as hopeful as expecting a gelding to foal.' But you must not say who gave you this advice."

So it was. As the king was walking along he saw the farmer fishing on the dry road. He asked him why he was fishing there.

"Why not?" said he, "it's as hopeful as expecting a gelding to foal."

The king at once began to rate the farmer. "That's not out of your own head," he said, and he kept at the farmer until he let the secret out.

So the king came home, summoned the queen, and said to her: "You have been with me for a long time, and you have given advice in spite of all, so you must go to-morrow. But I will allow you to take with you the thing you like best."

It was no good arguing. So the king invited all his courtiers and prepared a splendid banquet. When the banquet was finished, the queen said to the king: "Before we part, you must drink this glass of wine to my health," and she had put some opium into the wine on the sly.

The king drank it at a draught and fell asleep at once. A carriage was got ready, and the queen put the king in it and drove to her father's old hut. There she laid the king on the straw, and, when he woke up, he asked where he was.

"You are with me. Didn't you tell me that I could take the thing I liked best with me?"

The king saw how clever she was, and he said: "Now you can give advice to anybody you like."

And so they drove home again, and he was king and she queen again.

A Soldier and the Devil

A DISCHARGED SOLDIER WAS GOING HOME. He had only threepence in his pocket. As he was going through a forest he met a beggar. The beggar asked him for a penny. The soldier gave him one, and went on his way. Then he met another beggar. This beggar was very ill, and he asked the soldier for a penny. So the soldier gave him the other penny. Then he met a third beggar. This beggar was half-dead. The soldier took pity on him and gave him the third penny. Soon after he had left the forest our Lord appeared to him, and in return for those three pennies He granted him three boons. For the first boon

the soldier chose a pipe that should be full of tobacco whenever he wished, so that he might always have a smoke handy. The second boon he asked was that, if he wanted to put any one in his knapsack, they should be in it as soon as he said: "Leap into that knapsack." The third boon was that his purse should be full of gold coins whenever he knocked on it.

Our Lord said: "So be it!"

Soon afterwards he came to a mill and asked for a night's lodging. They said that they only had one room for themselves; the other one was haunted by a devil every midnight. But the soldier wasn't afraid. He said that they could leave him there alone; he didn't mind a bit.

He sat down at the table and played cards. When midnight came there was a terrible noise, and the devil appeared, sure enough. When he saw the soldier playing cards he grinned; he was sure he had him. So he sat down opposite him and began to play too. It was nearly one o'clock at last, time for him to go, so he caught hold of the soldier and tried to tear him in pieces. But he had no success. For the soldier said: "Leap into my knapsack," and the devil was in it. Then the soldier threw the sack with the devil in it under the bed, and went to sleep in the bed.

In the morning, as soon as he had got up, the millers went to see if the soldier was still alive. They were greatly surprised to find him all right. They said they would give him anything he wanted, but he wouldn't take anything. Off he went, and called at a blacksmith's. He told the blacksmith to give the devil in the sack a good hammering, and then he let the devil go.

After that he came into a town. He heard that there was a count's daughter there who was an accomplished cardplayer. She won everybody's money from them. He went to her palace and asked her if she would play with him. She was ready. So they played and played, but she couldn't win all his money from him, for his purse was always fuller than before. It was late by now and the lady was sick of the game, so he went to bed. He put the three precious gifts on the table, but when he got up in the morning they were gone; the lady had stolen them from him. He grieved over his bad luck, but it was no use, and he had to leave the palace.

As he went on his way, he saw a fine apple-tree by the side of the road with delicious apples on it. So he took an apple and ate half of it. Then he went on his way, but he was surprised to see that everybody who looked at him ran away from him. So he went to a well and saw that he had horns on his head; that came from his eating the apple. Back he went, and he found a pear-tree; he ate half of a pear and the horns fell off.

He thought that he would give the other half of the apple to the lady, and perhaps she would get horns too. So he went and gave her the half apple. She enjoyed it very well, but soon horns grew on her head. The count called together all the doctors and asked them to operate on the horns. But the more they cut at the horns the longer they grew. So the king proclaimed that she would marry the man who should rid her of the horns, but if he failed, his life should be forfeit. So the soldier came back and told the lady that he would rid her of the horns if she would give him his three treasures back. She agreed at once. So he gave her the other half of the pear; she ate it, and the horns fell off.

The soldier was quite happy now. One day he met Death, and he said to him: "Leap into my knapsack." And Death was immediately imprisoned in the knapsack.

The soldier was carrying Death about for some time, until at last the Lord appeared to him and told him he must not do that: he must let Death go, for people could not die, and there would soon be too many of them in the world. So he let Death go. He wanted to go to Heaven himself. But he went to Hell, and as he drew near Hell the devils closed the gate, they were so frightened of him. When he reached the gate of Heaven, he knocked. St. Peter opened the gate, but he wouldn't let him in. The soldier asked him to let him have just one peep, so that at least he might know what Heaven looked like.

Now, he remembered that he still had his soldier's cloak in his knapsack, so he took it out of the knapsack and threw it into Heaven. Then he jumped after it and sat down on it, and then he said he was sitting on his own property. He sat there for a full hundred years, though it only seemed a short time to him. But he couldn't come to an agreement with St. Peter on the case, so our Lord told him that he must first die, for no living people were admitted into Heaven. So the soldier had to leave the premises. He returned to this world, and afterwards he went to Heaven again, and there he is still, as right as rain.

The Golden Spinning Wheel

THERE WAS ONCE a poor woman who had twin daughters. The girls were exactly alike in face and feature but utterly different in disposition. Dobrunka was kind, industrious, obedient, and everything a good girl ought to be. Zloboha, her sister, was spiteful, disobedient, lazy, and proud. In fact, she had just about as many faults as a person could have. Yet strange to say the mother loved Zloboha much better and made everything easy for her.

They lived in a cottage a few miles from town. The cottage stood by itself in a little clearing in the woods. Hardly any one ever passed it except occasionally some man who had lost his way in the woods.

The mother put her favorite, Zloboha, out to service so that she might learn city ways, but she kept Dobrunka at home to do the housework and take care of the garden. Dobrunka always began the day by feeding the goats, then she prepared the breakfast, swept the kitchen, and when everything else was done she sat down at her spinning wheel and spun.

She seldom benefited from the yarn she spun so carefully, for her mother always sold it in town and spent the money on clothes for Zloboha. Yet Dobrunka loved her mother although she never had a kind word or a kind look from her the whole day long. She always obeyed her mother instantly and without a frown and no one ever heard her complain about all the work she had to do.

One day when her mother was going to town Dobrunka went part of the way with her, carrying her yarn wrapped up in a kerchief.

"Now see that you're not lazy while I'm away," her mother said, crossly.

"You know, mother, you never have to nag at me. Today when I finish the housework, I'll spin so industriously that you'll be more than satisfied when you get home."

She handed her yarn to her mother and went back to the cottage. Then when she had put the kitchen in order, she sat down to her wheel and began to spin. Dobrunka had a pretty voice, as pretty as any of the song-birds in the forest, and always when she was alone she sang. So today as she sat spinning she sang all the songs she knew, one after the other.

Suddenly she heard outside the trample of a horse. "Some one is coming," she thought to herself, "someone who has lost his way in the woods. I'll go see."

She got up from her wheel and peeped out through the small window. A young man was just dismounting from a spirited horse.

"Oh," thought Dobrunka to herself, "what a handsome young lord he is! How well his leather coat fits him! How well his cap with its white feather looks on his black hair! Ah, he is tying his horse and is coming in. I must slip back to my spinning."

The next moment the young man opened the door and stepped into the kitchen. All this happened a long time ago, you see, when there were no locks or bars on the doors, and there didn't have to be because nothing was ever stolen.

"Good day to you, my girl," the young man said to Dobrunka.

"Good day, sir," Dobrunka answered. "What is it, sir, you want?"

"Will you please get me a little water. I'm very thirsty."

"Certainly," Dobrunka said. "Won't you sit down while I'm getting it?"

She ran off, got the pitcher, rinsed it out, and drew some fresh water from the well.

"I wish I could give you something better, sir."

"Nothing could taste better than this," he said, handing her back the empty pitcher. "See, I have taken it all."

Dobrunka put the pitcher away and the young man, while her back was turned, slipped a leather bag, full of money, into the bed.

"I thank you for the drink," he said, as he rose to go. "I'll come again tomorrow if you'll let me."

"Come if you want to," Dobrunka said, modestly.

He took her hand, held it a moment, then leaped upon his horse and galloped off.

Dobrunka sat down again to her wheel and tried to work, but her mind wandered. The image of the young man kept rising before her eyes and I have to confess that, for an expert spinner, she broke her thread pretty often.

Her mother came home in the evening full of praises of Zloboha, who, she said, was growing prettier day by day. Everybody in town admired her and she was fast learning city ways and city manners. It was Zloboha this and Zloboha that for hours.

Finally the old woman remarked: "They say there was a great hunting party out today. Did you hear anything of it?"

"Oh, yes," Dobrunka said. "I forgot to tell you that a young huntsman stopped here to ask for a drink. He was handsomely dressed in leather. You know once when I was in town with you we saw a whole company of men in leather coats with white feathers in their caps. No doubt this young man belonged to the hunting party. When he had his drink, he jumped on his horse and rode off."

Dobrunka forgot to mention that he had taken her hand in parting and promised to come back next day.

When Dobrunka was preparing the bed for the night, the bag of money fell out. In great surprise she picked it up and handed it to her mother.

The old woman looked at her sharply.

"Dobrunka, who gave you all this money?"

"Nobody gave it to me, mother. Perhaps the huntsman slipped it into the bed. I don't know where else it could have come from."

The old woman emptied the bag on the table. They were all gold pieces.

"Good heavens, so much!" she murmured in amazement. "He must be a very rich young lord! Perhaps he saw how poor we were and thought to do a kind deed. May God grant him happiness!"

She gathered the money together and hid it in the chest.

Usually when Dobrunka went to bed after her day's work she fell asleep at once, but tonight she lay awake thinking of the handsome young rider. When she did at last fall asleep it was to dream of him. He was a powerful young lord, it seemed to her, in her dream. He lived in a great palace and she, Dobrunka, was his wife. She thought that they were giving a fine banquet to which all the nobles in the land had been invited. She and her husband arose from the table and went together into another room. He was about to put his arms about her and embrace her when suddenly a black cat sprang between them and buried its claws in Dobrunka's breast. Her heart's blood spurted out and stained her white dress. She cried out in fright and pain and the cry awoke her.

"What a strange dream," she thought to herself. "I wonder what it means. It began so beautifully but the cruel cat spoiled it all. I fear it bodes something ill."

In the morning when she got up, she was still thinking of it.

On other mornings it didn't take Dobrunka long to dress but this morning she was very slow. She shook out her fresh skirt again and again. She had the greatest trouble in putting on her bodice just right. She spent much time on her hair, into which she plaited the red ribbon that she usually kept for holidays. When at last she was dressed and ready to go about her household duties she looked very fresh and sweet.

As midday came, she found it hard to sit still at her wheel, but kept jumping up on any pretext whatever to run outdoors a moment to see if the young horseman was in sight.

At last she did see him at a distance and, oh, how she hurried back to her stool so that he would never think that she was watching for him.

He rode into the yard, tied his horse, and came into the cottage.

"Good day, Dobrunka," he said, speaking very gently and very respectfully.

Dobrunka's heart was beating so fast that she feared it would jump out of her body. Her mother was in the woods gathering fagots, so she was again alone with him. She managed to return his greeting and to ask him to sit down. Then she went back to her spinning.

The young man came over to her and took her hand.

"How did you sleep, Dobrunka?"

"Very well, sir."

"Did you dream?"

"Yes, I had a very strange dream."

"Tell me about it. I can explain dreams very well."

"But I can't tell this dream to you," Dobrunka said.

"Why not?"

"Because it's about you."

"That's the very reason you ought to tell me," the young man said.

He urged her and begged her until at last Dobrunka did tell him the dream.

"Well now," he said, "that dream of yours except the part about the cat can be realized easily enough."

Dobrunka laughed. "How could I ever become a fine lady?"

"By marrying me," the young man said.

Dobrunka blushed. "Now, sir, you are joking."

"No, Dobrunka, this is no joke. I really mean it. I came back this morning to ask you to marry me. Will you?"

Dobrunka was too surprised to speak, but when the young man took her hand she did not withdraw it.

Just then the old woman came in. The young man greeted her and without any delay declared his intentions. He said he loved Dobrunka and wished to make her his wife and that all he and Dobrunka were waiting for was the mother's consent.

"I have my own house," he added, "and am well able to take care of a wife. And for you too, dear mother, there will always be room in my house and at my table."

The old woman listened to all he had to say and then very promptly gave her blessing.

"Then, my dear one," the young man said to Dobrunka, "go back to your spinning and when you have spun enough for your wedding shift, I shall come for you."

He kissed her, gave his hand to her mother, and, springing on his horse, rode away.

From that time the old woman treated Dobrunka more kindly. She even went so far as to spend on Dobrunka a little of the money the young man had given them, but most of it, of course, went for clothes for Zloboha.

But in those happy days Dobrunka wasn't worrying about anything as unimportant as money. She sat at her wheel and spun away thinking all the while of her fine young lover. Time sped quickly and before she knew it she had spun enough for her wedding shift.

The very day she was finished her lover came. She heard the trample of his horse and ran out to meet him.

"Have you spun enough for your wedding shift?" he asked her as he took her to his heart.

"Yes," Dobrunka said, "I have."

"Then you can ride away with me this moment."

"This moment!" Dobrunka gasped. "Why so quickly?"

"It has to be, my dear one. Tomorrow I go off to war and want you to take my place at home. Then when I come back you'll be there to greet me as my wife."

"But what will my mother say to this?"

"She will have to consent."

They went into the cottage and spoke to the old woman. She was far from pleased with this arrangement, for she had worked out a very different plan in her mind. But what could she do? A rich young bridegroom always has his own way. So she hid her disappointment with a false smile and gave them her blessing.

Then the young man said to her: "Get your things together, mother, and follow Dobrunka, for I don't want her to be lonely while I'm gone. When you get to the city, go to the palace and ask for Dobromil. The people there will tell you where to go."

Dobrunka with tears streaming down her cheeks bid her mother good-by. Dobromil lifted her to the saddle in front of him and away they went like the wind.

The town was in great excitement. There was much hurrying to and fro as the troops were being put in readiness for the morrow. A crowd had gathered at the palace gates and as a young man came galloping up, holding in front of him a lady lovely as the day, the shout went up:

"Here he is! Here he is!"

The people in the courtyard took up the cry and as Dobromil rode through the gate all of them with one voice shouted out:

"Long live our beautiful queen! Long live our noble king!"

Dobrunka was struck with amazement.

"Are you really the king, Dobromil?" she asked, looking into his proud and happy face.

"Yes," he said. "Aren't you glad that I am?"

"I love you," Dobrunka said, "and so whatever you are makes no difference to me. But why did you deceive me?"

"I did not deceive you. I told you that your dream would be realized if you took me for your husband."

In those early times marriage was a simple affair. When a man and woman loved each other and their parents consented to their union, they were looked upon as married. So Dobromil now was able to present Dobrunka to his people as his wife.

There was great rejoicing, music played, and there was feasting and drinking in the banquet hall until dawn. The next day the young husband kissed his lovely bride farewell and rode off to war.

Left alone the young queen strayed through the magnificent palace like a lost lamb. She would have felt more at home rambling through the woods and awaiting the return of her husband in a little cottage than here where she was a lonely stranger. Yet she was not a stranger long, for within half a day she had won every heart by her sweetness and goodness.

The next day she sent for her mother and the old woman soon arrived bringing with her Dobrunka's spinning wheel. So now there was no more excuse for loneliness.

Dobrunka supposed that her mother would be made very happy to find what good fortune had befallen her daughter. The old woman pretended she was, but in her heart she was furious that a king had married Dobrunka and not Zloboha.

After a few days she said, very artfully, to Dobrunka: "I know, my dear daughter, that you think your sister, Zloboha, was not always kind to you in times past. She's sorry now and I want you to forgive her and invite her here to the palace."

"I should have asked her before this," said Dobrunka, "but I didn't suppose she wanted to come. If you wish it, we'll go for her at once."

"Yes, dear daughter, I do wish it."

So the queen ordered the carriage and off they went to fetch Zloboha. When they came to the edge of the woods they alighted and ordered the coachman to await them there. They went on afoot to the cottage where Zloboha was expecting them.

Zloboha came running out to meet them. She threw her arms about her sister's neck and kissed her and wished her happiness. Then the wicked sister and the wicked mother led poor unsuspecting Dobrunka into the house. Once inside Zloboha took a knife that she had ready and struck Dobrunka. Then they cut off Dobrunka's hands and feet, gouged out her eyes, and hid her poor mutilated body in the woods. Zloboha and her mother wrapped up the hands and the feet and the eyes to carry them back with them to the palace because they believed that it would be easier for them to deceive the king if they had with them something that had belonged to Dobrunka.

Then Zloboha put on Dobrunka's clothes and she and her mother rode back to town in the carriage and nobody could tell that she wasn't Dobrunka. In the palace the attendants soon whispered to each other that their mistress was kinder to them at first, but they suspected nothing.

In the meantime poor Dobrunka, who was not quite dead, had been found by a hermit and carried by him to a cave. She awoke to feel a kind hand soothing her wounds and putting some reviving drops between her lips. Of course, she could not see who it was, for she had no eyes. As she regained consciousness she remembered what had happened and began bitterly to upbraid her unnatural mother and her cruel sister.

"Be quiet. Do not complain," a low voice said. "All will yet be well."

"How can all be well," wept poor Dobrunka, "when I have no eyes and no feet and no hands? I shall never again see the bright sun and the green woods. I shall never again hold in my arms my beloved Dobromil. Nor shall I be able to spin fine flax for his shirts! Oh, what did I ever do to you, wicked mother, or to you, cruel sister, that you have done this to me?"

The hermit went to the entrance of the cave and called three times. Soon a boy came running in answer to the call.

"Wait here till I come back," the hermit said.

He returned in a short time with a golden spinning wheel in his arms. He said to the boy:

"My son, take this spinning wheel to town to the king's palace. Sit down in the courtyard near the gate and if any one asks you for how much you will sell the wheel, say: 'For two eyes.' Unless you are offered two eyes for it bring it back."

The boy took the spinning wheel and carried it to town as the hermit directed. He went to the palace and sat down in the courtyard near the gate, just as Zloboha and her mother were returning from a walk.

"Look, mother!" Zloboha cried. "What a gorgeous spinning wheel! I could spin on that myself! Wait. I'll ask whether it's for sale."

She went over to the boy and asked him would he sell the spinning wheel.

"Yes," he said, "if I get what I want."

"What do you want?"

"I want two eyes."

"Two eyes?"

"Yes, two eyes. My father told me to accept nothing for it but two eyes. So I can't sell it for money."

The longer Zloboha looked at the spinning wheel the more beautiful it seemed to her and the more she wanted it. Suddenly she remembered Dobrunka's eyes that she had hidden away.

"Mother," she said, "as a queen I ought to have something no one else has. When the king comes home he will want me to spin, and just think how lovely I should look sitting at this golden wheel. Now we've got those eyes of Dobrunka's. Let us exchange them for the golden spinning wheel. We'll still have the hands and feet."

The mother, who was as foolish as the daughter, agreed. So Zloboha got the eyes and gave them to the boy for the spinning wheel.

The boy hurried back to the forest and handed the eyes to the hermit. The old man took them and gently put them into place. Instantly Dobrunka could see.

The first thing she saw was the old hermit himself with his tall spare figure and long white beard. The last rays of the setting sun shone through the opening of the cave and lighted up his grave and gentle face. He looked to Dobrunka like one of God's own saints.

"How can I ever repay you?" she said, "for all your loving kindness? Oh, that I could cover your hands with kisses!"

"Be quiet, my child," the old man said. "If you are patient all will yet be well."

He went out and soon returned with some delicious fruit on a wooden plate. This he carried over to the bed of leaves and moss upon which Dobrunka was lying and with his own hands he fed Dobrunka as a mother would feed her helpless child. Then he gave her a drink from a wooden cup.

Early the next morning the hermit again called three times and the boy came running at once. This time the hermit handed him a golden distaff and said:

"Take this distaff and go to the palace. Sit down in the courtyard near the gate. If any one asks you what you want for the distaff, say two feet and don't exchange it for anything else."

Zloboha was standing at a window of the palace looking down into the courtyard when she saw the boy with a golden distaff.

"Mother!" she cried. "Come and see! There's that boy again sitting near the gate and this time he has a golden distaff!"

Mother and daughter at once went out to question the boy.

"What do you want for the distaff?" Zloboha asked.

"Two feet," the boy said.

"Two feet?"

"Yes, two feet."

"Tell me, what will your father do with two feet?"

"I don't know. I never ask my father what he does with anything. But whatever he tells me to do, I do. That is why I can't exchange the distaff for anything but two feet."

"Listen, mother," Zloboha said, "now that I have a golden spinning wheel, I ought to have a golden distaff to go with it. You know we have those two feet of Dobrunka's hidden away. What if I gave them to the boy? We shall still have Dobrunka's hands."

"Well, do as you please," the old woman said.

So Zloboha went and got Dobrunka's feet, wrapped them up, and gave them to the boy in exchange for the distaff. Delighted with her bargain, Zloboha went to her chamber and the boy hurried back to the forest.

He gave the feet to the hermit and the old man carried them at once inside the cave. Then he rubbed Dobrunka's wounds with some healing salve and stuck on the feet. Dobrunka wanted to jump up from the couch and walk but the old man restrained her.

"Lie quiet where you are until you are all well and then I'll let you get up."

Dobrunka knew that whatever the old hermit said was for her good, so she rested as he ordered.

On the third morning the hermit called the boy and gave him a golden spindle.

"Go to the palace again," he said, "and today offer this spindle for sale. If any one asks you what you want for the spindle, say two hands. Don't accept anything else."

The boy took the golden spindle and when he reached the palace and sat down in the courtyard near the gate, Zloboha ran up to him at once.

"What do you want for that spindle?" she asked.

"Two hands," the boy said.

"It's a strange thing you won't sell anything for money."

"I have to ask what my father tells me to ask."

Zloboha was in a quandary. She wanted the golden spindle, for it was very beautiful. It would go well with the spinning wheel and would be something to be proud of. Yet she didn't want to be left without anything that had belonged to Dobrunka.

"But really, mother," she whined, "I don't see why I have to keep something of Dobrunka's so that Dobromil will love me as he loved her. I'm sure I'm as pretty as Dobrunka ever was."

"Well," said the old woman, "it would be better if you kept them. I've often heard that's a good way to guard a man's love. However, do as you like."

For a moment Zloboha was undecided. Then, tossing her head, she ran and got the hands and gave them to the boy.

Zloboha took the spindle and, delighted with her bargain, carried it into her chamber where she had the wheel and distaff. The old woman was a little troubled, for she feared Zloboha had acted foolishly. But Zloboha, confident of her beauty and her ability to charm the king, only laughed at her.

As soon as the boy had delivered the hands to the hermit, the old man carried them into the cave. Then he anointed the wounds on Dobrunka's arms with the same healing salve that he used before, and stuck on the hands.

As soon as Dobrunka could move them she jumped up from the couch and, falling at the hermit's feet, she kissed the hands that had been so good to her.

"A thousand thanks to you, my benefactor!" she cried with tears of joy in her eyes. "I can never repay you, I know that, but ask of me anything I can do and I'll do it."

"I ask nothing," the old man said, gently raising her to her feet. "What I did for you I would do for any one. I only did my duty. So say no more about it. And now, my child, farewell. You are to stay here until some one comes for you. Have no concern for food. I shall send you what you need."

Dobrunka wanted to say something to him, but he disappeared and she never saw him again.

Now she was able to run out of the cave and look once more upon God's green world. Now for the first time in her life she knew what it meant to be strong and well. She threw herself on the ground and kissed it. She hugged the slender birches and danced around them, simply bursting with love for every living thing. She reached out longing hands towards the town and would probably have gone there running all the distance but she remembered the words of the old hermit and knew that she must stay where she was.

Meanwhile strange things were happening at the palace. Messengers brought word that the king was returning from war and there was great rejoicing on every side. The king's own household was particularly happy, for service under the new mistress was growing more unpleasant every day. As for Zloboha and her mother, it must be confessed that they were a little frightened over the outcome of their plot.

Finally the king arrived. Zloboha with smiling face went to meet him. He took her to his heart with great tenderness and from that moment Zloboha had no fear that he would recognize her.

A great feast was at once prepared, for the king had brought home with him many of his nobles to rest and make merry after the hardships of war.

Zloboha as she sat at Dobromil's side could not take her eyes off him. The handsome young soldier caught her fancy and she was rejoiced that she had put Dobrunka out of the way.

When they finished feasting, Dobromil asked her: "What have you been doing all this time, my dear Dobrunka? I'm sure you've been spinning."

"That's true, my dear husband," Zloboha said in a flattering tone. "My old spinning wheel got broken, so I bought a new one, a lovely golden one."

"You must show me it at once," the king said, and he took Zloboha's arm and led her away.

He went with her to her chamber where she had the golden spinning wheel and she took it out and showed it to him. Dobromil admired it greatly.

"Sit down, Dobrunka," he said, "and spin. I should like to see you again at the distaff."

Zloboha at once sat down behind the wheel. She put her foot to the treadle and started the wheel. Instantly the wheel sang out and this is what it sang:

> *"Master, master, don't believe her!*
> *She's a cruel and base deceiver!*
> *She is not your own sweet wife!*
> *She destroyed Dobrunka's life!"*

Zloboha sat stunned and motionless while the king looked wildly about to see where the song came from.

When he could see nothing, he told her to spin some more. Trembling, she obeyed. Hardly had she put her foot to the treadle when the voice again sang out:

> *"Master, master, don't believe her!*
> *She's a cruel and base deceiver!*
> *She has killed her sister good*
> *And hid her body in the wood!"*

Beside herself with fright, Zloboha wanted to flee the spinning wheel, but Dobromil restrained her. Suddenly her face grew so hideous with fear that Dobromil saw she was not his own gentle Dobrunka. With a rough hand he forced her back to the stool and in a stern voice ordered her to spin.

Again she turned the fatal wheel and then for the third time the voice sang out:

> *"Master, master, haste away!*
> *To the wood without delay!*
> *In a cave your wife, restored,*
> *Yearns for you, her own true lord!"*

At those words Dobromil released Zloboha and ran like mad out of the chamber and down into the courtyard where he ordered his swiftest horse to be saddled instantly. The attendants, frightened by his appearance, lost no time and almost at once Dobromil was on his horse and flying over hill and dale so fast that the horse's hoofs scarcely touched the earth.

When he reached the forest he did not know where to look for the cave. He rode straight into the wood until a white doe crossed his path. Then the horse in fright plunged to one side and pushed through bushes and undergrowth to the base of a big rock. Dobromil dismounted and tied the horse to a tree.

He climbed the rock and there he saw something white gleaming among the trees. He crept forward cautiously and suddenly found himself in front of a cave. Imagine then his joy, when he enters and finds his own dear wife Dobrunka.

As he kisses her and looks into her sweet gentle face he says: "Where were my eyes that I was deceived for an instant by your wicked sister?"

"What have you heard about my sister?" asked Dobrunka, who as yet knew nothing of the magic spinning wheel.

So the king told her all that had happened and she in turn told him what had befallen her.

"And from the time the hermit disappeared," she said in conclusion, "the little boy has brought me food every day."

They sat down on the grass and together they ate some fruit from the wooden plate. When they rose to go they took the wooden plate and the cup away with them as keepsakes.

Dobromil seated his wife in front of him on the horse and sped homewards with her. All his people were at the palace gate waiting to tell him what had happened in his absence.

It seems that the devil himself had come and before their very eyes had carried off his wife and mother-in-law. They looked at each other in amazement as Dobromil rode up with what seemed to be the same wife whom the devil had so recently carried off.

Dobromil explained to them what had happened and with one voice they called down punishment on the head of the wicked sister.

The golden spinning wheel had vanished. So Dobrunka hunted out her old one and set to work at once to spin for her husband's shirts. No one in the kingdom had such fine shirts as Dobromil and no one was happier.

The Natural World

THE STORIES in this volume are all of Czech, Moravian, and Slovak origin, and are to be found in many versions in the books of folktales collected by Erben, Nemcova, Kulda, Dobsinsky, Rimavsky, Benes-Trebizsky, and Miksicek among others.

Some of the stories in this section – such as Nemcova's very beautiful 'The Twelve Months' and Erben's spirited 'Zlatovlaska the Golden-haired' – are in such definitive form that it feels as though they have been told for the very last time. But variants of most of the tales are, of course, to be found in other countries. Grimm's 'The White Snake', for instance, is a variant of 'Zlatovlaska'.

The Twelve Months

ONCE UPON A TIME there lived a mother who had two daughters. One was her own child, the other her stepdaughter. She was very fond of her own daughter, but she would not so much as look at her stepdaughter. The only reason was that Maruša, the stepdaughter, was prettier than her own daughter, Holena. The gentle-hearted Maruša did not know how beautiful she was, and so she could never make out why her mother was so cross with her whenever she looked at her. She had to do all the housework, tidying up the cottage, cooking, washing, and sewing, and then she had to take the hay to the cow and look after her. She did all this work alone, while Holena spent the time adorning herself and lazing about. But Maruša liked work, for she was a patient girl, and when her mother scolded and rated her, she bore it like a lamb. It was no good, however, for they grew crueller and crueller every day, only because Maruša was growing prettier and Holena uglier every day.

At last the mother thought: "Why should I keep a pretty stepdaughter in my house? When the lads come courting here, they will fall in love with Maruša and they won't look at Holena."

From that moment the stepmother and her daughter were constantly scheming how to get rid of poor Maruša. They starved her and they beat her. But she bore it all, and in spite of all she kept on growing prettier every day. They invented torments that the cruellest of men would never have thought of.

One day – it was in the middle of January – Holena felt a longing for the scent of violets.

"Go, Maruša, and get me some violets from the forest; I want to wear them at my waist and to smell them," she said to her sister.

"Great heavens! sister. What a strange notion! Who ever heard of violets growing under the snow?" said poor Maruša.

"You wretched tatterdemalion! how dare you argue when I tell you to do something? Off you go at once, and if you don't bring me violets from the forest I'll kill you!" said Holena threateningly.

The stepmother caught hold of Maruša, turned her out of the door, and slammed it to after her. She went into the forest weeping bitterly. The snow lay deep, and there wasn't a human footprint to be seen. Maruša wandered about for a long time, tortured by hunger and trembling with cold. She begged God to take her from the world.

At last she saw a light in the distance. She went towards the glow, and came at last to the top of a mountain. A big fire was burning there, and round the fire were twelve stones with twelve men sitting on them. Three of them had snow-white beards, three were not so old, and three were still younger. The three youngest were the handsomest of them all. They were not speaking, but all sitting silent. These twelve men were the twelve months. Great January sat highest of all; his hair and beard were as white as snow, and in his hand he held a club.

Maruša was frightened. She stood still for a time in terror, but, growing bolder, she went up to them and said: "Please, kind sirs, let me warm my hands at your fire. I am trembling with the cold."

Great January nodded, and asked her: "Why have you come here, my dear little girl? What are you looking for?"

"I am looking for violets," answered Maruša.

"This is no time to be looking for violets, for everything is covered with snow," answered Great January.

"Yes, I know; but my sister Holena and my stepmother said that I must bring them some violets from the forest. If I don't bring them, they'll kill me. Tell me, fathers, please tell me where I can find them."

Great January stood up and went to one of the younger months – it was March – and, giving him the club, he said: "Brother, take the high seat."

March took the high seat upon the stone and waved the club over the fire. The fire blazed up, the snow began to melt, the trees began to bud, and the ground under the young beech-trees was at once covered with grass and the crimson daisy buds began to peep through the grass. It was springtime. Under the bushes the violets were blooming among their little leaves, and before Maruša had time to think, so many of them had sprung up that they looked like a blue cloth spread out on the ground.

"Pick them quickly, Maruša!" commanded March.

Maruša picked them joyfully till she had a big bunch. Then she thanked the months with all her heart and scampered merrily home.

Holena and the stepmother wondered when they saw Maruša bringing the violets. They opened the door to her, and the scent of violets filled all the cottage.

"Where did you get them?" asked Holena sulkily.

"They are growing under the bushes in a forest on the high mountains."

Holena put them in her waistband. She let her mother smell them, but she did not say to her sister: "Smell them."

Another day she was lolling near the stove, and now she longed for some strawberries. So she called to her sister and said: "Go, Maruša, and get me some strawberries from the forest."

"Alas! dear sister, where could I find any strawberries? Who ever heard of strawberries growing under the snow?" said Maruša.

"You wretched little tatterdemalion, how dare you argue when I tell you to do a thing? Go at once and get me the strawberries, or I'll kill you!"

The stepmother caught hold of Maruša and pushed her out of the door and shut it after her. Maruša went to the forest weeping bitterly. The snow was lying deep, and there wasn't a human footprint to be seen anywhere. She wandered about for a long time, tortured by hunger and trembling with cold. At last she saw the light she had seen the other day. Overjoyed, she went towards it. She came to the great fire with the twelve months sitting round it.

"Please, kind sirs, let me warm my hands at the fire. I am trembling with cold."

Great January nodded, and asked her: "Why have you come again, and what are you looking for here?"

"I am looking for strawberries."

"But it is winter now, and strawberries don't grow on the snow," said January.

"Yes, I know," said Maruša sadly; "but my sister Holena and my stepmother bade me bring them some strawberries, and if I don't bring them, they will kill me. Tell me, fathers, tell me, please, where I can find them."

Great January arose. He went over to the month sitting opposite to him – it was June – and handed the club to him, saying: "Brother, take the high seat."

June took the high seat upon the stone and swung the club over the fire. The fire shot up, and its heat melted the snow in a moment. The ground was all green, the trees were covered with leaves, the birds began to sing, and the forest was filled with all kinds of flowers. It was summer. The ground under the bushes was covered with white starlets, the starry blossoms were turning into strawberries every minute. They ripened at once, and before Maruša had time to think, there were so many of them that it looked as though blood had been sprinkled on the ground.

"Pick them at once, Maruša!" commanded June.

Maruša picked them joyfully till she had filled her apron full. Then she thanked the months with all her heart and scampered merrily home. Holena and the stepmother wondered when they saw Maruša bringing the strawberries. Her apron was full of them. They ran to open the door for her, and the scent of the strawberries filled the whole cottage.

"Where did you pick them?" asked Holena sulkily.

"There are plenty of them growing under the young beech-trees in the forest on the high mountains."

Holena took the strawberries, and went on eating them till she could eat no more. So did the stepmother too, but they didn't say to Maruša: "Here is one for you."

When Holena had enjoyed the strawberries, she grew greedy for other dainties, and so on the third day she longed for some red apples.

"Maruša, go into the forest and get me some red apples," she said to her sister.

"Alas! sister dear, how am I to get apples for you in winter?" protested Maruša.

"You wretched little tatterdemalion, how dare you argue when I tell you to do a thing? Go to the forest at once, and if you don't bring me the apples I will kill you!" threatened Holena.

The stepmother caught hold of Maruša and pushed her out of the door and shut it after her. Maruša went to the forest weeping bitterly. The snow was lying deep; there wasn't a human footprint to be seen anywhere. But she didn't wander about this time. She ran straight to the top of the mountain where the big fire was burning. The twelve months were sitting round the fire; yes, there they certainly were, and Great January was sitting on the high seat.

"Please, kind sirs, let me warm my hands at the fire. I am trembling with cold."

Great January nodded, and asked her: "Why have you come here, and what are you looking for?"

"I am looking for red apples."

"It is winter now, and red apples don't grow in winter," answered January.

"Yes, I know," said Maruša sadly; "but my sister and my stepmother, too, bade me bring them some red apples from the forest. If I don't bring them, they will kill me. Tell me, father, tell me, please, where I could find them."

Great January rose up. He went over to one of the older months – it was September. He handed the club to him and said: "Brother, take the high seat."

Month September took the high seat upon the stone and swung the club over the fire. The fire began to burn with a red flame, the snow began to melt. But the trees were not covered with leaves; the leaves were wavering down one after the other, and the cold wind was driving them to and fro over the yellowing ground. This time Maruša did not see so many flowers. Only red pinks were blooming on the hillside, and meadow saffrons were flowering in the valley. High fern and thick ivy were growing under the young beech-trees. But Maruša was only looking for red apples, and at last she saw an apple-tree with red apples hanging high among its branches.

"Shake the tree at once, Maruša!" commanded the month.

Right gladly Maruša shook the tree, and one apple fell down. She shook it a second time, and another apple fell down.

"Now, Maruša, run home quickly!" shouted the month.

Maruša obeyed at once. She picked up the apples, thanked the months with all her heart, and ran merrily home.

Holena and the stepmother wondered when they saw Maruša bringing the apples. They ran to open the door for her, and she gave them two apples.

"Where did you get them?" asked Holena.

"There are plenty of them in the forest on the high mountain."

"And why didn't you bring more? Or did you eat them on the way home?" said Holena harshly.

"Alas! sister dear, I didn't eat a single one. But when I had shaken the tree once, one apple fell down, and when I shook it a second time, another apple fell down, and they wouldn't let me shake it again. They shouted to me to go straight home," protested Maruša.

Holena began to curse her: "May you be struck to death by lightning!" and she was going to beat her.

Maruša began to cry bitterly, and she prayed to God to take her to Himself, or she would be killed by her wicked sister and her stepmother. She ran away into the kitchen.

Greedy Holena stopped cursing and began to eat the apple. It tasted so delicious that she told her mother she had never tasted anything so nice in all her life. The stepmother liked it too. When they had finished, they wanted some more.

"Mother, give me my fur coat. I'll go to the forest myself. That ragged little wretch would eat them all up again on her way home. I'll find the place all right, and I'll shake them all down, however they shout at me."

Her mother tried to dissuade her, but it was no good. She took her fur coat, wrapped a cloth round her head, and off she went to the forest. Her mother stood on the threshold, watching to see how Holena would manage to walk in the wintry weather.

The snow lay deep, and there wasn't a human footprint to be seen anywhere. Holena wandered about for a long time, but the desire of the sweet apple kept driving her on. At last she saw a light in the distance.

She went towards it, and climbed to the top of the mountain where the big fire was burning, and round the fire on twelve stones the twelve months were sitting. She was terrified at first, but she soon recovered. She stepped up to the fire and stretched out her hands to warm them, but she didn't say as much as "By your leave" to the twelve months; no, she didn't say a single word to them.

"Why have you come here, and what are you looking for?" asked Great January crossly.

"Why do you want to know, you old fool? It's no business of yours," replied Holena angrily, and she turned away from the fire and went into the forest.

Great January frowned and swung the club over his head. The sky grew dark in a moment, the fire burned low, the snow began to fall as thick as if the feathers had been shaken out of a down quilt, and an icy wind began to blow through the forest. Holena couldn't see one step in front of her; she lost her way altogether, and several times she fell into snowdrifts. Then her limbs grew weak and began slowly to stiffen. The snow kept on falling and the icy wind blew more icily than ever. Holena began to curse Maruša and the Lord God. Her limbs began to freeze, despite her fur coat.

Her mother was waiting for Holena; she kept on looking out for her, first at the window, then outside the door, but all in vain.

"Does she like the apples so much that she can't leave them, or what is the matter? I must see for myself where she is," decided the stepmother at last. So she put on her fur coat, she wrapped a shawl round her head, and went out to look for Holena. The snow was lying deep; there wasn't a human footprint to be seen; the snow fell fast, and the icy wind was blowing through the forest.

Maruša had cooked the dinner, she had seen to the cow, and yet Holena and her mother did not come back. "Where are they staying so long?" thought Maruša, as she sat down to work at the distaff. The spindle was full already and it was quite dark in the room, and yet Holena and the stepmother had not come back.

"Alas, Lord! what has come to them?" cried Maruša, peering anxiously through the window. The sky was bright and the earth was all glittering, but there wasn't a human soul to be seen.... Sadly she shut the window; she crossed herself, and prayed for her sister and her mother.... In the morning she waited with breakfast, she waited with dinner; but however much she waited, it was no good. Neither her mother nor her sister ever came back. Both of them were frozen to death in the forest.

So good Maruša inherited the cottage, a piece of ploughland and the cow. She married a kind husband, and they both lived happily ever after.

Three Doves

ACERTAIN MERCHANT DIED. His son was nineteen years old at the time. He said to his mother: "Mother dear, I'm going to try my luck in the world."

His mother answered: "Go, dear son, but don't stay long there, for I am old, and should like some help in my old age." She fitted him out for the journey, and said good-bye to him.

Out into the world went the son, and he travelled on till he came into a forest. He had been going through it for three days, and no end appeared. On the third day he kept on and came at last to a cottage. He went into the cottage and he saw a horrible being seated on a stool. The fellow asked him where he was going.

"I don't know where I am going. I'm seeking my fortune in some service."

"Well, if you like, you can enter my service."

The lad was very hungry, so he took service with the other.

His master said to him: "You must serve me for a year at least."

So he served him for a year. He was treated very well, and he was a faithful servant to his master. The master was a sorcerer, but he didn't do any harm to the lad. He had a big pond, and three doves used to come there to bathe. Each of them had three golden feathers. These three doves were three enchanted princesses.

When the year's service was ended, the sorcerer said: "What wages shall I give you?"

The lad said he left it to him.

"You're a good lad," said the sorcerer. "Come with me to my cellar and take as much money as you like, gold or silver, just as you wish."

So the lad took as much as he could carry, and the sorcerer gave him one of the three doves too, saying:

"When you get home, if you haven't got a house of your own, have one built, and then pluck those three feathers out of the dove, and hide them away so carefully that no human eye can see them. The dove will turn into a lovely princess and you may marry her."

So he took the dove and returned home. He had a house built and made a secret place in one of the walls for the three feathers. When he plucked out the feathers the dove became a beautiful princess, but she did not know where the feathers were. But his mother knew quite well, for he had told her all and showed her where the feathers were hidden.

When they had been living together for three years he went a-hunting one day with another lord, and his mother stayed at home with her daughter-in-law. The mother said to her: "Dear daughter-in-law, I can't tell you how beautiful I think you. If one were to search the whole world through, one couldn't find so beautiful a woman."

The daughter-in-law answered: "Dear lady, the beauty I have now is nothing to what I should have had I but one of my golden feathers."

The mother went straight off, fetched one of the feathers, and gave it to her.

She thrust it into her skin, and she was immediately far more beautiful than before. The mother kept looking at her, and said: "If you had the others as well, you would be even more beautiful." Then she fetched the other two feathers and gave them to her.

She thrust them into her skin, and behold! she was a dove again. She flew off through the window, thanking her mother-in-law: "Thank you, dearest mother, for giving me these three feathers. I will wait a little for my husband, to say good-bye to him."

So she perched on the roof to wait till her husband should return from the forest.

Now, the husband's nose fell to bleeding violently. He grew frightened, and began to wonder what great misfortune had befallen him at home. He mounted his horse and hastened home. As he was approaching the door the dove called out: "Good-bye, dear husband. I thank you for your true love, but you will never see me more."

Then the dove flew away, and the husband began to weep and to wail. Of course, he was very angry with his mother, and he decided to go away again and follow wherever his eyes might lead him. So he started off, and he went back to the sorcerer in whose service he had been before. As soon as he entered the sorcerer said:

"Aha! you have not followed my advice. I won't help you this time; the three doves are gone from here. But go to my brother, for all the birds and animals are under his power, and perhaps some of them might know where the doves are. I will give you a ball, and when you roll it three times, you will get there this evening. You must ask him whether he knows anything about the doves, and you must tell him, too, that I sent you to him."

The lad thanked him heartily and went on his way. He rolled the ball thrice and reached the other brother's by evening. He told him that his brother had asked to be remembered kindly to him, and then he asked whether he knew where the doves that used to bathe in his brother's pond were.

The brother answered: "My good lad, I know nothing at all about them. You must wait till morning. All the birds and animals are under my power, and if they know anything about it, it will be all right."

In the morning they went to the forest. The brother blew a whistle, and instantly swarms of birds gathered round, asking what was their master's will.

He said: "Tell me, does any one of you know about those three golden doves which used to bathe in my brother's pond?"

None of them knew, so he blew his whistle again and all manner of animals gathered round him: bears, lions, squirrels, wolves, every kind of wild animal, and they asked what was their master's will.

He said: "I would know whether any one of you knows anything about three golden doves which used to bathe in my brother's pond."

None of them knew. So he said:

"My dear lad, I cannot help you any more in this matter, but I have another brother, and, if he cannot tell you anything about them, then you will never hear of them any more. He dwells twice seventy miles from here, and all the devils of Hell are subjected to him. I will give you another ball like the one you had yesterday, and, when you have rolled it thrice, you will get there before evening."

He rolled the ball thrice and got there the same evening. The sorcerer was sitting in his garden on the grass. His hair was all dishevelled like a mop, his paunch was bare like a pail, his nose reached to his middle, and was as bare as a stick – in fact, his appearance was terrible.

The lad was terrified, but the sorcerer said: "Don't be frightened, my boy; though I look so hideous, yet I have a good heart. What do you want?"

"I have come from your brother to ask whether you can tell me about the three doves which used to bathe in your brother's pond."

"My dear lad, I know nothing about them, but as soon as you get up in the morning I will call my apprentices, to find if any one of them knows anything about the doves."

In the morning they got up and went into the forest. The sorcerer blew a whistle, and at once hosts of devils appeared, such a multitude that they darkened the whole forest.

The lad was frightened, but the sorcerer said: "Don't be afraid; not a hair of your head shall be harmed."

The devils asked what was their master's will.

He said: "Does any one of you know anything, about the three doves which used to bathe in my brother's pond?"

None of them knew anything. The sorcerer looked about him and asked: "Where is the lame one?"

The lame one had been left behind, but he was hurrying up for fear he should be too late. He came and asked what was his master's will. The sorcerer answered: "I want to find out whether you know anything about those three doves that used to bathe in my brother's pond."

"Of course I know about them, for I have been driving them before me. They are bathing in the Red Sea now."

The sorcerer said: "You must take up this man and carry him as far as their gold-roofed palace," and he took the lad aside and whispered in his ear:

"When the devil asks you how quick he is to take you, if he says: 'As quickly as the wind blows?' say 'No'; and if he says, 'As quickly as the step goes?' say 'No' again. But if he says, 'As quickly as the air goes?' say 'Even so.' If your cap falls, do not look after it, and don't tell the devil about it, or he will let you fall and won't carry you the palace. When you are seven miles from the palace you will see it, and the devil will ask you if you see it; but shut your eyes tight and say that you can't see it. When you are three miles from it, you will see it quite plainly, and he will ask you again whether you see it. But you must shut your eyes tight and say that you can't see it. Then you will be above the palace roof, and he will ask you again whether you see it. You must say again that you can't see it, or he will let you drop on the roof and you won't be able to get down."

The devil took the man and flew with him as the air goes. When they were seven miles from the palace, the devil asked: "Do you see the palace now? It is quite plain to see now."

The lad shut his eyes tight and said that he couldn't see it. So they flew on, and when they were three miles from the castle the devil asked him did he see it now. He shut his eyes tight and said that he couldn't see it. When they were right over the roof, the devil asked: "Surely you must see it now; we are just over the roof."

But he shut his eyes tight and said: "I don't see it."

The devil said angrily: "You must be blind if you can't see it; we are just above the roof." And he seized him in anger, and set him on the golden table in that royal castle.

The three princesses were sitting at the table, knitting with golden thread. His own wife was the middle one, and she knew him at once. She sprang up right gladly and welcomed him with joy. She nearly fainted, she was so pleased that he had been able to come so many miles in such a short time.

"Welcome, dear husband, welcome! Welcome, our deliverer! You will save us from the enchantment under which we are in this castle."

The time passed very slowly there. So one day his wife brought him the keys and showed him through all the rooms and closets, letting him see everything except one room, which she would not open for him.

The three princesses had to take the shape of doves for two hours in the morning and three hours before the evening, and they had to go to the Red Sea to bathe there. One day when they had gone out to bathe he thought: "Why don't you want to open that room for me?" So he went and searched among the other keys for the key, and opened the room for himself.

In the room he saw a three-headed dragon, and each of its heads was stuck upon a hook so that it hung down from it. Under the dragon were placed three glasses of water. The lad was terrified and started to run away. But the dragon kept on calling out: "Don't be frightened, don't run away, but come back again and give me that glass of water. Your life shall be spared this once."

So he gave him the glass of water; the dragon drained it up, and instantly one of the heads fell from the hook. He begged again: "Now give me that other glass of water, and your life shall be spared a second time."

He gave it him; the dragon drank it up, and immediately the second head fell from the hook. Then the dragon said: "Now do as you like. But you must give me the third glass of water, whether you like it or not!"

In terror he gave him the third glass; the third head drank it up and fell from its hook. Now the dragon was quite free, and instantly he made for the Red Sea, and began to chase after the three doves until he caught one of them. It was the lad's wife.

The other two princesses came back again and began to weep and to wail.

"Thou luckless fellow! we were happy in the hope that thou wouldst deliver us, and now we are worse off than ever – now our torments will last till doomsday!"

He, too, burst into tears, for he was sad at heart that the dragon had carried off his wife, whom he had won at the risk of his life.

The princesses' three brothers were under enchantment too. One of them was in the castle, changed into the shape of a horse. One day the horse said to the sorrowing husband: "The dragon is away from home now. Let us go and steal the princess."

So they went to the dragon's castle, carried off the princess, and ran for home. The other brother of the three princesses was in the dragon's castle under enchantment in the shape of a horse.

When the dragon came home, he said to the horse: "Where is my princess?"

The horse answered: "They came and carried her away."

The dragon mounted the horse at once and said: "Now we'll ride as fast as we can. We must overtake them."

The horse answered: "We cannot possibly overtake them."

But the dragon said: "Only let us start; we shall overtake them."

They started, and they overtook them near the castle. The dragon snapped the princess away at once, saying to the lad: "I promised to spare your life in return for that glass of water; now I have spared it, but don't dare to come to my castle ever again."

And with that the dragon rode home, carrying the princess with him.

Some time after that the horse said to the sorrowing husband: "The dragon is away from home again. Let us go and steal the princess."

So they went and stole her again.

The dragon came home and asked the horse: "Where is my princess?"

The horse answered: "Hibad! They have stolen her again, but we cannot overtake them this time."

The dragon said: "We must overtake them."

He mounted the horse, and they went flying after them till at last they overtook them. The dragon snapped away the princess, saying to the lad: "There's your life spared for the second glass. But if you come again, I'll tear you to pieces."

The lad was sorrowful, and wept and bewailed his fate because he had lost his wife for ever. But the horse said:

"I will give you one more counsel. I know a place where there are some young ravens. We will go there, and you must take the young ravens from their nest on the tree. The old ones will fly at you and peck you – they won't want to let you have their young chicks; but tell them that you won't give them back their chicks unless they bring you the healing water and the water of life.

"When they bring the water, take one of the young ravens and pull its head off; then dip it in the healing water and put the head to the body again. That's how you will be certain that they have brought you the real water of life. If the wound grows together again, you may be sure it is the real water of life. As soon as the wound has grown together, take the water of life and pour some of it into the raven's bill, and when the bird revives, you will know quite certainly that it is the water of life."

The lad did all this. The old ravens brought him the water in leather bottles. He took one of the chicks, pulled its head off, dipped it into the healing water, and the wound grew together again. Then he poured some of the water of life into its bill, and it came alive again. Then he put the young ravens back into the nest again, took the water, and went home.

When he got there, the horse said to him: "The dragon is away from home to-day. Let us go and see if we can get the princess."

So off they went and carried away the princess. They ran off as fast as they could.

The dragon came home and asked the horse: "Where is my princess?"

The horse replied: "She's gone from us. They've carried her off again, and this time we shall never catch up with them."

The dragon said in a rage: "What should prevent us from getting her back? Let's go at once."

So they flew after them, and they reached the castle just as the fugitives were going in through the gate.

The dragon snapped the princess away, saying to the lad: "You rascal! I told you I would tear you to pieces if you came a third time for her."

So he caught hold of him, and took a foot in each claw, and tore him in two. Then he went off with the princess and the horse.

The lad's horse took the healing water, dipped the two halves into it, put the one against the other, and they grew together. Then he took the water of life and poured it into the lad's mouth, and he was alive again. Then they went into the castle.

The lad was weeping bitterly and crying out that all was over, that now he would be separated from his wife for ever. But the horse gave him comfort, saying:

"Well, I really don't know what advice I ought to give you now. We have been three times, and he caught up with us every time. And the last time you were torn in pieces. I don't know how things will turn out. But I have another brother across the Red Sea, and he is stronger than I or the dragon. If we could only get him, we should be sure to kill the dragon. But it's a hard thing to do, for he is in service with the Devil's grandmother. We will try it together, if only we can manage to cross the Red Sea. And, if you follow the advice I give you, you will get the horse.

"You must serve the Devil's grandmother for three days, and, when you have served the three days, you must ask for that lean horse as wages. You will have to herd twelve horses for three days. Nobody has ever managed to do it yet. When the first day's service is done, on the next day the Devil's grandmother always cuts off the servant's head and hangs it on a hook. Now, listen carefully. While you are herding the horses, anything the hag gives you to eat at home, eat your fill of it. But, if she gives you anything to eat in the field, do not eat it, but throw it away. If you were to eat it, sleep would come down on you, your horses would stray, and the Devil's grandmother would cut off your head and hang it upon a hook."

So off they went together till they came to the Red Sea. As they were drawing near to the sea, they saw a huge fly entangled in a cobweb and struggling to free itself. So the lad went up to it and said: "Poor fly! You can't get out of that cobweb; wait a bit, and I will help you."

The cobweb was as big as a sheet, but he tore it in two and the fly crept out.

The fly said: "Thank you for helping me out of the cobweb. Tear one of my feet from under my belly, and, whenever you are in need, think of me, and I will help you."

The lad thought: "Poor fly! how could you help me?" Nevertheless, he tore off one of her feet and kept it.

Then he went on his way, and he saw a wolf with his tail trapped under a heavy log, and he was unable to help himself, for wolves have stiff backs, and no wolf has ever been able to turn. The lad rolled the log away and released the wolf.

The wolf said: "Thank you for helping me. Take one of my claws, and, whenever you are in sore need, think of me, and I will help you." So the lad took one of his claws and kept it.

When he got quite close to the sea, he saw a crab as big as a barrel. The crab was lying on the sand with his belly upwards, and he couldn't manage to turn himself over again. So the lad went and turned the crab over again. The crab asked him where he was going. He said he was going to the Devil's grandmother across the Red Sea.

The crab said: "My dear lad, I'll make a bridge for you across the sea, so that you will be able to get across. But, besides that, you must pluck off one of my claws from under my belly, and when you are in sore need, think of me, and I will help you."

So he plucked off one of the claws and kept it. The crab sidled into the sea, and immediately all the crabs of the sea came together, and they closed in on one another so that they made a bridge across the sea. The lad crossed the bridge and came to the Devil's grandmother. She was standing waiting for him in the doorway of her house, and welcomed him. He'd just come at the right time; she wanted him to herd her horses. She gave him plenty of good food to eat, and sent him out to the fields. She put twelve horses in his charge, and said to him:

"Look to it that you herd them well, for if you lose one of them you will lose your head. Just look here at these twenty-four posts, with a hook on each one of them. There are heads on twenty-three of them. The last hook is waiting for your head. If you herd my horses badly, that hook is waiting for your head."

Then she fitted him out for herding the horses. She gave him a piece of bread, so that he might have enough to eat and not starve. He meant to follow the horse's advice, and threw the bread away. But a fierce hunger came upon him, and he had to go and look for the bread and eat it up.

The moment he had eaten it he fell asleep and all the horses were lost. When he awoke there wasn't a single horse there. Sorrowfully he said: "The Devil's grandmother was right; my head will hang from that hook." In his grief he thought of the fly, and it came flying up and called out: "Why are you weeping and wailing?"

He said that he had been hungry, and had been forced to eat the bread, so that he fell asleep and all the horses were lost.

The fly tried to comfort him, saying: "Don't be troubled, dear lad; I will help you."

So she called together all the flies, and they flew everywhere looking for the horses, and when they found them, they buzzed round them and plagued them till they drove them up to the herdsman. He drove them joyfully home.

The Devil's grandmother welcomed them, and when she saw that all the horses were there, she said: "You've herded them well enough, for you have brought them all back." Then she seized a hatchet and began to beat the horses with it, and most of all the lean one, till the flesh hung in strips from its body. The lad was sorry for the horse, for the hag was beating it hardest and it was the leanest of them all. But the Devil's grandmother took a salve and anointed the horses' wounds, and they were healed by morning.

The next day she fitted him out again for herding the horses, and gave him some more of the bread, telling him to eat it all. But when he came to the pasture he crumbled the bread and trampled the crumbs into the ground, so that it should be uneatable. But it was no good. He was forced to dig it up and eat it, earth and all, so great was the hunger that the Devil's grandmother had sent against him. In a moment he fell asleep and all the horses were lost.

When he woke he saw that there were no horses there. He wept and wailed. But he thought of the wolf, and the wolf came running up and asked him: "Why are you weeping and wailing? Don't be troubled; I will help you."

He went and summoned all the wolves. A great flock of wolves ran up, and they scattered everywhere, looking for the horses. When they found them, they drove them to the herdsman, each horse with a wolf at its side leading it by the ear. The herdsman was overjoyed, and took the horses and drove them home.

The Devil's grandmother was waiting for him in front of the house. She said: "Indeed you have herded them well; this is the second day that you have brought them all home." But she beat the horses with the hatchet far worse than the day before; then she anointed their wounds with the salve, so that they should be healed by morning.

On the third day she sent him out again to herd the horses, and gave him some more of the bread, telling him to eat it and not to throw it away. But when he came to the pasture he threw the bread down on the sand and trampled it in, so that it should be uneatable. But he had to search it out again, so great was the hunger the Devil's grandmother sent against him. The moment he had finished it he fell asleep and the horses were lost. When he woke he burst into tears. This time it was all up with him; the fly and the wolf had helped him before, but the crab had already made a bridge for him, so there was nobody to help him. The horses didn't know where to hide themselves to save themselves from being beaten by the Devil's grandmother, so they leapt into the sea, where nobody could find them.

The herdsman was in agony, and he kept on wailing that now his head must hang upon that hook. At last he thought of the crab. The crab turned round in the sea, and instantly all the crabs collected and began searching the sea for the horses, and they pinched them until they drove them out of the sea. But the lean one, since he couldn't think of a better hiding-place, crouched under the crab's belly. The other crabs set to work to look for him, and at last they found him. The big crab had to turn over, and then they drove the lean horse out. The herdsman took the horses and drove them home joyfully, because his three days of service were now over.

The Devil's grandmother was waiting for him, and she beat the horses with the hatchet so fiercely that their flesh hung in strips from their bodies. Then she anointed them with the salve, and the wounds healed by morning. In the morning she asked the herdsman what wages he wanted. He answered: "I want nothing but that lean old horse."

She said: "It would be a sorry thing to give you such a wretched horse in return for such good service; I will give you the best horse."

He answered: "I won't take any horse but the lean one."

She asked him why he wanted the leanest one. He replied: "Because I am sorry for him, for he always gets the worst beating. I will have that one, and no other."

So she said: "Well, I will give him to you, if you must have him, but I will give you this fat one too. You can ride on his back home and lead the lean one with you."

He mounted the fat horse and rode off. But when they were drawing near to the gate, the lean horse said: "Get down from that horse and mount me, or you will be the worse for it."

So he jumped down from the fat horse and mounted the lean one.

The fat horse growled: "It's the Devil gave you that advice."

And the lean horse said: "If you had gone under the gate on that horse's back, he would have dashed you against the vault of the gate, so that your head would have been knocked off, and you would have been killed."

So they came safely home. When the princesses saw him come back they were delighted.

The other horse said: "Now, brother, let us go. The dragon is away from home, and the princess will be ours." So they went and carried off the princess.

When the dragon came home, he asked his horse: "Where is my princess?"

The horse replied: "She has gone, and this time we shan't get her back. The horse from the Red Sea has come, and he will get the better of us all."

The dragon took no heed of that, but flew after them and caught them up just by the gate. He was going to snap the princess away, but this time he could not do it. For the horse from over the Red Sea kicked his nose with his hoof, so that the dragon fell down from his horse, and the other two horses fell upon him, and between them they killed the dragon.

They came to the castle with the princess, and they were congratulating one another on their victory over their enemy. Then the horse which had been giving good advice to his rider all the time said: "Now, dear brother-in-law, take my sword there hanging from the ceiling and cut my head off."

He was sad and said: "How could I do that, after all the acts of kindness you have done for me?"

The horse said: "My good friend, I cannot tell you why you must behead me, but you would do me a great wrong if you did not do it."

So he hesitated no longer, but cut his head off. The blood spurted up twelve feet high, and instantly the horse became a beautiful youth. Seeing that, the lad was quick to behead the other horses, and they all turned into handsome princes like the first one.

They all thanked him for delivering them, and they made him king of that castle, and there he lived with his wife and her two sisters in all happiness and harmony till they died. The three brothers took possession of the dragon's castle.

The Bear, the Eagle and the Fish

ONCE THERE WAS there was a count and he had three daughters. All of them were young and as pretty as peacocks, but the youngest was the loveliest of them all. The count had little money to spend, for he had lost it all by gambling. And so – since he had to spend the time in some way or other – he used to go hunting. One day, when he was out hunting he lost his way in a forest, and he could not find his way out of it. Suddenly a big bear rushed out at him, shouting at the top of his voice. He said he would show him the way out of the forest and, besides, he would give him as much gold and silver as he wanted on one condition, and that condition was that the count should give him one of his daughters in marriage. The count was terrified. But after thinking it over for a time, he consented at last. The bear showed him the way out of the forest and gave him everything he had promised, and so the count was pleased.

He spent his time eating and drinking and gambling, till all the money melted away. He never so much as gave a thought to the bear, until one day, when the eldest daughter was marriageable, a carriage came rolling up. The carriage was drawn by a pair of raven-black horses, and in it sat a prince with cheeks of white and red, whose robes blazed with gold. He came and took the eldest daughter and drove off. The countess wept, but the count did not mind a bit, but being short of money, he began hunting again.

One day he lost his way again, and this time an eagle flew down to him and promised to show him the way out of the forest, and to give him heaps of money into the bargain, if he would only give him his second daughter in return. The bargain was made and the eagle fetched away the second daughter, and only the youngest was left at home. Yet even her the count sold, and it was a fish that got her.

So the count and the countess were left alone. They were very sad, but after a time a boy was born to them, and they watched over him like the apple of their eye. When the boy was grown up, he saw that the countess looked sad sometimes, and he gave her no rest till she had told him everything. When he had heard the story, he put his best clothes on, took his sword, mounted his horse, and said good-bye to his parents, telling them that he was going to search for his lost sisters.

So he rode on till he came to the eldest sister. Her he found playing with three little bear cubs, for these were her babies. He met his brother-in-law, who gave him three hairs and told him to rub those hairs with his fingers if he found himself in any difficulty. Then he went to the second sister, and found her with two eaglets and the old eagle, his brother-in-law, as well. The eagle gave him three feathers, saying they would be of help to him in time of need. He thanked the eagle for that and went on his way, and at last he came to his youngest sister. It was not so easy to get to her, for she dwelt under the water, and he had to drop into her house through the chimney. He would have missed the chimney if it hadn't been for the smoke from it: it was bluish smoke, hardly visible. His sister welcomed him heartily and showed him her baby, a pretty little fish, and her husband, a giant fish. The lad got three fish-scales from the husband to use in time of trouble.

He learned that the bear and the eagle were the brothers of the fish. They were sons of a powerful king, but they had been enchanted by an envious magician and turned into these shapes. The sorcerer could take different forms. But the brother must not let that dismay him. He must get hold of a golden egg which was hidden in the sorcerer and throw it on the ground. If he began to grow faint and did not know what to do, he must call one of his brothers-in-law, and he would advise him what to do.

And so it was. The young count attacked the magician, who turned into a bull. But the young count was not afraid: he rubbed the bear's hair; the bear came running up and tore the bull in pieces. But out of the bull flew a wild duck and tried to escape. Then the count thought of the eagle feathers, and immediately the eagle flew up, and he tore the duck to pieces. But a golden egg fell from the duck and it rolled into the pond. But that too was of no avail, for the count rubbed the fish scales, and after a while the fish threw the egg upon the bank. The count caught it and flung it to the ground so that it was smashed into many pieces.

At once all around was changed. The pond turned into a meadow upon which a beautiful castle was shining. The castle was full of servants and the three princes, with their wives and children, were just walking out of it. All were overjoyed to be so happily delivered, and, when they had enough of rejoicing, they started off to find their parents.

Their first journey was to the old count and countess, so that they might enjoy the sight of their children and grandchildren. Afterwards they hastened to the old king. He ordered many cannon to be fired, and prepared a splendid banquet. And he gave the kingdom to his eldest son. The second son went to the land of the count, and it was divided between him and his brother-in-law. And the youngest went to the disenchanted castle. All of them reigned prosperously and wisely in their several realms and, if they haven't died since, they are reigning still.

The Three Roses

ONCE UPON A TIME there was a mother who had three daughters. There was to be a market in the next town, and she said she would go to it. She asked the daughters what she should bring them back. Two of them named a great number of things; she must buy all of them, they said. You know the sort of women, and the sort of things they would want. Well, when they had asked for more than enough, the mother asked the third daughter:

"And you, don't you want anything?"

"No, I don't want anything; but, if you like, you can bring me three roses, please."

If she wanted no more than that, her mother was ready to bring them.

When the mother knew all she wanted, she went off to market. She bought all she could, piled it all on her back, and started for home. But she was overtaken by nightfall, and the poor mother completely lost her way and could go no farther. She wandered through the forest till she was quite worn out, and at last she came to a palace, though she had never before heard of any palace there. There was a large garden full of roses, so beautiful that no painter alive could paint them, and all the roses were smiling at her. So she remembered her youngest daughter, who had wished for just such roses. She had forgotten it entirely till then. Surely that was because she was so old! Now she thought: "There are plenty of roses here, so I will take these three."

So she went into the garden and took the roses. At once a basilisk came and demanded her daughter in exchange for the roses. The mother was terrified and wanted to throw the flowers away. But the basilisk said that wouldn't be any use, and he threatened to tear her to pieces. So she had to promise him her daughter. There was no help for it, and so she went home.

She took the three roses to her daughter and said: "Here are the roses, but I had to pay dearly for them. You must go to yonder castle in payment for them, and I don't even know whether you will ever come back."

But Mary seemed as though she didn't mind at all, and she said she would go. So the mother took her to the castle. There was everything she wanted there. Soon the basilisk appeared and told Mary that she must nurse him in her lap for three hours every day. There was no way out, do it she must, and so the basilisk came and she nursed him for three hours. Then he went out, but he came next day and the day after that. On the third day he brought a sword and told poor Mary to cut his head off.

She protested that she wasn't used to doing things like that, and do it she could not. But the basilisk said in a rage that, if that was so, he would tear her to pieces. As there was no choice, she went up to him and cut his head off. And as the basilisk's head rolled on the ground, there came forth from his body a long serpent, hissing horribly. He asked her to cut his head off again. Mary did not hesitate this time, but cut his head off at once.

The serpent (by the way, he held the golden keys of that palace in his mouth) was immediately changed into a beautiful youth, and he said in a pleasant voice: "This castle belongs to me, and, as you have delivered me, there is no help for it: I must marry you."

So there was a great wedding, the castle was full of their attendants, and they all had to play and dance. But the floor was of paper, so I fell through it, and here I am now.

Zlatovlaska the Golden-Haired

THERE WAS ONCE an old king who was so wise that he was able to understand the speech of all the animals in the world. This is how it happened. An old woman came to him one day bringing him a snake in a basket.

"If you have this snake cooked," she told him, "and eat it as you would a fish, then you will be able to understand the birds of the air, the beasts of the earth, and the fishes of the sea."

The king was delighted. He made the old wise woman a handsome present and at once ordered his cook, a youth named Yirik, to prepare the "fish" for dinner.

"But understand, Yirik," he said severely, "you're to cook this 'fish,' not eat it! You're not to taste one morsel of it! If you do, you forfeit your head!"

Yirik thought this a strange order.

"What kind of a cook am I," he said to himself, "that I'm not to sample my own cooking?"

When he opened the basket and saw the "fish," he was further mystified.

"Um," he murmured, "it looks like a snake to me."

He put it on the fire and, when it was broiled to a turn, he ate a morsel. It had a fine flavor. He was about to take a second bite when suddenly he heard a little voice that buzzed in his ear these words:

"Give us some, too! Give us some, too!"

He looked around to see who was speaking but there was no one in the kitchen. Only some flies were buzzing about.

Just then outside a hissing voice called out:

"Where shall we go? Where shall we go?"

A higher voice answered:

"To the miller's barley field! To the miller's barley field!"

Yirik looked out the window and saw a gander with a flock of geese.

"Oho!" he said to himself, shaking his head. "Now I understand! Now I know what kind of 'fish' this is! Now I know why the poor cook was not to take a bite!"

He slipped another morsel into his mouth, garnished the "fish" carefully on a platter, and carried it to the king.

After dinner the king ordered his horse and told Yirik to come with him for a ride. The king rode on ahead and Yirik followed.

As they cantered across a green meadow, Yirik's horse began to prance and neigh.

"Ho! Ho!" he said. "I feel so light that I could jump over a mountain!"

"So could I," the king's horse said, "but I have to remember the old bag of bones that is perched on my back. If I were to jump he'd tumble off and break his neck."

"And a good thing, too!" said Yirik's horse. "Why not? Then instead of such an old bag of bones you'd get a young man to ride you like Yirik."

Yirik almost burst out laughing as he listened to the horses' talk, but he suppressed his merriment lest the king should know that he had eaten some of the magic snake.

Now of course the king, too, understood what the horses were saying. He glanced apprehensively at Yirik and it seemed to him that Yirik was grinning.

"What are you laughing at, Yirik?"

"Me?" Yirik said. "I'm not laughing. I was just thinking of something funny."

"Um," said the king.

His suspicions against Yirik were aroused. Moreover he was afraid to trust himself to his horse any longer. So he turned back to the palace at once.

There he ordered Yirik to pour him out a goblet of wine.

"And I warn you," he said, "that you forfeit your head if you pour a drop too much or too little."

Yirik carefully tilted a great tankard and began filling a goblet. As he poured a bird suddenly flew into the window pursued by another bird. The first bird had in its beak three golden hairs.

"Give them to me! Give them to me! They're mine!" screamed the second bird.

"I won't! I won't! They're mine!" the first bird answered. "I picked them up!"

"Yes, but I saw them first!" the other cried. "I saw them fall as the maiden sat and combed her golden tresses. Give me two of them and I'll let you keep the third."

"No! No! No! I won't let you have one of them!"

The second bird darted angrily at the first and after a struggle succeeded in capturing one of the golden hairs. One hair dropped to the marble floor, making as it struck a musical tinkle, and the first bird escaped still holding in its bill a single hair.

In his excitement over the struggle, Yirik overflowed the goblet.

"Ha! Ha!" said the king. "See what you've done! You forfeit your head! However, I'll suspend sentence on condition that you find this golden-haired maiden and bring her to me for a wife."

Poor Yirik didn't know who the maiden was nor where she lived. But what could he say? If he wanted to keep his head, he must undertake the quest. So he saddled his horse and started off at random.

His road led him through a forest. Here he came upon a bush under which some shepherds had kindled a fire. Sparks were falling on an anthill nearby and the ants in great excitement were running hither and thither with their eggs.

"Yirik!" they cried. "Help! Help, or we shall all be burned to death, we and our young ones in the eggs!"

Yirik instantly dismounted, cut down the burning bush, and put out the fire.

"Thank you, Yirik, thank you!" the ants said. "Your kindness to us this day will not go unrewarded. If ever you are in trouble, think of us and we will help you."

As Yirik rode on through the forest, he came upon two fledgling ravens lying by the path.

"Help us, Yirik, help us!" they cawed. "Our father and mother have thrown us out of the nest in yonder tall fir tree to fend for ourselves. We are young and helpless and not yet able to fly. Give us some meat to eat or we shall perish with hunger."

The sight of the helpless fledglings touched Yirik to pity. He dismounted instantly, drew his sword, and killed his horse. Then he fed the starving birds the meat they needed.

"Thank you, Yirik, thank you!" the little ravens croaked. "You have saved our lives this day. Your kindness will not go unrewarded. If ever you are in trouble, think of us and we will help you."

Yirik left the young ravens and pushed on afoot. The path through the forest was long and wearisome. It led out finally on the seashore.

On the beach two fishermen were quarreling over a big fish with golden scales that lay gasping on the sand.

"It's mine, I tell you!" one of the men was shouting. "It was caught in my net, so of course it's mine!"

To this the other one shouted back:

"But your net would never have caught a fish if you hadn't been out in my boat and if I hadn't helped you!"

"Give me this one," the first man said, "and I'll let you have the next one."

"No! You take the next one!" the other said. "This one's mine!"

So they kept on arguing to no purpose until Yirik went up to them and said:

"Let me decide this for you. Suppose you sell me the fish and then divide the money."

He offered them all the money the king had given him for his journey. The fishermen, delighted at the offer, at once agreed. Yirik handed them over the money and then, taking the gasping fish in his hand, he threw it back into the sea.

When the fish had caught its breath, it rose on a wave and called out to Yirik:

"Thank you, Yirik, thank you. You have saved my life this day. Your kindness will not go unrewarded. If ever you are in trouble, think of me and I will help you."

With that the golden fish flicked its tail and disappeared in the water.

"Where are you going, Yirik?" the fishermen asked.

"I'm going in quest of a golden-haired maiden whom my master, the king, wished to make his wife."

"He must mean the Princess Zlatovlaska," the fishermen said to each other.

"The Princess Zlatovlaska?" Yirik repeated. "Who is she?"

"She's the golden-haired daughter of the King of the Crystal Palace. Do you see the faint outlines of an island over yonder? That's where she lives. The king has twelve daughters but Zlatovlaska alone has golden hair. Each morning at dawn a wonderful glow spreads over land and sea. That's Zlatovlaska combing her golden hair."

The fishermen conferred apart for a moment and then said:

"Yirik, you settled our dispute for us and now in return we'll row you over to the island."

So they rowed Yirik over to the Island of the Crystal Palace and left him there with the warning that the king would probably try to palm off on him one of the dark-haired princesses.

Yirik at once presented himself at the palace, got an audience with the king, and declared his mission.

"H'm," the king said. "So your master desires the hand of my daughter, the Princess Zlatovlaska, eh? H'm, h'm. Well, I see no objection to your master as a son-in-law, but of course before I entrust the princess into your hands you must prove yourself worthy. I tell you what I'll do: I'll give you three tasks to perform. Be ready for the first one tomorrow."

Early the next day the king said to Yirik:

"My daughter, Zlatovlaska, had a precious necklace of pearls. She was walking in the meadow over yonder when the string broke and the pearls rolled away in the tall grasses. Now your first task is to gather up every last one of those pearls and hand them to me before sundown."

Yirik went to the meadow and when he saw how broad it was and how thickly covered with tall grasses his heart sank for he realized that he could never search over the whole of it in one day. However, he got down on his hands and knees and began to hunt.

Midday came and he had not yet found a single pearl.

"Oh dear," he thought to himself in despair, "if only my ants were here, they could help me!"

He had no sooner spoken than a million little voices answered:

"We are here and we're here to help you!"

And sure enough there they were, the very ants that he supposed were far away!

"What do you want us to do?" they asked.

"Find me all the pearls that are scattered in this meadow. I can't find one of them."

Instantly the ants scurried hither and thither and soon they began bringing him the pearls one by one. Yirik strung them together until the necklace seemed complete.

"Are there any more?" he asked.

He was about to tie the string together when a lame ant, whose foot had been burned in the fire, hobbled up, crying:

"Wait, Yirik, don't tie the string yet! Here's the last pearl!"

Yirik thanked the ants for their help and at sundown carried the string of pearls to the king. The king counted the pearls and, to his surprise, found that not one was missing.

"You've done this well," he said. "Tomorrow I'll give you your second task."

The next day when Yirik presented himself, the king said:

"While my daughter, Zlatovlaska, was bathing in the sea, a golden ring slipped from her finger and disappeared. Your task is to find me this ring before sundown."

Yirik went down to the seashore and as he walked along the beach his heart grew heavy as he realized the difficulty of the task before him. The sea was clear but so deep that he couldn't even see the bottom. How then could he find the ring?

"Oh dear," he said aloud, "if only the golden fish were here! It could help me."

"I am here," a voice said, "and I'm here to help you."

And there was the golden fish on the crest of a wave, gleaming like a flash of fire!

"What do you want me to do?" it said.

"Find me a golden ring that lies somewhere on the bottom of the sea."

"Ah, a golden ring? A moment ago I met a pike," the fish said, "that had just such a golden ring. Wait for me here and I'll go find the pike."

In a few moments the golden fish returned with the pike and sure enough it was Zlatovlaska's ring that the pike was carrying.

That evening at sundown the king acknowledged that Yirik had accomplished his second task.

The next day the king said:

"I could never allow my daughter, Zlatovlaska, the Golden-Haired, to go to the kingdom of your master unless she carried with her two flasks, one filled with the Water of Life, the other with the Water of Death. So today for a third task I set you this: to bring the princess a flask of the Water of Life and a flask of the Water of Death."

Yirik had no idea which way to turn. He had heard of the Waters of Life and Death, but all he knew about them was that their springs were far away beyond the Red Sea. He left the Crystal Palace and walked off aimlessly until his feet had carried him of themselves into a dark forest.

"If only those young ravens were here," he said aloud, "they could help me!"

Instantly he heard a loud, "Caw! Caw!" and two ravens flew down to him, saying:

"We are here! We are here to help you! What do you want us to do?"

"I have to bring the king a flask of the Water of Life and a flask of the Water of Death and I don't know where the springs are. Do you know?"

"Yes, we know," the ravens said. "Wait here and we'll soon fetch you water from both springs."

They flew off and in a short time returned, each bearing a gourd of the precious water.

Yirik thanked the ravens and carefully filled his two flasks.

As he was leaving the forest, he came upon a great spider web. An ugly spider sat in the middle of it sucking a fly. Yirik took a drop of the Water of Death and flicked it on the spider. The spider doubled up dead and fell to the ground like a ripe cherry.

Then Yirik sprinkled a drop of Living Water on the fly. The fly instantly revived, pulled itself out of the web, and flew about happy and free once again.

"Thank you, Yirik," it buzzed, "thank you for bringing me back to life. You won't be sorry. Just wait and you'll soon see that I'll reward you!"

When Yirik returned to the palace and presented the two flasks, the king said:

"But one thing yet remains. You may take Zlatovlaska, the Golden-Haired, but you must yourself pick her out from among the twelve sisters."

The king led Yirik into a great hall. The twelve princesses were seated about a table, beautiful maidens all and each looking much like the others. Yirik could not tell which was Zlatovlaska, the Golden-Haired, for each princess wore a long heavy white veil so draped over her head and shoulders that it completely covered her hair.

"Here are my twelve daughters," the king said. "One of them is Zlatovlaska, the Golden-Haired. Pick her out and you may lead her at once to your master. If you fail to pick her out, then you must depart without her."

In dismay Yirik looked from sister to sister. There was nothing to show him which was Zlatovlaska, the Golden-Haired. How was he to find out?

Suddenly he heard a buzzing in his ear and a little voice whispered:

"Courage, Yirik, courage! I'll help you!"

He turned his head quickly and there was the fly he had rescued from the spider.

"Walk slowly by each princess," the fly said, "and I'll tell you when you come to Zlatovlaska, the Golden-Haired."

Yirik did as the fly ordered. He stopped a moment before the first princess until the fly buzzed:

"Not that one! Not that one!"

He went on to the next princess and again the fly buzzed:

"Not that one! Not that one!"

So he went on from princess to princess until at last the fly buzzed out:

"Yes, that one! That one!"

So Yirik remained standing where he was and said to the king:

"This, I think, is Zlatovlaska, the Golden-Haired."

"You have guessed right," the king said.

At that Zlatovlaska removed the white veil from her head and her lovely hair tumbled down to her feet like a golden cascade. It shimmered and glowed like the sun in the early morning when he peeps over the mountain top. Yirik stared until the brightness dimmed his sight.

The king immediately prepared Zlatovlaska, the Golden-Haired, for her journey. He gave her the two precious flasks of water; he arranged a fitting escort; and then with his blessing he sent her forth under Yirik's care.

Yirik conducted her safely to his master.

When the old king saw the lovely princess that Yirik had found for him, his eyes blinked with satisfaction, he capered about like a spring lamb, and he ordered that immediate preparations be made for the wedding. He was most grateful to Yirik and thanked him again and again.

"My dear boy," he said, "I had expected to have you hanged for your disobedience and let the ravens pick your bones. But now, to show you how grateful I am for the beautiful bride you have found me, I'm not going to have you hanged at all. Instead, I shall have you beheaded and then given a decent burial."

The execution took place at once in order to be out of the way before the wedding.

"It's a great pity he had to die," the king said as the executioner cut off Yirik's head. "He has certainly been a faithful servant."

Zlatovlaska, the Golden-Haired, asked if she might have his severed head and body. The king who was too madly in love to refuse her anything said: "Yes."

So Zlatovlaska took the body and the head and put them together. Then she sprinkled them with the Water of Death. Instantly the wound closed and soon it healed so completely that there wasn't even a scar left.

Yirik lay there lifeless but looking merely as if he were asleep. Zlatovlaska sprinkled him with the Water of Life and immediately his dead limbs stirred. Then he opened his eyes and sat up. Life poured through his veins and he sprang to his feet younger, fresher, handsomer than before.

The old king was filled with envy.

"I, too," he cried, "wish to be made young and handsome!"

He commanded the executioner to cut off his head and he told Zlatovlaska to sprinkle him afterwards with the Water of Life.

The executioner did as he was told. Then Zlatovlaska sprinkled the old king's head and body with the Water of Life. Nothing happened. Zlatovlaska kept on sprinkling the Water of Life until there was no more left.

"Do you know," the princess said to Yirik, "I believe I should have used the Water of Death first."

So now she sprinkled the body and head with the Water of Death and, sure enough, they grew together at once. But of course there was no life in them. And of course there was no possible way of putting life into them because the Water of Life was all gone. So the old king remained dead.

"This will never do," the people said. "We must have a king. And with the wedding feast and everything prepared we simply must have a wedding, too. If Zlatovlaska, the Golden-Haired, cannot marry the old king, she'll have to marry some one else. Now who shall it be?"

Some one suggested Yirik because he was young and handsome and because, like the old king, he could understand the birds and the beasts.

"Yirik!" the people cried. "Let Yirik be our king!"

And Zlatovlaska, the Golden-Haired, who had long since fallen in love with handsome Yirik, consented to have the wedding at once in order that the feast already prepared might not be wasted.

So Yirik and Zlatovlaska, the Golden-Haired, were married and they ruled so well and they lived so happily that to this day when people say of some one: "He's as happy as a king," they are thinking of King Yirik, and when they say of some one: "She's as beautiful as a queen," they are thinking of Zlatovlaska, the Golden-Haired.

The Betrothal Gifts

A FARMER who had three sons was much troubled in his mind as to how he should leave his property. "My farm is too small to divide," he kept thinking to himself. "If I divide it into three equal parts and give each of my sons one part, they will all be poor cottagers, and yet, if I give it all to one son, I shall be unjust to the other two. My grandfather always said that it is a father's duty to treat all his children alike and I'm sure I don't want to depart from his teachings."

At last he called his sons together and said: "I have hit upon a plan whereby fate shall decide which of you shall be my heir. You must all go out into the world and find brides, and he who brings back as a betrothal gift the most beautiful ring shall have the farm."

The king was delighted. He made the old wise woman a handsome present and at once ordered his cook, a youth named Yirik, to prepare the "fish" for dinner.

The sons agreed to this plan and the next day they all set out in different directions in quest of brides.

Now the youngest son, whose name was Kubik, was not considered as bright as his brothers, for he was kind to beggars and he never drove a hard bargain. His brothers often laughed at him and his father pitied him, for he thought that Kubik was too gentle to make his way in the world.

Kubik's path took him into a deep forest. He walked on and on until suddenly a little frog hopped up in front of him and said:

"Where are you going, Kubik?"

Now Kubik had never in all his life heard of a frog that could talk. At first he was frightened but even so he was too polite not to answer a civil question. So he told the frog about his father and the farm and the quest for betrothal gifts upon which he and his brothers were bound.

The frog listened and when he was finished she said: "Come with me, Kubik, and my daughter, Kachenka, will give you a more beautiful ring than any your father or brothers have ever seen."

Kubik hesitated, but at last not to hurt the frog's feelings he agreed. "But if your daughter Kachenka looks like you," he thought to himself, "Heaven help me, for she'll be a pretty dear price to pay for a farm!"

The frog led him to a deep valley at one side of which rose a high rocky cliff that was honey-combed with caverns. The frog hopped into one of these and called out:

"Kachenka, my child, where are you? Here is Kubik come to woo you and to beg a betrothal gift. Bring out your little box of rings."

Instantly a second frog appeared dragging a heavy jewel casket. Kachenka, alas, was a hundred times uglier than her mother. Her legs were crooked, her face was all covered with spots, and when she spoke her voice was hoarse and croaking.

For a moment Kubik shivered and turned away in disgust, but only for a moment until he remembered that it wasn't Kachenka's fault that she was a frog.

The two frogs put the casket before him and opened it and Kubik saw that it was filled with a collection of the rarest and most beautiful rings in the world.

"Make your own choice, Kubik," the old frog said.

Kubik selected as plain a ring as there was, for he was ashamed to take one of the handsomest.

"Not that one!" the old frog said, "unless you want your brothers to laugh at you."

Thereupon she herself picked out the ring that had the biggest diamond of them all, wrapped it up carefully in paper, and handed it to Kubik.

"Now hurry home," she said, "for your brothers are already there and your father is waiting for you."

As soon as Kubik reached home the farmer called his three sons together and demanded to be shown their betrothal gifts.

All the eldest son had was a common brass ring.

"Um," the farmer said, shaking his head. "Well, put it away for a keepsake."

The second son showed a silver ring that was worth a few cents more.

"A little better," the old man mumbled, "but not good enough for a farmer. Put it away for a keepsake. And now," he said, turning to his youngest son, "let us see what Kubik has brought from his promised bride."

They all looked at Kubik, and Kubik blushed as he felt in his pocket for the little package.

"Ho, ho!" his brothers laughed. "Kubik has such a fine ring that he has to keep it wrapped up."

But when he opened the paper they stopped laughing, and well they might, for there was a great diamond that sparkled and blazed until it seemed that the sun was shining in the room.

"Kubik!" the farmer cried when at last he found his voice, "where did you get that ring? You must have stolen it, you wicked boy!" And without waiting to hear what Kubik had to say, he reached for a whip and trounced the poor lad to within an inch of his life. Then he took the ring and hid it carefully away.

"Now, my boys," he said to his sons, "you will all have to make another trial. This time ask of your promised brides the gift of an embroidered kerchief and he who brings back the most beautiful kerchief shall be my heir."

So the next day the three sons again started out, each in a different direction.

Kubik thought to himself: "I won't go the way I went yesterday or I may meet that old frog again and then, when I get home, the only prize I'll get will be another beating."

So he took a different path but he hadn't gone far before the old frog hopped up in front of him.

"What's the matter, Kubik?" she asked.

At first Kubik didn't want to tell her but she questioned him and finally, not to seem rude, he told her about the beating his father had given him on account of Kachenka's ring and about the new quest for embroidered kerchiefs upon which his father was now sending him and his brothers.

"Now don't think any more about that whipping," the old frog advised him. "And as for an embroidered kerchief, why, Kachenka is the very girl for that! She will give you one that will make your brothers open their eyes!"

Kubik wasn't sure that he wanted to accept another of Kachenka's gifts, but the old frog urged him and at last he agreed. So again they took the path to the rocky cliff. The old frog called her daughter out as before and presently Kachenka appeared dragging a chest that was filled with the most wonderful of kerchiefs, all of fine silk and all richly embroidered and so large that they were more like shawls than kerchiefs.

Kubik reached in and took the first that came to hand.

"Tut, tut!" the old frog said. "That's no way to select a kerchief."

Then she herself picked out the biggest and the most richly

embroidered of them all and wrapped it up in paper. She gave it to Kubik and said:

"Now hurry home, for your brothers are already there and your father is waiting for you."

As soon as Kubik reached home the farmer called his three sons together and demanded to be shown their betrothal gifts.

All the eldest one had was a small cheap kerchief of no value whatever.

"Um," the farmer said, shaking his head. "Well, put it away for a keepsake."

The kerchief of the second had cost a few cents more.

"A little better," the old man mumbled. "Perhaps it's good enough for a farmer. And now," he said, turning to his youngest son, "let us see what Kubik has brought from his promised bride."

They all looked at Kubik, and Kubik blushed as he pulled out a parcel from under his shirt.

"Ho, ho!" his brothers laughed. "Kubik has such a fine kerchief that he has to keep it wrapped up in paper!"

But when Kubik opened the paper they stopped laughing, and well they might, for there was a silken kerchief so big that it could have covered the whole room and so richly embroidered that any princess in the world would have been proud to own it.

"Kubik!" the farmer cried when at last he was able to speak, "where did you get that kerchief? You must have stolen it, you wicked boy!"

And without waiting to hear what Kubik had to say, he reached down the whip again and trounced the poor boy to within an inch of his life. Then he took the kerchief and hid it carefully away.

"Now, my sons," he said, "you will all have to make another trial. But this time it will not be for a ring or a kerchief. This time bring home your brides and he whose bride is the most beautiful shall be my heir."

So the next day the three sons again started out, each in a different direction.

"I don't want to see Kachenka again," poor Kubik said to himself. "Twice I've brought back the best betrothal gift and each time I've got a beating for it. I wonder what they would say if I brought home a frog for a bride! Then they would have something to laugh at!"

So he took a different path through the forest but again he hadn't gone far before the old frog hopped up in front of him. This time Kubik turned and ran. The old frog called after him but the louder she called the faster he ran.

He ran on and on until suddenly a great snake stopped him. The snake reared high its head, then dropped into a coil. Again it reared up and swayed from side to side threatening to strike if Kubik went on. So Kubik saw that fate was determined that he should marry a frog and reluctantly he turned back.

The snake led him to the cliff, where the old frog greeted him kindly and thanked the snake for his faithful service.

Poor Kubik! He was very tired and very unhappy. When you come to think of it, who wouldn't be unhappy at the prospect of being united for life to a frog?

Kubik was so tired that presently he fell asleep and it was just as well he did, for at least in dreams he could forget his troubles.

The next morning when he woke and rubbed his eyes, he found himself lying on a soft feather bed, white as snow, in a splendid room with decorations that were fit for a king. A fine silken shirt lay spread out on a chair beside the bed and beyond the chair was a stand with a silver basin. When he got up attendants came running in carrying clothes of richly woven cloth of gold. They dressed Kubik and they combed his hair until they had him looking like a young prince. Then they brought him breakfast and there was cream with the coffee and I would have you know that this was only the second time in his life that Kubik had ever had cream with his coffee!

Kubik did not know what to think of it all. His head went round and round. When he looked out the window he saw no trace of cliff or caverns or forest. Instead he saw a big town with streets and houses and people going to and fro.

Presently music began to play under the window, a great crowd gathered and soon attendants came in to escort Lord Kubik out. As he reached the castle gate, the people cheered and a coach and six drove up. Two ladies were in it, a mother and daughter, both dressed in beautiful silks. They alighted from the coach and when they saw Kubik they smiled and came toward him with outstretched hands.

"You don't know us, do you, Kubik?" the older lady said. "I was that old frog who coaxed you to the cliff and this, my beautiful daughter, was the other little frog, the very ugly one, that you feared you would have to take home to your father's house as your bride. You see, Kubik, we were all under an evil enchantment. Many years ago a wicked magician brought ruin on us and our kingdom. He changed our subjects into snakes and us into frogs and turned our fine city into a rocky cliff. Nothing could break the enchantment until some one should come and ask a betrothal gift from my daughter. We lived in the forest for years and years and all those years I begged all the people who wandered by to help us but they only trod on us or turned away from us in disgust. You, Kubik, were the first not to scorn us for our ugly looks. By this you broke the evil spell that held us and now we are all free. As a reward you shall marry my daughter, the Princess Kachenka, and be made king!"

Then the old queen took Kubik by the hand and led him to the royal coach, where she made him sit between her and the princess. Music played and the people cheered, and in this style they drove to Kubik's native village and to his father's house.

The old man was in the yard chopping firewood and his older sons were helping him. They, too, had brought home their brides, plain country girls from poor farms, and at that moment they were all awaiting Kubik's arrival.

"Look, father," the oldest son cried, "some fine folk are turning in here!"

"We're not behind in our taxes, are we?" the second son asked.

"Hush!" the old man whispered. "I have nothing to fear. My affairs are all in good order."

He put his cap respectfully under his arm and stood bareheaded and both his sons followed his example.

The coach drove straight into the yard and a handsome young lord and two beautiful ladies alighted. The handsome young lord greeted the old man and his sons and they bowed and scraped and pressed their hats under their arms tighter and tighter.

Then they all stepped into the old kitchen that was black with the smoke of many years and the handsome young lord sat down on the bench behind the table as though that was where he always sat. The two brothers and their brides shrank back against the oven and held their breath.

Then the handsome young lord said to the old man: "Don't you know me?"

"Where could I ever have seen your lordship?" the farmer asked, humbly. He kept bobbing so low it was a wonder he didn't bump his head against the floor.

"And do neither of your sons know me? I think these are your sons, aren't they?"

The farmer kept on bowing and the two sons looked down, too embarrassed to speak.

At length the handsome young lord said: "What, don't you know your own son, Kubik, whom you used to beat for stealing when he showed you his betrothal gifts?"

At that the old man looked at him closely and cried out: "Bless my soul, I believe it is our Kubik! But who could recognize the boy!... And is this his bride? That settles it! Kubik shall have the farm! Kubik has brought home the most beautiful bride!"

"Kubik doesn't need the farm," the old queen said, "nor will you need it any longer nor your other sons. You will all come home with us to our kingdom over which Kubik is now king. And may God grant you many years to live on in peace and quiet."

The farmer was overjoyed at this arrangement. He embraced his son, and his son's bride, and his son's royal mother-in-law.

He gave his farm to the poorest man in the village and then he and his sons accompanied Kubik back to his kingdom. There he lived long in peace and comfort enjoying the thought that good fortune had come to them all on account of his determination not to divide the farm.

The poor man who inherited the farm prayed for him and his sons every night and never tired of telling the story of how Kubik became a king and his brothers courtiers.

So for many years the memory of Kubik was kept green. Now people are beginning to forget him, so I thought it was time that I tell his story again.

The Wood Maiden

BETUSHKA WAS A LITTLE GIRL. Her mother was a poor widow with nothing but a tumble-down cottage and two little nanny-goats. But poor as they were Betushka was always cheerful. From spring till autumn she pastured the goats in the birch wood. Every morning when she left home her mother gave her a little basket with a slice of bread and a spindle.

"See that you bring home a full spindle," her mother always said.

Betushka had no distaff, so she wound the flax around her head. Then she took the little basket and went romping and singing behind the goats to the birch wood. When they got there she sat down under a tree and pulled the fibers of the flax from her head with her left hand, and with her right hand let down the spindle so that it went humming along the ground. All the while she sang until the woods echoed and the little goats nibbled away at the leaves and grass.

When the sun showed midday, she put the spindle aside, called the goats and gave them a mouthful of bread so that they wouldn't stray, and ran off into the woods to hunt berries or any other wild fruit that was in season. Then when she had finished her bread and fruit, she jumped up, folded her arms, and danced and sang.

The sun smiled at her through the green of the trees and the little goats, resting on the grass, thought: "What a merry little shepherdess we have!"

After her dance she went back to her spinning and worked industriously. In the evening when she got home her mother never had to scold her because the spindle was empty.

One day at noon just after she had eaten and, as usual, was going to dance, there suddenly stood before her a most beautiful maiden. She was dressed in white gauze that was fine as a spider's web. Long golden hair fell down to her waist and on her head she wore a wreath of woodland flowers.

Betushka was speechless with surprise and alarm.

The maiden smiled at her and said in a sweet voice:

"Betushka, do you like to dance?"

Her manner was so gracious that Betushka no longer felt afraid, and answered:

"Oh, I could dance all day long!"

"Come, then, let us dance together," said the maiden. "I'll teach you."

With that she tucked up her skirt, put her arm about Betushka's waist, and they began to dance. At once such enchanting music sounded over their heads that Betushka's heart went one-two with the dancing. The musicians sat on the branches of the birch trees. They were clad in little frock coats, black and gray and many-colored. It was a carefully chosen orchestra that had gathered at the bidding of the beautiful maiden: larks, nightingales, finches, linnets, thrushes, blackbirds, and showy mocking-birds.

Betushka's cheeks burned, her eyes shone. She forgot her spinning, she forgot her goats. All she could do was gaze at her partner who was moving with such grace and lightness that the grass didn't seem to bend under her slender feet.

They danced from noon till sundown and yet Betushka wasn't the least bit tired. Then they stopped dancing, the music ceased, and the maiden disappeared as suddenly as she had come.

Betushka looked around. The sun was sinking behind the wood. She put her hands to the unspun flax on her head and remembered the spindle that was lying unfilled on the grass. She took down the flax and laid it with the spindle in the little basket. Then she called the goats and started home.

She reproached herself bitterly that she had allowed the beautiful maiden to beguile her and she told herself that another time she would not listen to her. She was so quiet that the little goats, missing her merry song, looked around to see whether it was really their own little shepherdess who was following them. Her mother, too, wondered why she didn't sing and questioned her.

"Are you sick, Betushka?"

"No, dear mother, I'm not sick, but I've been singing too much and my throat is dry."

She knew that her mother did not reel the yarn at once, so she hid the spindle and the unspun flax, hoping to make up tomorrow what she had not done today. She did not tell her mother one word about the beautiful maiden.

The next day she felt cheerful again and as she drove the goats to pasture she sang merrily. At the birch wood she sat down to her spinning, singing all the while, for with a song on the lips work falls from the hands more easily.

Noonday came. Betushka gave a bit of bread to each of the goats and ran off to the woods for her berries. Then she ate her luncheon.

"Ah, my little goats," she sighed, as she brushed up the crumbs for the birds, "I mustn't dance today."

"Why mustn't you dance today?" a sweet voice asked, and there stood the beautiful maiden as though she had fallen from the clouds.

Betushka was worse frightened than before and she closed her eyes tight. When the maiden repeated her question, Betushka answered timidly:

"Forgive me, beautiful lady, for not dancing with you. If I dance with you I cannot spin my stint and then my mother will scold me. Today before the sun sets I must make up for what I lost yesterday."

"Come, child, and dance," the maiden said. "Before the sun sets we'll find some way of getting that spinning done!"

She tucked up her skirt, put her arm about Betushka, the musicians in the treetops struck up, and off they whirled. The maiden danced more beautifully than ever. Betushka couldn't take her eyes from her. She forgot her goats, she forgot her spinning. All she wanted to do was to dance on forever.

At sundown the maiden paused and the music stopped. Then Betushka, clasping her hands to her head, where the unspun flax was twined, burst into tears. The beautiful maiden took the flax from her head, wound it round the stem of a slender birch, grasped the spindle, and began to spin. The spindle hummed along the ground and filled in no time. Before the sun sank behind the woods all the flax was spun, even that which was left over from the day before. The maiden handed Betushka the full spindle and said:

> "Remember my words:
> "Reel and grumble not!
> Reel and grumble not!"

When she said this, she vanished as if the earth had swallowed her.

Betushka was very happy now and she thought to herself on her way home: "Since she is so good and kind, I'll dance with her again if she asks me. Oh, how I hope she does!"

She sang her merry little song as usual and the goats trotted cheerfully along.

She found her mother vexed with her, for she had wanted to reel yesterday's yarn and had discovered that the spindle was not full.

"What were you doing yesterday," she scolded, "that you didn't spin your stint?"

Betushka hung her head. "Forgive me, mother. I danced too long." Then she showed her mother today's spindle and said: "See, today I more than made up for yesterday."

Her mother said no more but went to milk the goats and Betushka put away the spindle. She wanted to tell her mother her adventure, but she thought to herself: "No, I'll wait. If the beautiful lady comes again, I'll ask her who she is and then I'll tell mother." So she said nothing.

On the third morning she drove the goats as usual to the birch wood. The goats went to pasture and Betushka, sitting down under a tree, began to spin and sing. When the sun pointed to noon, she laid her spindle on the grass, gave the goats a mouthful of bread, gathered some strawberries, ate her luncheon, and then, giving the crumbs to the birds, she said cheerily:

"Today, my little goats, I will dance for you!"

She jumped up, folded her arms, and was about to see whether she could move as gracefully as the beautiful maiden, when the maiden herself stood before her.

"Let us dance together," she said. She smiled at Betushka, put her arm about her, and as the music above their heads began to play, they whirled round and round with flying feet. Again Betushka forgot the spindle and the goats. Again she saw nothing but the beautiful maiden whose body was lithe as a willow shoot. Again she heard nothing but the enchanting music to which her feet danced of themselves.

They danced from noon till sundown. Then the maiden paused and the music ceased. Betushka looked around. The sun was already set behind the woods. She clasped her hands to her head and looking down at the unfilled spindle she burst into tears.

"Oh, what will my mother say?" she cried.

"Give me your little basket," the maiden said, "and I will put something in it that will more than make up for today's stint."

Betushka handed her the basket and the maiden took it and vanished. In a moment she was back. She returned the basket and said:

"Look not inside until you're home!
Look not inside until you're home!"

As she said these words she was gone as if a wind had blown her away.

Betushka wanted awfully to peep inside but she was afraid to. The basket was so light that she wondered whether there was anything at all in it. Was the lovely lady only fooling her? Halfway home she peeped in to see.

Imagine her feelings when she found the basket was full of birch leaves! Then indeed did Betushka burst into tears and reproach herself for being so simple. In her vexation she threw out a handful of leaves and was going to empty the basket when she thought to herself:

"No, I'll keep what's left as litter for the goats."

She was almost afraid to go home. She was so quiet that again the little goats wondered what ailed their shepherdess.

Her mother was waiting for her in great excitement.

"For heaven's sake, Betushka, what kind of a spool did you bring home yesterday?"

"Why?" Betushka faltered.

"When you went away this morning I started to reel that yarn. I reeled and reeled and the spool remained full. One skein, two skeins, three skeins, and still the spool was full. 'What evil spirit has spun that?' I cried out impatiently, and instantly the yarn disappeared from the spindle as if blown away. Tell me, what does it mean?"

So Betushka confessed and told her mother all she knew about the beautiful maiden.

"Oh," cried her mother in amazement, "that was a wood maiden! At noon and midnight the wood maidens dance. It is well you are not a little boy or she might have danced you to death! But they are often kind to little girls and sometimes make them rich presents. Why didn't you tell me? If I hadn't grumbled, I could have had yarn enough to fill the house!"

Betushka thought of the little basket and wondered if there might be something under the leaves. She took out the spindle and unspun flax and looked in once more.

"Mother!" she cried. "Come here and see!"

Her mother looked and clapped her hands. The birch leaves were all turned to gold!

Betushka reproached herself bitterly: "She told me not to look inside until I got home, but I didn't obey."

"It's lucky you didn't empty the whole basket," her mother said.

The next morning she herself went to look for the handful of leaves that Betushka had thrown away. She found them still lying in the road but they were only birch leaves.

But the riches which Betushka brought home were enough. Her mother bought a farm with fields and cattle. Betushka had pretty clothes and no longer had to pasture goats.

But no matter what she did, no matter how cheerful and happy she was, still nothing ever again gave her quite so much pleasure as the dance with the wood maiden. She often went to the birch wood in the hope of seeing the maiden again. But she never did.

The Bird with the Golden Gizzard

THERE WAS ONCE a poor man who had a large family. He was so poor that he had nothing to feed the children. For three days they had had no food. On the third day as the father was out cutting osiers he saw, sitting in a bush, a small bird that shone like gold.

"If I could snare that bird," he thought to himself, "and take it home, the children would be amused and perhaps forget they were hungry."

So he caught the bird and carried it home and, sure enough, the children were so delighted that for two days they didn't cry for food.

On the third day the bird laid a golden egg. The oldest boy took the egg to the goldsmith to sell it. The goldsmith examined it and said:

"I don't believe I have money enough to buy this egg."

"Just give me some bread," the boy said. "That will be enough."

The goldsmith gave him two loaves of bread, one under each arm, and filled his pockets with golden ducats. So for once the whole family had all it could eat and still there was money left over.

Two days later the bird laid another golden egg which the boy carried to the goldsmith and sold for the same price.

Now the goldsmith had a son who said he would like to see this wonderful bird. So he went home with the boy. He looked the bird over very carefully and under its wings he discovered an inscription that no one else had seen. The inscription read:

Whoever eats my heart will become king.

Whoever eats my gizzard will find under his head each morning a heap of golden ducats.

The youth went home and told his father about the strange inscription. They talked the matter over and at last decided that it would be well for the young man to marry the poor man's oldest daughter provided he could get the golden bird as dowry.

The goldsmith went to see the girl's father and after some discussion the marriage was arranged.

The wedding day arrived. The bridegroom ordered the bird to be roasted and ready to be put on the table when the bridal party came home from church. It was his intention to eat the heart himself and have his bride eat the gizzard.

The children of the family cried bitterly at the thought of losing their pretty bird, but the bridegroom, of course, had his way.

Now two of the boys stayed home from the wedding and they decided that they would like very much to taste the roast bird if only they could find a piece that nobody would miss. They did not dare take a leg or a wing, but they thought it would be safe to pick out a morsel from the inside. So one boy ate the heart, the other the gizzard. Then they were so frightened at what they had done that they ran away and never came back.

When the bride and groom returned from church, the bird was carried to the table. The groom looked at once for the heart and the gizzard and was greatly shocked at their disappearance.

The two boys who had gone out into the world found work with a merchant. They slept together and every morning the merchant's wife found a heap of golden ducats under the feather bed. She didn't know to which boy they belonged. She took them and saved them for a whole year until they filled a hogshead.

At the end of a year the boys decided to go out again into the world. The merchant showed them all the ducats his wife had found in their bed and he said to them:

"Take with you as many as you want now and when you come back you may have the rest."

The brothers parted company and each set out alone, the one to the left, the other to the right.

The younger brother came to a tavern. The landlady had two daughters who were so sharp at cards that they very soon won all the money he had. When he was picked clean he asked them to stop playing until the next morning when he would again have plenty of money.

Sure enough in the morning when he got up he had all the money he wanted. The girls asked him where it came from and he told them.

When they heard about the gizzard he had swallowed, they put something in his wine that made him sick at his stomach and he threw up the gizzard. The younger girl instantly snatched it, washed it, and swallowed it herself. Then as he had no more money they drove the poor boy away.

As he wandered in the fields he grew very hungry. He came to a meadow where he found a kind of sorrel that he ate. As soon as he ate it he turned into a goat and went jumping about the bushes nibbling at the leaves. He chanced to eat a kind of leaf that changed him back into himself.

"Ah," he thought, "now I know what to do!"

He picked some of the sorrel and some of the other leaves and went straight back to the tavern. He told them there that he was bringing them a present of a new kind of spinach that tasted very good. They asked him would he cook it for them.

The cook tasted it and at once she turned into a goat. The serving maid came into the kitchen and when she saw a goat there she drove it out. The youth asked the maid would she like to taste the new spinach. She tasted it and immediately she turned into a goat. Then when the landlady and her two daughters tasted it they, too, turned into goats.

He fed the cook and the serving maid some of the other leaves and they turned back into themselves. But the other three he left as goats.

He made halters for them and then he hitched them up and drove off.

He drove on and on until he came to a town where the king was building himself a castle. Now this king was his brother who had eaten the magic bird's heart. The king's workmen were hauling stone for the new castle, so he decided to put his goats to work hauling stone. He loaded his cart heavier than all the other carts.

The king noticed him and recognized him and asked him where he got those goats. So he told the king the whole story. The king thought the goats had been punished long enough and begged his brother to have pity on them and restore them. He took the king's advice and did so.

When they were once more human beings, he married the girl who had swallowed the gizzard. They soon became very rich, for every morning there was a heap of golden ducats under her head.

The Supernatural & the Uncanny

THE CZECH PEOPLE have preserved their love for folktales, adapting them to be in keeping with higher morality and the national sentiment.

Many of their supernatural features are subtle, keeping understated and often within the strict limits of probability. It is the very same method which, for example, H.G. Wells employs in some of his novels.

Many of the tales here deal with the strange and the mysterious. They are unsettling in ways you cannot always fathom – particularly 'Gentle Dora' and 'Grandfather's Eyes'. Another story of note included in this section is 'Katcha and the Devil' as its keen humour is particularly Czech in character.

Gentle Dora

THERE WAS ONCE a young devil who, as he wandered over the earth, found a book. He slipped it carelessly into his pocket and carried it down to hell. Now this book contained a list of the good deeds of a rich man, and the account of a good deed is of course never allowed to enter hell.

The devils in hell when they opened the book were greatly incensed over their comrade's stupidity and at once they dragged him off to Prince Lucifer for punishment.

Lucifer when he heard the case shook his head gravely.

"This is a serious offense," he said to the culprit. "To atone you must do one of two things: every day for seven years you must bring a soul to hell, or you must remain on earth for seven years and take service among men. Which will you do?"

The young devil was a stupid fellow and he knew he would never be able to seduce a soul every day for seven years. So he said:

"If I must choose, Your Majesty, let it be exile on earth for seven years."

So Lucifer pronounced sentence and the young devil was driven out of hell and warned not to return until the seven years were up.

Sad and forlorn he wandered up and down the world looking for work. People everywhere were suspicious of his black face and turned him away.

One day he met a man to whom he told his story.

"And just because I'm a devil," he said in conclusion, "no one will hire me."

"I know where you can get work," the man told him. "Just beyond the next village there is a big farm which is owned by a woman. She's always in need of laborers for she has such a sharp tongue and such a mean disposition that no one can stay with her longer than a month. Her name is Dora and in mockery the people hereabouts call her Gentle Dora.

Why don't you take service with her? As you're a devil, you may be able to get the best of her."

The devil thanked the man for this suggestion and at once presented himself to Gentle Dora. Gentle Dora, as usual, was in need of laborers and so she employed the devil instantly in spite of his black face.

From the start she worked him like a slave from morning till night, scolded him incessantly, and didn't give him half enough to eat. The poor fellow grew thin and almost pale. The months went by and each new month was harder to live through than the one before.

"I can do a day's work with the best of them," the devil thought to himself, "but there is no one, either man or devil, who can stand this woman's everlasting nagging. Oh dear, oh dear, what shall I do?"

Now Gentle Dora was looking for a husband. She had already had five husbands all of whom she had nagged to death. On account of this record every bachelor and widower in the village was a little shy of proposing himself as a sixth husband.

The devil, who as I have told you was a simple fellow, finally decided that it would be a mighty clever thing for him to marry Gentle Dora. He felt sure that once he was her husband she would give him less work and more food. So he proposed to her.

The rich widow didn't much fancy his black face, but on the other hand she wanted a husband and so, as there was no other prospect in sight, she accepted him.

"At least," she thought to herself, "by making him my husband, I'll save his wages."

It wasn't long before the devil found out that life as a husband was even harder than life as a laborer. Now without wages he had ten times more to do while Gentle Dora did nothing but spend her time hunting work for him.

"Why do you think I've married," she would cry, "if it isn't to have some one take care of me!"

So she would stand over him and scold and scold and scold while he, poor devil, toiled and sweated, doing the work of six men.

Time went by and the devil grew thinner and thinner and paler and paler. Gentle Dora begrudged him every mouthful he ate and was forever harping on his enormous appetite.

At last one day she said to him:

"You're simply eating me out of house and home. From now on you will have to board yourself. As I'm an honest woman I'll treat you justly. This year we'll divide the harvest half and half. Which will you have: that which grows above the ground, or that which grows below the ground?"

This sounded fair enough and the devil said:

"Give me the part that grows above the ground."

Thereupon Gentle Dora had the whole farm planted in potatoes and beets and carrots. When the harvest came she gave the devil the tops and herself took all the tubers.

That winter the poor devil would have starved if the neighbors hadn't taken pity on him and fed him.

In the spring Gentle Dora asked him what part of the new crop he wanted.

"This time," he said, "give me the part that grows under the ground."

Gentle Dora agreed and then planted the entire farm in millet and rye and poppy seed. At the harvest she took all the grain as her share and told the devil that the worthless roots belonged to him.

"What chance has a poor devil with such a woman?" he thought to himself bitterly.

Discouraged and unhappy he went out to the roadside where he sat down. The troubles of domestic life pressed upon him so heavily that soon he began to cry.

Presently a journeyman shoemaker came by and said to him:

"Comrade, what ails you?"

The devil looked at the shoemaker and, when he saw that the shoemaker was a friendly sort of person, he told him his story.

"Why do you stand such treatment?" the shoemaker asked.

The devil snuffled.

"How can I help it? I'm married to her."

"How can you help it?" the shoemaker repeated. "Comrade, look at me. At home I have just such a wife as your Gentle Dora. There was no living with her in peace, so one morning bright and early I ups and puts my tool kit on my shoulder and leaves her. Now I wander about from place to place, mending a shoe here and a slipper there, and life is much pleasanter than it used to be. Why don't you leave your Gentle Dora and come along with me? We'll make out somehow."

The devil was overjoyed at the suggestion and without a moment's hesitation he tramped off with the shoemaker.

"You won't regret the kindness you've done me," the devil said. "I'm so thin and pale that probably you don't realize I'm a devil. But I am and I can reward you."

They wandered about together for a long time living on the shoemaker's earnings. At last one day the devil said:

"Comrade, you have befriended me long enough. It is now my turn to do something for you. I've got a fine idea. You see that big town we're coming to? Well, I'll hurry on ahead and take possession of the prince's young daughter. You come along more slowly and when you hear the proclamation that the prince will richly reward any one who will cure his daughter, present yourself at the palace. When they lead you to the princess, make mysterious passes over her and mumble some gibberish. Then I will quit her body and the prince will reward you."

The devil's scheme worked perfectly. When the shoemaker reached the town the herald was already proclaiming the sad news that the princess had been taken possession of by a devil and that the prince was in search of a capable exorcist.

The shoemaker presented himself at the palace, made mysterious passes over the princess's body, pretended to mumble magic incantations, and in a short time had apparently succeeded in exorcising the devil.

In his gratitude for the princess's recovery, the prince paid the shoemaker a hundred golden ducats.

The devil waited for the shoemaker outside the town gate.

"You see," he said when the shoemaker had shown him the money, "I'm not an ungrateful devil."

They turned the same trick in several other cities until the shoemaker had a heavy bag of gold.

"Now you're a rich man," the devil said, "and we can part company. My seven years are up and I am going soon to return to hell. But before I go I'm going to take possession of one more princess. I served Gentle Dora so long that it's a pleasant change to rule some one. This time don't you try to exorcise me. You're famous now and the princess's father will probably hunt you out and beg you to cure his daughter, but you must excuse yourself. This is all I ask of you. If you allow yourself to be persuaded, I'll punish you by taking possession of your body. Don't forget!"

They bade each other good-bye and parted, the shoemaker going west and the devil east.

Soon word began to pass up and down the land that there was a great king toward the east who needed the services of the famous exorcist to restore his daughter. Emissaries of the king found the shoemaker and against his will dragged him to court. He declared he was powerless to help the princess but the king wouldn't listen to him and threatened him with torture and death if he refused to make the effort.

"Well then," the shoemaker said, after much thought, "chain the princess to her bed, order out all the attendants, and let me see her alone."

The king had these conditions fulfilled and the shoemaker went boldly into the princess's chamber.

"Hist! Devil!" he called softly.

Instantly the devil jumped out of the princess's mouth and when he saw the shoemaker he stamped his foot in anger.

"What!" he cried. "You've come after my warning! Don't you remember what I told you?"

The shoemaker put his finger to his lips and winked.

"Softly, comrade," he whispered, "softly! I'm not come to exorcise you but to warn you. You know that precious wife of yours, Gentle Dora? Well, she's traced you here and she's down in the courtyard now waiting for you."

The devil turned white with fright.

"Gentle Dora!" he gasped. "Lucifer, help me!"

Without another word he jumped out the window and flew straight down to hell as fast as the wind could carry him. And so great is his fear of Gentle Dora that he has never dared to show his face on earth again.

The king rewarded the shoemaker royally and to this day the shoemaker is wandering merrily about from place to place. Whenever he hears of a woman who is a scold, he says:

"Why, she's a regular Gentle Dora, isn't she?"

And when people ask him: "Who's Gentle Dora?" he tells them this story.

The Witch and the Horseshoes

ONCE THERE WAS a farmer's wife – I can't tell you which one – who was a witch. Now these folks used to have a feast every Eve of St. Philip and St. James.

As soon as they began to burn the brooms she couldn't rest: go she must. So she stripped her clothes off, and, standing under the chimney, she anointed herself with some ointment. When she had finished, she said: "Fly, but don't touch anything." And away she flew in the twinkling of an eye. Yes, that was just how it was.

But the farmhand was watching all this from the stables, and he watched carefully where she put the ointment. So he went in too, stripped his clothes off, and anointed himself. He said: "Fly, but don't touch anything." And off he flew till he came to the place where the witches were having their feast. Now, when he came there, the farmer's wife knew him, and, to hide herself from him, she turned herself into a white horse. But he did not lose sight of the horse. He mounted it and went to the smith with it, and told him to shoe it. Next day the woman had four horseshoes on, two on her hands and two on her feet. And she had to stay like that always!

The Haunted Mill

THERE WAS a haunted mill, and, dear me, what was it like! A rope-dancer came there with some monkeys. In the evening the Waternick came with a basketful of fishes. He made a fire and fried the fishes.

Meanwhile the monkeys had been sitting behind the stove, but when the Nick put the fishes in the pan and was tasting whether they were done, the monkeys came from behind the stove, and one of them put its paw into the pan. The man smacked him over the paw and said: "Get away, pussy! You didn't catch them, so don't eat them." And the monkey ran away.

After awhile comes another monkey and puts his paw in the pan. He smacked him too and said the same. But the rope-dancer had a bear, too, which was lying under the table all the time; and, when he heard the Waternick speak, he came from under the table, ran straight to the pan, and put his paw into it. The Waternick did the same to him as he had done to the monkeys. But the bear couldn't stand that. He sprang upon the poor Waternick and gave him a good beating. The Waternick had to run off, leaving the fishes behind. He didn't haunt the mill any more, and that's how they got rid of him.

The Flaming Horse

THERE WAS ONCE a land that was dreary and dark as the grave, for the sun of heaven never shone upon it. The king of the country had a wonderful horse that had, growing right on his forehead, a flaming sun. In order that his subjects might have the light that is necessary for life, the king had this

horse led back and forth from one end of his dark kingdom to the other. Wherever he went his flaming head shone out and it seemed like beautiful day.

Suddenly this wonderful horse disappeared. Heavy darkness that nothing could dispel settled down on the country. Fear spread among the people and soon they were suffering terrible poverty, for they were unable to cultivate the fields or do anything else that would earn them a livelihood. Confusion increased until the king saw that the whole country was likely to perish. In order then, if possible, to save his people, he gathered his army together and set out in search of the missing horse.

Through heavy darkness they groped their way slowly and with difficulty to the far boundaries of the kingdom. At last they reached the ancient forests that bordered the neighboring state and they saw gleaming through the trees faint rays of the sunshine with which that kingdom was blessed.

Here they came upon a small lonely cottage which the king entered in order to find out where he was and to ask directions for moving forward.

A man was sitting at the table reading diligently from a large open book. When the king bowed to him, he raised his eyes, returned the greeting, and stood up. His whole appearance showed that he was no ordinary man but a seer.

"I was just reading about you," he said to the king, "that you were gone in search of the flaming horse. Exert yourself no further, for you will never find him. But trust the enterprise to me and I will get him for you."

"If you do that, my man," the king said, "I will pay you royally."

"I seek no reward. Return home at once with your army, for your people need you. Only leave here with me one of your serving men."

The king did exactly as the seer advised and went home at once.

The next day the seer and his man set forth. They journeyed far and long until they had crossed six different countries. Then they went on into the seventh country which was ruled over by three brothers who had married three sisters, the daughters of a witch.

They made their way to the front of the royal palace, where the seer said to his man: "Do you stay here while I go in and find out whether the kings are at home. It is they who stole the flaming horse and the youngest brother rides him."

Then the seer transformed himself into a green bird and flew up to the window of the eldest queen and flitted about and pecked until she opened the window and let him into her chamber. When she let him in, he alighted on her white hand and the queen was as happy as a child.

"You pretty thing!" she said, playing with him. "If my husband were home how pleased he would be! But he's off visiting a third of his kingdom and he won't be home until evening."

Suddenly the old witch came into the room and as soon as she saw the bird she shrieked to her daughter: "Wring the neck of that cursed bird, or it will stain you with blood!"

"Why should it stain me with blood, the dear innocent thing?"

"Dear innocent mischief!" shrieked the witch. "Here, give it to me and I'll wring its neck!"

She tried to catch the bird, but the bird changed itself into a man and was already out of the door before they knew what had become of him.

After that he changed himself again into a green bird and flew up to the window of the second sister. He pecked at it until she opened it and let him in. Then he flitted about her, settling first on one of her white hands, then on the other.

"What a dear bird you are!" cried the queen. "How you would please my husband if he were at home. But he's off visiting two-thirds of his kingdom and he won't be back until tomorrow evening."

At that moment the witch ran into the room and as soon as she saw the bird she shrieked out: "Wring the neck of that wretched bird, or it will stain you with blood!"

"Why should it stain me with blood?" the daughter answered. "The dear innocent thing!"

"Dear innocent mischief!" shrieked the witch. "Here, give it to me and I'll wring its neck!"

She reached out to catch the bird, but in less time than it takes to clap a hand, the bird had changed itself into a man who ran through the door and was gone before they knew where he was.

A moment later he again changed himself into a green bird and flew up to the window of the youngest queen. He flitted about and pecked until she opened the window and let him in. Then he alighted at once on her white hand and this pleased her so much that she laughed like a child and played with him.

"Oh, what a dear bird you are!" she cried. "How you would delight my husband if he were home. But he's off visiting all three parts of his kingdom and he won't be back until the day after tomorrow in the evening."

At that moment the old witch rushed into the room. "Wring the neck of that cursed bird!" she shrieked, "or it will stain you with blood."

"My dear mother," the queen answered, "why should it stain me with blood – beautiful innocent creature that it is?"

"Beautiful innocent mischief!" shrieked the witch. "Here, give it to me and I'll wring its neck!"

But at that moment the bird changed itself into a man, disappeared through the door, and they never saw him again.

The seer knew now where the kings were and when they would come home. So he made his plans accordingly. He ordered his servant to follow him and they set out from the city at a quick pace. They went on until they came to a bridge which the three kings as they came back would have to cross.

The seer and his man hid themselves under the bridge and lay there in wait until evening. As the sun sank behind the mountains, they heard the clatter of hoofs approaching the bridge. It was the eldest king returning home. At the bridge his horse stumbled on a log which the seer had rolled there.

"What scoundrel has thrown a log here?" cried the king angrily.

Instantly the seer leaped out from under the bridge and demanded of the king how he dared to call him a scoundrel. Clamoring for satisfaction he drew his sword and attacked the king. The king, too, drew sword and defended himself, but after a short struggle he fell from his horse dead.

The seer bound the dead king to his horse and then with a cut of the whip started the horse homewards.

The seer hid himself again and he and his man lay in wait until the next evening.

On that evening near sunset the second king came riding up to the bridge. When he saw the ground sprinkled with blood, he cried out: "Surely there has been a murder here! Who has dared to commit such a crime in my kingdom!"

At these words the seer leaped out from under the bridge, drew his sword, and shouted: "How dare you insult me? Defend yourself as best you can!"

The king drew, but after a short struggle he, too, yielded up his life to the sword of the seer.

The seer bound the dead king to his horse and with a cut of the whip started the horse homewards.

Then the seer hid himself again under the bridge and he and his man lay there in wait until the third evening.

On the third evening just at sunset the youngest king came galloping home on the flaming steed. He was hurrying fast because he had been delayed. But when he saw red blood at the bridge he stopped short and looked around.

"What audacious villain," he cried, "has dared to kill a man in my kingdom!"

Hardly had he spoken when the seer stood before him with drawn sword demanding satisfaction for the insult of his words.

"I don't know how I've insulted you," the king said, "unless you're the murderer."

When the seer refused to parley, the king, too, drew his sword and defended himself.

To overcome the first two kings had been mere play for the seer, but it was no play this time. They both fought until their swords were broken and still victory was doubtful.

"We shall accomplish nothing with swords," the seer said. "That is plain. I tell you what: let us turn ourselves into wheels and start rolling down the hill and the wheel that gets broken let him yield."

"Good!" said the king. "I'll be a cartwheel and you be a lighter wheel."

"No, no," the seer answered quickly. "You be the light wheel and I'll be the cartwheel."

To this the king agreed. So they went up the hill, turned themselves into wheels and started rolling down. The cartwheel went whizzing into the lighter wheel and broke its spokes.

"There!" cried the seer, rising up from the cartwheel. "I am victor!"

"Not so, brother, not so!" said the king, standing before the seer. "You only broke my fingers! Now I tell you what: let us change ourselves into two flames and let the flame that burns up the other be victor. I'll be a red flame and do you be a white one."

"Oh, no," the seer interrupted. "You be the white flame and I'll be the red one."

The king agreed to this. So they went back to the road that led to the bridge, turned themselves into flames, and began burning each other mercilessly. But neither was able to burn up the other.

Suddenly a beggar came down the road, an old man with a long gray beard and a bald head, with a scrip at his side and a heavy staff in his hand.

"Father," the white flame said, "get some water and pour it on the red flame and I'll give you a penny."

But the red flame called out quickly: "Not so, father! Get some water and pour it on the white flame and I'll give you a shilling!"

Now of course the shilling appealed to the beggar more than the penny. So he got some water, poured it on the white flame and that was the end of the king.

The red flame turned into a man who seized the flaming horse by the bridle, mounted him and, after he had rewarded the beggar, called his servant and rode off.

Meanwhile at the royal palace there was deep sorrow for the murdered kings. The halls were draped in black and people came from miles around to gaze at the mutilated bodies of the two elder brothers which the horses had carried home.

The old witch was beside herself with rage. As soon as she had devised a plan whereby she could avenge the murder of her sons-in-law, she took her three daughters under her arm, mounted an iron rake, and sailed off through the air.

The seer and his man had already covered a good part of their journey and were hurrying on over rough mountains and across desert plains, when the servant was taken with a terrible hunger. There wasn't anything in sight that he could eat, not even a wild berry. Then suddenly they came upon an apple tree that was bending beneath a load of ripe fruit. The apples were red and pleasant to the sight and sent out a fragrance that was most inviting.

The servant was delighted. "Glory to God!" he cried. "Now I can feast to my heart's content on these apples!"

He was already running to the tree when the seer called him back.

"Wait! Don't touch them! I will pick them for you myself!"

But instead of picking an apple, the seer drew his sword and struck a mighty blow into the apple tree. Red blood gushed forth.

"Just see, my man! You would have perished if you had eaten one apple. This apple tree is the eldest queen, whom her mother, the witch, placed here for our destruction."

Presently they came to a spring. Its water bubbled up clear as crystal and most tempting to the tired traveler.

"Ah," said the servant, "since we can get nothing better, at least we can take a drink of this good water."

"Wait!" cried the seer. "I will draw some for you."

But instead of drawing water he plunged his naked sword into the middle of the spring. Instantly it was covered with blood and blood began to spurt from the spring in thick streams.

"This is the second queen, whom her mother, the witch, placed here to work our doom."

Presently they came to a rosebush covered with beautiful red roses that scented all the air with their fragrance.

"What beautiful roses!" said the servant. "I have never seen any such in all my life. I'll go pluck a few. As I can't eat or drink, I'll comfort myself with roses."

"Don't dare to pluck them!" cried the seer. "I'll pluck them for you."

With that he cut into the bush with his sword and red blood spurted out as though he had cut a human vein.

"This is the youngest queen," said the seer, "whom her mother, the witch, placed here in the hope of revenging herself on us for the death of her sons-in-law."

After that they proceeded without further adventures.

When they crossed the boundaries of the dark kingdom, the sun in the horse's forehead sent out its blessed rays in all directions. Everything came to life. The earth rejoiced and covered itself with flowers.

The king felt he could never thank the seer enough and he offered him the half of his kingdom.

But the seer replied: "You are the king. Keep on ruling over the whole of your kingdom and let me return to my cottage in peace."

He bade the king farewell and departed.

Grandfather's Eyes

ONCE UPON A TIME there was a poor boy whom everybody called Yanechek. His father and mother were dead and he was forced to start out alone in the world to make a living. For a long time he could find nothing to do. He wandered on and on and at last he came to a little house that stood by itself near the edge of the woods. An old man sat on the doorstep and Yanechek could see that he was blind, for there were empty holes where his eyes used to be.

Some goats that were penned in a shed near the house began bleating and the old man said:

"You poor things, you want to go to pasture, don't you? But I can't see to drive you and I have no one else to send."

"Send me, grandfather," Yanechek said. "Take me as your goatherd and let me work for you."

"Who are you?" the old man asked.

Yanechek told him who he was and the old man agreed to take him.

"And now," he said, "drive the goats to pasture. But one thing, Yanechek: don't take them to the hill over there in the woods or the Yezinkas may get you! That's where they caught me!"

Now Yanechek knew that the Yezinkas were wicked witches who lived in a cave in the woods and went about in the guise of beautiful young women. If they met you they would greet you modestly and say something like "God bless you!" to make you think they were good and kind and then, once they had you in their power, they would put you to sleep and gouge out your eyes! Oh, yes, Yanechek knew about the Yezinkas.

"Never fear, grandfather, the Yezinkas won't get me!"

The first day and the second day Yanechek kept the goats near home. But the third day he said to himself: "I think I'll try the hill in the woods. There's better grass there and I'm not afraid of the Yezinkas."

Before he started out he cut three long slender switches from a blackberry bramble, wound them into small coils, and hid them in the crown of his hat. Then he drove the goats through the woods where they nibbled at leaves and branches, beside a deep river where they paused to drink, and up the grassy slopes of the hill.

There the goats scattered this way and that and Yanechek sat down on a stone in the shade. He was hardly seated when he looked up and there before him, dressed all in white, stood the most beautiful maiden in the world. Her skin was red as roses and white as milk, her eyes were black as sloe berries, and her hair, dark as the raven's wing, fell about her shoulders in long waving tresses. She smiled and offered Yanechek a big red apple.

"God bless you, shepherd boy," she said. "Here's something for you that grew in my own garden."

But Yanechek knew that she must be a Yezinka and that, if he ate the apple, he would fall asleep and then she would gouge out his eyes. So he said, politely: "No, thank you, beautiful maiden. My master has a tree in his garden with apples that are bigger than yours and I have eaten as many as I want."

When the maiden saw that Yanechek was not to be coaxed, she disappeared.

Presently a second maiden came, more beautiful, if possible, than the first. In her hand she carried a lovely red rose.

"God bless you, shepherd boy," she said. "Isn't this a lovely rose? I picked it myself from the hedge. How fragrant it is! Will you smell it?"

She offered him the rose but Yanechek refused it.

"No, thank you, beautiful maiden. My master's garden is full of roses much sweeter than yours and I smell roses all the time."

At that the second maiden shrugged her shoulders and disappeared.

Presently a third one came, the youngest and most beautiful of them all. In her hand she carried a golden comb.

"God bless you, shepherd boy."

"Good day to you, beautiful maiden."

She smiled at Yanechek and said: "Truly you are a handsome lad, but you would be handsomer still if your hair were nicely combed. Come, let me comb it for you."

Yanechek said nothing but he took off his hat without letting the maiden see what was hidden in its crown. She came up close to him and then, just as she was about to comb his hair, he whipped out one of the long blackberry switches and struck her over the hands. She screamed and tried to escape but she could not because it is the fate of a Yezinka not to be able to move if ever a human being strikes her over the hands with a switch of bramble.

So Yanechek took her two hands and bound them together with the long thorny switch while she wept and struggled.

"Help, sisters! Help!" she cried.

At that the two other Yezinkas came running and when they saw what had happened they, too, began to weep and to beg Yanechek to unbind their sister's hands and let her go.

But Yanechek only laughed and said: "No. You unbind them."

"But, Yanechek, how can we? Our hands are soft and the thorns will prick us."

However, when they saw that Yanechek was not to be moved, they went to their sister and tried to help her. Whereupon Yanechek whipped out the other two blackberry switches and struck them also on their soft pretty hands, first one and then the other. After that they, too, could not move and it was easy enough to bind them and make them prisoners.

"Now I've got the three of you, you wicked Yezinkas!" Yanechek said. "It was you who gouged out my poor old master's eyes, you know it was! And you shall not escape until you do as I ask."

He left them there and ran home to his master to whom he said: "Come, grandfather, for I have found a means of restoring your eyes!"

He took the old man by the hand and led him through the woods, along the bank of the river, and up the grassy hillside where the three Yezinkas were still struggling and weeping.

Then he said to the first of them: "Tell me now where my master's eyes are. If you don't tell me, I'll throw you into the river."

The first Yezinka pretended she didn't know. So Yanechek lifted her up and started down the hill toward the river.

That frightened the maiden and she cried out: "Don't throw me into the river, Yanechek, and I'll find you your master's eyes, I promise you I will!"

So Yanechek put her down and she led him to a cave in the hillside where she and her wicked sisters had piled up a great heap of eyes – all kinds of eyes they were: big eyes, little eyes, black eyes, red eyes, blue eyes, green eyes – every kind of eye in the world that you can think of.

She went to the heap and picked out two eyes which she said were the right ones. But when the poor old man tried to look through them, he cried out in fright:

"I see nothing but dark treetops with sleeping birds and flying bats! These are not my eyes! They are owls' eyes! Take them out! Take them out!"

When Yanechek saw how the first Yezinka had deceived him, without another word he picked her up, threw her into the river, and that was the end of her.

Then he said to the second sister: "Now you tell me where my master's eyes are."

At first she, too, pretended she didn't know, but when Yanechek threatened to throw her likewise into the river, she was glad enough to lead him back to the cave and pick out two eyes that she said were the right ones.

But when the poor old man tried to look through them, again he cried out in fright: "I see nothing but tangled underbrush and snapping teeth and hot red tongues! These are not my eyes! They are wolves' eyes! Take them out! Take them out!"

When Yanechek saw how the second Yezinka had deceived him, without another word he picked her up, and threw her also into the river, and that was the end of her.

Then Yanechek said to the third sister: "Now you tell me where my master's eyes are."

At first she, too, pretended she didn't know, but when Yanechek threatened to throw her likewise into the river, she was glad enough to lead him to the cave and pick out two eyes that she said were the right ones.

But when the poor old man tried to look through them, again he cried out in fright: "I see nothing but swirling waters and flashing fins! These are not my eyes! They are fishes' eyes! Take them out! Take them out!"

When Yanechek saw how the third Yezinka had deceived him, without another word he was ready to serve her as he had served her sisters. But she begged him not to drown her and she said:

"Let me try again, Yanechek, and I'll find you the right eyes, I promise you I will!"

So Yanechek let her try again and from the very bottom of the heap she picked out two more eyes that she swore were the right ones.

When the old man looked through them, he clapped his hands and said: "These are my own eyes, praise God! Now I can see as well as ever!"

After that the old man and Yanechek lived on happily together. Yanechek pastured the goats and the old man made cheeses at home and they ate them together. And you may be sure that the third Yezinka never showed herself again on that hill!

The Devil's Gifts

THERE WERE ONCE TWO MEN, a shoemaker and a farmer, who had been close friends in youth. The shoemaker married and had many children to whom the farmer stood godfather. For this reason the two men called each other "Godfather." When they met it was "Godfather, this," and "Godfather, that." The shoemaker was an industrious little man and yet with so many mouths to fill he remained poor. The farmer on the other hand soon grew rich for he had no children to eat into his savings.

Years went by and money and possessions began to change the farmer's disposition. The more he accumulated, the more he wanted, until people were whispering behind his back that he was miserly and avaricious. His wife was like him. She, too, saved and skimped although, as I have told you, they had neither chick nor child to provide for.

The richer the farmer grew, the less he cared for his poor friend and his poor friend's children. Now when they called him "Godfather," he frowned impatiently, and whenever he saw any of them he pretended to be very busy for fear they should ask him a favor.

One day when he had slaughtered beef, the poor shoemaker came to him and said:

"My dear Godfather, you have just made a killing. Won't you please give me a little piece of meat? My wife and children are hungry."

"No!" roared the rich man. "Why should I feed your family? You ought to save as I do and then you wouldn't have to ask favors of any one."

Humiliated by the refusal, the shoemaker went home and told his wife what his friend had said.

"Go back to him," his wife insisted, "and tell him again that his godchildren are hungry. I don't think he understood you."

So the poor little shoemaker returned to the rich man. He cleared his throat apologetically and stammered:

"Dear Godfather, you – you don't want your poor godchildren to go hungry, do you? Give me just one small piece of meat – that's all I ask."

In a rage, the rich man picked up a hunk of meat and threw it at his poor friend.

"There!" he shouted. "And now go to hell, you and the meat with you, and tell the Devil I sent you."

The shoemaker picked up the piece of meat. It was all fat and gristle.

"No use carrying this home," he thought to himself. "I think I better do as Godfather says. Yes, I'll go to hell and give it to the Devil."

So he tramped down to hell and presented himself at the gate. The little devil who stood on guard greeted him merrily.

"Hello, shoemaker! What do you want here?"

"I have a present for the Devil, a piece of meat that Godfather gave me."

The little devil of a guard nodded his head understandingly.

"I see, I see. Very well then, come with me and I'll lead you to Prince Lucifer. But I'll give you a bit of advice first. When the Prince asks you what present you'd like in return, tell him you'd like the tablecloth off his own table."

The little devil of a guard then conducted the shoemaker into Prince Lucifer's presence and the Prince received him with every mark of consideration. The shoemaker told him what Godfather had said and presented him the hunk of meat. Lucifer received it most graciously. Then he said:

"Now, my dear shoemaker, let me make you a little present in return. Do you see anything here that you'd like?"

"If it pleases your Highness," the shoemaker said, "give me that cloth that is spread over your table."

Lucifer at once handed him the cloth and dismissed him with many wishes for a pleasant journey back to earth.

As the shoemaker was leaving the friendly little devil of a guard said to him:

"I just want to tell you that's no ordinary tablecloth that the Prince has given you. No, indeed! Whenever you're hungry, all you've got to do is spread out that cloth and say: 'Meat and drink for one!' or, for as many as you want, and instantly you will have what you ask."

Overjoyed at his good fortune the little shoemaker hurried back to earth. As night came on he stopped at a tavern. He thought this was a good place to try the tablecloth. So he took it out of his bag, spread it over the table, and said:

"Meat and drink for one!"

Instantly a fine supper appeared and the shoemaker ate and drank his fill.

Now the landlord of the tavern was an evil, covetous fellow and when he saw how the tablecloth worked his fingers itched to own it. He called his wife aside and told her in guarded whispers what he had seen.

Her eyes, too, filled with greed.

"Husband," she whispered back, "we've got to get possession of that tablecloth! Think what a help it would be to us in our business! I tell you what we'll do: tonight when the shoemaker is asleep we'll steal his tablecloth and slip in one of our own in its place. He's a simple fellow and will never know the difference."

So that night while the shoemaker was asleep, they tip-toed in, stole the magic tablecloth out of the bag, and substituted one of their own.

The next morning when the shoemaker awoke and spread out the cloth which he found in his bag and said: "Meat and drink for one!" of course nothing happened.

"That's strange," he thought to himself. "I'll have to take this back to the Devil and ask him to give me something else."

So instead of going home he went back to hell and knocked at the gate.

"Hello, shoemaker!" the little devil of a guard said. "What do you want now?"

"Well, you see it's this way," the shoemaker explained: "this tablecloth of the Devil's worked all right last night but it doesn't work this morning."

The little devil grinned.

"Oh, I see. And you want Prince Lucifer to take it back and give you something else, eh? Well, I'm sure he will. If you want my advice, I should say to ask him for that red rooster that sits in the chimney corner."

The Prince received the shoemaker as kindly as before and was perfectly willing to exchange the tablecloth for the red rooster.

When the shoemaker got back to the gate, the little devil of a guard said:

"I see you've got the red rooster. Now I just want to tell you that's no ordinary rooster. Whenever you need money, all you have to do is put that rooster on the table and say: 'Crow, rooster, crow!' He'll crow and as he crows a golden ducat will drop from his bill!"

"What a lucky fellow I am!" the little shoemaker thought to himself as he hurried back to earth.

As night came on he stopped again at the same tavern and, when it was time to pay for his supper, he put the red rooster on the table and said:

"Crow, rooster, crow!"

The rooster crowed and sure enough a golden ducat dropped from his bill.

The covetous landlord licked his greedy lips and hurried off to his wife.

"We've got a red rooster," the wife said. "I'll tell you what we'll do: when the shoemaker's asleep we'll trade roosters. He's a simple fellow and will never know the difference."

So the next morning after breakfast, when the shoemaker put what he thought was his own rooster on the table and said: "Crow, rooster, crow!" of course nothing happened.

"I wonder what's the matter with you," he said to the rooster. "I'll have to take you back to the Devil."

So again he tramped down to hell and explained to the little devil of a guard that the rooster no longer dropped golden ducats from his bill.

The little devil listened and grinned.

"I suppose you want Prince Lucifer to give you something else, eh?"

The shoemaker nodded.

"I'm sure he will," the little devil said. "He seems to have taken quite a fancy to you. Now take my advice and ask him for the pair of clubs that are lying under the oven."

So the shoemaker when he was led again into Lucifer's presence explained to the Prince that the red rooster no longer worked and please would His Highness give him something else instead.

The Prince was most affable.

"Certainly," he said.

"Well then, Your Highness, I'd like that pair of clubs I see under the oven."

Lucifer gave him the clubs and wished him a pleasant journey home.

When the shoemaker got back to the gate, the little devil of a guard wagged his head and blinked his eyes.

"Shoemaker," he said, "those are fine clubs! You don't know how fine they are! Why, they'll do anything you tell them! If you point to a man and say to them: 'Tickle that fellow!' they'll jump about and tickle him under the ribs. If you say: 'Strike that fellow!' they'll hit him. And if you say: 'Beat him!' they'll give him a terrible drubbing. Now I want you to try these clubs on that landlord and his wife for they have been playing tricks on you. They stole your tablecloth and your rooster. When you reach the tavern tonight, they'll be entertaining a wedding party and they'll say they haven't any room for you. Don't argue but quietly take out your clubs and order them to knock about among the wedding guests. Then order them to beat the landlord and his wife and those two will soon cry for mercy and be more than willing to return you your property."

The shoemaker thanked the little devil of a guard for his good advice and, putting the clubs in his bag, climbed back to earth. When he reached the tavern, sure enough he found a wedding party feasting and dancing.

"Get out of here!" the landlord cried. "There's no room for you!"

Without a word the shoemaker took out his clubs and said:

"Clubs, knock around among the wedding guests!"

Instantly the two clubs went knocking about among the wedding guests, tickling some and throwing down others, until the place was in an uproar.

"Now beat the landlord and his wife!" the shoemaker cried.

At that the clubs hopped over to the landlord and his wife and began beating them over the head and shoulders until they both dropped on their knees before the shoemaker and begged for mercy.

"Are you ready to give me back my tablecloth and rooster?" the shoemaker asked.

"Yes, yes!" they cried. "Only call off your clubs and we'll give you back your tablecloth and rooster – we swear we will!"

When he thought he had punished them enough, the shoemaker ordered the clubs to stop and the landlord and his wife tottered off as fast as their trembling legs could carry them. Presently they returned with the tablecloth and the rooster.

So the shoemaker, when he got home, had all three of the Devil's presents tucked safely away in his bag.

"Now, wife!" he cried. "Now, children! Now we are going to have a feast!"

He spread out the tablecloth and said:

"Meat and drink for ten!"

Instantly such a feast appeared that for a moment the poor wife and the hungry children couldn't believe their eyes. Then they set to, and, oh! I can't begin to tell you all they ate!

When they could eat no more, the shoemaker said:

"That isn't all. I've got something else in my bag."

He took out the clubs and said:

"Clubs, tickle the children!"

Instantly the clubs hopped around among the children and tickled them under the ribs until they were all roaring with laughter.

"And that isn't all!" the shoemaker said. "I've got something else in my bag."

He pulled out the red rooster, put him on the table, and said:

"Crow, rooster, crow!"

The rooster crowed and a golden ducat dropped from his bill.

"Oh!" the children cried, and the youngest one begged: "Make him do it again! Make him do it again!"

So again the shoemaker said: "Crow, rooster, crow!" and again a golden ducat dropped from the rooster's bill.

The children were so amused that the shoemaker kept the rooster crowing all night long until the room was overflowing with a great heap of shining ducats.

The next day the shoemaker said to his wife:

"We must measure our money and see how much we have. Send one of the children over to Godfather to borrow a bushel measure."

So the youngest child ran over to the rich man's house and said:

"Godfather, my father says will you please lend us a bushel measure to measure our money."

"Measure your money!" the rich man growled. "Pooh, pooh, what nonsense! Wife, where's that old worn-out measure that we're going to throw away? It's the very thing to lend these beggars."

The woman who was just as disagreeable as the man handed the child an old broken measure and said, severely:

"See you bring it back at once!"

In a short time the little girl returned the measure.

"Thanks, Godfather," she said. "We've got a hundred bushels."

"A hundred bushels!" the farmer repeated scornfully after the child was gone. "A hundred bushels of what? Look inside the measure, wife, and see if you find a trace of anything."

The woman peered inside the measure and found a golden ducat lodged in a slit. She took it out and the mere sight of it made her face and her husband's face turn sick and pale with envy.

"Do you suppose those beggars really have got some money?" he said. "We better go over at once and see."

So they hurried over to the shoemaker's cottage and they shook hands with him and his wife most effusively and they rubbed their hands together and they smiled and they smiled and the rich man said:

"Dear Godfather, how are you? And how are all my dear godchildren? And what is this good fortune that has come to you?"

"I owe it all to you," the shoemaker said.

"To me?" the farmer repeated and, although he began to feel sick inside to think that any one had benefited through him, he kept on smiling and rubbing his hands. "Tell me about it, dear Godfather."

"You know that piece of meat you gave me," the shoemaker said. "You told me to give it to the Devil. I took your advice and made the Devil a present of it and he gave me all these wonderful things in return."

The shoemaker made the tablecloth spread itself, he made the rooster crow and drop a golden ducat, and he made the clubs dance merrily around the room and tickle the children under the ribs.

The farmer and his wife grew sicker and sicker with envy but they kept on smiling and rubbing their hands and asking questions.

"Tell us, dear Godfather," they said, "what road do you take to go to hell? Of course we're not expecting to go ourselves but we'd just like to know."

The shoemaker told them the way and they hurried home. They slaughtered their finest cattle and then, packing on their backs all the choicest cuts of the meat, they staggered down to hell.

When the little devil of a guard saw them coming, he grinned and chuckled.

"Welcome!" he cried. "We've been waiting for you a long time! Come right in!"

He led them to Prince Lucifer and the Prince recognized them instantly.

"It's very good of you coming before you had to," he said. "This saves me a trip to earth. I was thinking just the other day it was time to go after you. And see all that fine meat you've brought with you! I certainly am glad to see you! It isn't often I have the pleasure of meeting people as avaricious, as greedy, as mean, as you two have been. In fact, both of you are such ornaments to hell that I think I'll just have to keep you here forever!"

So the rich farmer and his wife were never again seen on earth.

As for the shoemaker – he and his family lived long and merrily. They shared their good fortune with others, never forgetting the time when they, too, suffered from poverty. And because they were good and kind, the Devil's gifts brought them only happiness.

The Devil's Match

ONCE UPON A TIME there was a poor farmer who lived in a wretched tumble-down cottage beyond the village and whose farm consisted of a miserable little field no bigger than your hand. His children were ragged and hungry and his wife was always worried over getting them enough to eat.

Yet the farmer was a clever fellow with a quick shrewd wit and people used to say that he'd be able to fool the devil if ever he had the chance. One day the chance came.

His wife had sent him into the forest to gather a bundle of faggots. Suddenly without any warning a young man with black face and shiny eyes stood before him.

"It's a devil, of course," the farmer told himself. "But even so there's no use being frightened."

So he wished the devil a civil good-day and the devil, who was really a very simple fellow indeed, returned his greeting and asked him what he was doing in the forest.

Now the farmer suddenly remembered that his grandmother had once told him devils were afraid of lime trees because the bast from lime trees is the one thing in the world they are unable to break. That's why, when you catch a devil, you must tie his hands together with bast.

So the farmer, recalling what his grandmother had said, remarked casually:

"Oh, I'm looking for a lime tree. I want to strip off some bast. Then I'm going after them" – and when he said them he paused significantly – "and tie them hand and foot."

He peeped at the devil out of the corner of his eye and saw that the devil had turned almost white under his black skin.

"He is a foolish one!" he thought to himself.

"Oh, don't do that!" the devil cried. "What have we ever done to you?"

The farmer pretended to be firm and repeated that that was just what he was going to do.

"Please listen to me," the devil begged. "If you promise to let us alone I tell you what I'll do: I'll bring you such a big bag of gold that it will make you a rich man."

At first the farmer, being a shrewd fellow, pretended that he cared nothing for money. Then gradually he let himself be persuaded and at last said:

"Very well. If you bring me the gold within an hour I won't bind you with bast. But don't keep me waiting or I may change my mind."

The young devil – oh, you never saw a more stupid young fellow! – scurried off and, long before the hour was up, he came panting back with a great big bag of gold.

"Is that enough?" he asked.

The farmer who had really never seen so much money in all his life hemmed and hawed but finally said:

"Well, it isn't as much as I expected but I'll accept it."

The young devil, delighted with his bargain, hurried back to hell and told all his black comrades how grateful they ought to be to him for saving them from the farmer who was planning to bind them, hand and foot, with bast.

When the other devils heard the whole story, they laughed at him loud and long.

"You are certainly the stupidest devil in hell!" they said. "Why, that man has made a fool of you!"

They discussed the matter among themselves and decided that the devil would have to get back the bag of gold or the story would leak out and thereafter the people on earth would have no more respect for devils.

"Go back to the farmer," they said, "and dare him to a wrestling match. Tell him that whoever wins the match is to keep the gold."

So the young devil went back to earth and dared the farmer to a wrestling match. The farmer, who saw how things were, said:

"My dear young friend, if I were to wrestle with you I'm afraid I'd hurt you for I'm awfully strong. I tell you what I'll do: I'll let you wrestle with my old grandfather. He's ninety-nine years old but even so he's more nearly in your class."

The devil agreed to this and the farmer – oh, but that farmer was a sly one! – led him out into the forest to a cave where a big brown bear lay asleep.

"There's my grandfather," the farmer said. "Go wake him up and make him wrestle."

The devil shook the bear and said:

"Wake up, old man! Wake up! We're going to wrestle!"

The bear opened his little eyes, stood up on his hind legs, and taking the devil in his arms hugged him until the devil thought his bones would all be crushed. It was as much as the devil could do to escape with his life.

"Oh, my poor ribs! My poor ribs!" he gasped when he was safely back in hell. "He's a terrible man – that farmer! Why, even his old grandfather is so strong that I thought he'd squeeze me to death!"

But when he had told his full story the other devils laughed at him louder than before and told him that the farmer had again fooled him.

"You've got to try another match with him," they said. "This time dare him to a foot race and mind you don't let him fool you."

So in a day or two when the soreness was gone from his bones the devil went back to earth and dared the farmer to run a foot race with him.

"Certainly," the farmer said, "but it's hardly fair to let you run against me because I go like the wind. I tell you what I'll do: I'll let you race with my small son. He's only a year old and perhaps you can beat him."

The devil – I never knew a more stupid fellow in my life! – agreed to this and the farmer took him out to a meadow. Under some bushes he showed him a rabbit's hole.

"My little boy's asleep in there," he said. "Call him out."

"Little boy!" the devil called. "Come out and run a race with me!"

Instantly a rabbit jumped out of the hole and went hoppetylop across the meadow. The devil tried hard to overtake him but couldn't. He ran on and on. They came at last to a deep ravine. The rabbit leaped across but the devil, when he tried to do the same, slipped and fell and went rolling down over stones and brambles, down, down, down, into a brook. When he had dragged himself out of the water, bruised and scratched, the rabbit had disappeared.

"I've had enough of that farmer," the devil said when he got back to hell. "Why, do you know, he has a small boy just one year old and I tell you there isn't one of you can beat that boy running!"

But the devils when they heard the rest of the story only laughed and jeered and told their comrade that the farmer had again tricked him.

"You've got to go back to him another time," they said. "It will never do for people to get the idea that devils are such fools."

"But I tell you I won't dare him to another wrestling match," the young devil said, "nor to a foot race, either."

"Try whistling this time," his comrades told him. "You ought to be able to beat him whistling. Now have your wits about you and don't let him fool you again."

So the devil went back to earth and said to the farmer:

"We've got to have another contest for that bag of money. This time let's try whistling."

"Very well," the farmer said. "We'll have a whistling match."

They went off into the forest and the farmer told the devil to whistle first.

The devil whistled and all the leaves on the trees shook and trembled. He whistled again and the twigs began to crackle and break. He whistled a third time and big branches snapped off and fell to the ground.

"There!" the devil exclaimed, "Can you beat that?"

"My poor boy," the farmer said. (Oh, but that farmer was a tricky one!) "Is that the best you can do? Why, when I whistle, if you don't cover up your ears you'll be deafened! And as likely as not a tree will fall on you and kill you! Now shall I begin?"

"Wait a minute!" the devil begged. "Won't you please tie up my ears before you begin because I don't want to be deafened."

This was just what the farmer was hoping the devil would say. So he took out a big kerchief and put it over the devil's ears and also over his eyes and tied it behind in a hard knot.

"Now then!" he shouted. "Take care!"

With that he began to whistle and as he whistled he picked up a big branch off the ground and gave the devil an awful crack over the head.

"My head! My head!" the devil cried.

"My poor fellow!" the farmer said, pretending to be very sympathetic. "I hope that tree as it fell down didn't hurt you! Now I'm going to whistle again and you must be more careful."

This time when he whistled the farmer struck the devil over the head harder than before.

"That's enough!" the devil shouted. "Another tree has fallen on me! Stop! Stop!"

"No," the farmer insisted. "You whistled three times and I'm going to whistle three times. Are you ready?"

The poor devil had to say: "Yes," and thereupon the farmer began to whistle and at the same time to beat the devil over his head and shoulders until the devil supposed that the whole forest was falling on him.

"Stop whistling!" he shouted. "Stop or I'll be killed!"

But the farmer wouldn't stop until he was too exhausted to beat the devil any longer.

Then he paused and asked:

"Shall I whistle some more?"

"No! No! No!" the devil roared. "Undo the kerchief and let me go and I swear I'll never come back!"

So the farmer undid the kerchief and the devil fled, too terrified to stop even long enough to look around for all those fallen trees.

He never came back and the farmer was left in undisputed possession of the gold.

"I owe all my good fortune to my old grandmother," the farmer used to say, "for she it was who told me to tie *them* with bast."

The Devil's Little Brother-in-Law

ONCE UPON A TIME there was a youth named Peter. He was the son of a rich farmer but on his father's death his stepmother robbed him of his inheritance and drove him out into the world, penniless and destitute.

"Begone with you now!" she shouted. "Never let me see your face again!"

"Where shall I go?" Peter asked.

"Go to the Devil, for all I care!" the stepmother cried and slammed the door in his face.

Peter felt very sad at being driven away from the farm that had always been his home, but he was an able-bodied lad, industrious and energetic, and he thought he would have no trouble making his way in the world.

He tramped to the next village and stopped at a big farmhouse. The farmer was standing at the door, eating a great hunk of buttered bread.

Peter touched his hat respectfully and said:

"Let every one praise Lord Jesus!"

With his mouth stuffed full, the farmer responded:

"Until the Day of Judgment!" Then in a different tone he demanded: "What do you want?"

"I'm looking for work," Peter said. "Do you need a laborer?"

Peter was well dressed for he had on the last clothes his kind father had given him. The farmer looked him over and sneered.

"A fine laborer you would make! You would do good work at meals – I see that, and spend the rest of your time at cards and teasing the maids! I know your kind!"

Peter tried to tell the farmer that he was industrious and steady but with an oath the farmer told him to go to the Devil. Then stepping inside the house he slammed the door in Peter's face.

In the next village he applied for work at the bailiff's house. The bailiff's wife answered his knock.

"The master is playing cards with two of his friends," she said. "I'll go in and ask him if he has anything for you to do."

Peter heard her speak to some one inside and then a rough voice bellowed out:

"No! How often have I told you not to interrupt me when I'm busy! Tell the fellow to go to the Devil!"

Without waiting for the bailiff's wife, Peter turned away. Tired and discouraged he took a path into the woods and sat down.

"There doesn't seem to be any place for me in all the world," he thought to himself. "They all tell me to go to the Devil – my stepmother, the farmer, and now the bailiff. If I knew the way to hell I think I'd take their advice. I'm sure the Devil would treat me better than they do!"

Just then a handsome gentleman, dressed in green, walked by. Peter touched his hat politely and said:

"Let every one praise Lord Jesus."

The man passed him without responding. Then he looked back and asked Peter why he looked so discouraged.

"I have reason to look discouraged," Peter said. "Everywhere I ask for work they tell me to go to the Devil. If I knew the way to hell I think I'd take their advice and go."

The stranger smiled.

"But if you saw the Devil, don't you think you'd be afraid of him?"

Peter shook his head.

"He can't be any worse than my stepmother, or the farmer, or the bailiff."

The man suddenly turned black.

"Look at me!" he cried. "Here I am, the very person we've been talking about!"

With no show of fear Peter looked the Devil up and down.

Then the Devil said that if Peter still wished to enter his service, he would take him. The work would be light, the Devil said, and the hours good, and if Peter did as he was told he would have a pleasant time. The Devil promised to keep him seven years and at the end of that time to make him a handsome present and set him free.

Peter shook hands on the bargain and the Devil, taking him about the waist, whisked him up into the air, and, pst! before Peter knew what was happening, they were in hell.

The Devil gave Peter a leather apron and led him into a room where there were three big cauldrons.

"Now it's your duty," the Devil said, "to keep the fires under these cauldrons always burning. Keep four logs under the first cauldron, eight logs under the second, and twelve under the third. Be careful never to let the fires go out. And another thing, Peter: you're never to peep inside the cauldrons. If you do I'll drive you away without a cent of wages. Don't forget!"

So Peter began working for the Devil and the treatment he received was so much better than that which he had had on earth that, sometimes, it seemed to him he was in heaven rather than hell. He had plenty of good food and drink and, as the Devil had promised him, the work was not heavy.

For companions he had the young apprentice devils, a merry black crew, who told droll stories and played amusing pranks.

Time passed quickly. Peter was faithful at his work and never once peeped under the lids of his three cauldrons.

At last he began to grow homesick for the world and one day he asked the Devil how much longer he had still to serve.

"Tomorrow," the Devil told him, "your seven years are up."

The next day while Peter was piling fresh logs under the cauldrons, the Devil came to him and said:

"Today, Peter, you are free. You have served me faithfully and well and I am going to reward you handsomely. Money would be too heavy for you to carry, so I am going to give you this bag which is a magic bag. Whenever you open it and say: 'Bag, I need some ducats,' the bag will always have just as many as you need. Good luck go with you, Peter. However, I don't believe you'll have a very good time at first for people will think you're a devil. You know you do look pretty black for you haven't washed for seven years and you haven't cut your hair or nails."

"That's true," said Peter. "I just remember I haven't washed ever since I've been down here. I certainly must take a bath and get my hair cut and my nails trimmed."

The Devil shook his head.

"No, Peter, one bath won't do it. Water won't wash off the kind of black you get down here. I know what you must do but I won't tell you just yet. Go up into the world as you are and, if ever you need me, call me. If the people up there ask you who you are, tell them you're the Devil's little brother-in-law. This isn't a joke. It's true as you'll find out some day."

Peter then took leave of all the little black apprentices and the Devil, lifting him on his back, whisked him up to earth and set him down in the forest on exactly the same spot where they had met seven years before.

The Devil disappeared and Peter, stuffing the magic bag in his pocket, walked to the nearest village.

His appearance created a panic. On sight of him the children ran screaming home, crying out:

"The Devil! The Devil is coming!"

Mothers and fathers ran out of the houses to see what was the matter but on sight of Peter they ran in again, barred all the doors and windows, and making the sign of the cross prayed God Almighty to protect them.

Peter went on to the tavern. The landlord and his wife were standing in the doorway. As Peter came toward them, they cried out in fright:

"O Lord, forgive us our sins! The Devil is coming!"

They tried to run away but they tripped over each other and fell down, and before they could scramble to their feet Peter stood before them.

He looked at them for a moment and laughed. Then he went inside the tavern, sat down, and said:

"Landlord, bring me a drink!"

Quaking with fright the landlord went to the cellar and drew a pitcher of beer. Then he called the little herd who was working in the stable.

"Yirik," he said to the boy, "take this beer into the house. There's a man in there waiting for it. He's a little strange looking but you needn't be afraid. He won't hurt you."

Yirik took the pitcher of beer and started in. He opened the door and then, as he caught sight of Peter, he dropped the pitcher and fled.

The landlord scolded him angrily.

"What do you mean," he shouted, "not giving the gentleman his beer? And breaking the pitcher, too! The price of it will be deducted from your wages! Draw another pitcher of beer and place it at once before the gentleman."

Yirik feared Peter but he feared the landlord more. He was an orphan, poor lad, and served the landlord for his keep and three dollars a year.

So with trembling fingers he drew a pitcher of beer and then, breathing a prayer to his patron saint, he slowly dragged himself into the tavern.

"There, there, boy," Peter called out kindly. "You needn't be afraid. I'm not going to hurt you. I'm not the Devil. I'm only his little brother-in-law."

Yirik took heart and placed the beer in front of Peter. Then he stood still, not daring to raise his eyes.

Peter began asking him about himself, who he was, how he came to be working for the landlord, and what kind of treatment he was receiving. Yirik stammered out his story and as he talked he forgot his fear, he forgot that Peter looked like a devil, and presently he was talking to him freely as one friend to another.

Peter was touched by the orphan's story and, pulling out his magic money bag, he filled Yirik's cap with golden ducats. The boy danced about the room with delight. Then he ran outside and showed the landlord and the people who had gathered the present which the strange gentleman had made him.

"And he says he's not the Devil," Yirik reported, "but only his brother-in-law."

When the landlord heard that Peter really hadn't any horns or a flaming tongue, he picked up courage and going inside he begged Peter to give him, too, a few golden ducats. But Peter only laughed at him.

Peter stayed at the tavern overnight. Just as he fell asleep some one shook his hand and, as he opened his eyes, he saw his old master standing beside him.

"Quick!" the Devil whispered. "Get up and hurry out to the shed! The landlord is about to murder the orphan for his money."

Peter jumped out of bed and ran outside to the shed where Yirik slept. He burst open the door just as the landlord was ready to stab the sleeping boy with a dagger.

"You sinner!" Peter cried. "I've caught you at last! Off to hell you go with me this instant to stew forever in boiling oil!"

The landlord fainted with terror. Peter dragged him senseless into the house. When he came to himself he fell on his knees before Peter and begged for mercy. He offered Peter everything he possessed if only Peter would grant him another chance and he solemnly vowed that he would repent and give up his evil ways.

At last Peter said:

"Very well. I'll give you another chance provided that, from this time on, you treat Yirik as your son. Be kind to him and send him to school. The moment you forget your promise and treat him cruelly, I'll come and carry you off to hell! Remember!"

There was no need to urge the landlord to remember. From that night he was a changed man. He became honest in all his dealings and he really did treat Yirik as though he were his own son.

Peter stayed on at the tavern and stories about him and his golden ducats began to spread through the country-side. The prince of the land heard of him and sent word that he would like to see him at the castle. Peter answered the prince's messenger that if the prince wished to see him he could come to the tavern.

"Who is this prince of yours," Peter asked the landlord, "and why does he want to see me?"

"He'd probably like to borrow some money from you," the landlord said. "He's deep in debt for he has two of the wickedest, most extravagant daughters in the world. They're the children of his first marriage. They are proud and haughty and they waste the money of the realm as though it were so much sand. The people are crying out against them and their wasteful ways but the prince seems unable to curb them. The prince has a third daughter, the child of his second wife. Her name is Angelina and she certainly is as good and beautiful as an angel. We call her the Princess Linka. There isn't a man in the country that wouldn't go through fire and water for her – God bless her! As for the other two – may the Devil take them!"

Suddenly remembering himself, the landlord clapped his hand to his mouth in alarm.

Peter laughed good-humoredly.

"That's all right, landlord. Don't mind me. As I've told you before I'm not the Devil. I'm only his little brother-in-law."

The landlord shook his head.

"Yes, I know, but I must say it seems much the same to me."

One afternoon the prince came riding down to the tavern and asked for Peter. He was horrified at first by Peter's appearance, but he treated him most politely, invited him to the castle, and ended by begging the loan of a large sum of money.

Peter said to the prince:

"I'll give you as much money as you want provided you let me marry one of your daughters."

The prince wasn't prepared for this but he needed money so badly that he said:

"H'm, which one of them?"

"I'm not particular," Peter answered. "Any of them will do."

When he gave the prince some money in advance, the prince agreed and Peter promised to come to the castle the next day to meet his bride to be.

The prince when he got home told his daughters that he had seen Peter. They questioned him about Peter's appearance and asked him what sort of a looking person this brother-in-law of the Devil was.

"He isn't so very ugly," the prince said, "really he isn't. If he washed his face and trimmed his hair and nails he'd be fairly good-looking. In fact I rather like him."

He then talked to them very seriously about the state of the treasury and he told them that unless he could raise a large sum of money shortly there was danger of an uprising among the people.

"If you, my daughters, wish to see the peace of the country preserved, if you want to make me happy in my old age, one of you will have to marry this young man, for I see no other way to raise the money."

At this the two older princesses tossed their heads scornfully and laughed loud and long.

"You may rest assured, dear father, that neither of us will marry such a creature! We are the daughters of a prince and won't marry beneath us, no, not even to save the country from ruin!"

"Then I don't know what I'll do," the prince said.

"Father," whispered Linka, the youngest. Her voice quavered and her face turned pale. "Father, if your happiness and the peace of the country depend on this marriage, I will sacrifice myself, God help me!"

"My child! My dear child!" the prince cried, taking Linka in his arms and kissing her tenderly.

The two elder sisters jeered and ha-ha-ed.

"Little sister-in-law of the Devil!" they said mockingly. "Now if you were to marry Prince Lucifer himself that would be something, for at least you would be a princess! But only to be his sister-in-law – ha! ha! – what does that amount to?"

And they laughed with amusement and made nasty evil jokes until poor little Linka had to put her hands to her ears not to hear them.

The next day Peter came to the castle. The older sisters when they saw how black he was were glad enough they had refused to marry him. As for Linka, the moment she looked at him she fainted dead away.

When she revived the prince led her over to Peter and gave Peter her hand. She was trembling violently and her hand was cold as marble.

"Don't be afraid, little princess," Peter whispered to her gently. "I know how awful I look. But perhaps I won't always be so ugly. I promise you, if you marry me, I shall always love you dearly."

Linka was greatly comforted by the sound of his pleasant voice, but each time she looked at him she was terrified anew.

Peter saw this and made his visit short. He handed out to the prince as much money as he needed and then, after agreeing to return in eight days for the wedding, he hurried off.

He went to the place where he had met the Devil the first time and called him by name with all his might.

The Devil instantly appeared.

"What do you want, little brother-in-law?"

"I want to look like myself again," Peter said. "What good will it do me to marry a sweet little princess and then have the poor girl faint away every time she looks at me!"

"Very well, brother-in-law. If that is how you feel about it, come along with me and I'll soon make you into a handsome young man."

Peter leaped on the Devil's back and off they flew over mountains and forests and distant countries.

They alighted in a deep forest beside a bubbling spring.

"Now, little brother-in-law," the Devil said, "wash in this water and see how handsome you'll soon be."

Peter threw off his clothes and jumped into the water and when he came out his skin was as beautiful and fresh as a girl's. He looked at his own reflection in the spring and it made him so happy that he said to the Devil:

"Brother-in-law, I'm more grateful to you for this than for all the money you've given me. Now my dear Linka will love me!"

He put his arms about the Devil's neck and off they flew once again. This time they went to a big city where Peter bought beautiful clothes and jewels and coaches and horses. He engaged servants in fine livery and, when he was ready to go to his bride, he had a following that was worthy of any prince.

At the castle the Princess Linka paced her chamber pale and trembling. The two older sisters were with her, laughing heartlessly and making evil jokes, and running every moment to the window to see if the groom were coming.

At last they saw in the distance a long line of shining coaches with outriders in rich livery. The coaches drew up at the castle gate and from the first one a handsome youth, arrayed like a prince, alighted. He hurried into the castle and ran straight upstairs to Linka's chamber.

At first Linka was afraid to look at him for she supposed he was still black. But when he took her hand and whispered: "Dear Linka, look at me now and you won't be frightened," she looked and it seemed to her that Peter was the very handsomest young man in all the world. She fell in love with him on sight and I might as well tell you she's been in love with him ever since.

The two older sisters stood at the window frozen stiff with envy and surprise. Suddenly they felt some one clutch them from behind.

They turned in fright and who did they see standing there but the Devil himself!

"Don't be afraid, my dear brides," he said. "I'm not a common fellow. I'm Prince Lucifer himself. So, in becoming my brides you are not losing rank!"

Then he turned to Peter and chuckled.

"You see now, Peter, why you are my brother-in-law. You're marrying one sister and I'm taking the other two!"

With that he picked up the two wicked sisters under his arm and puff! with a whiff of sulphur they all three disappeared through the ceiling.

The Princess Linka as she clung to her young husband asked a little fearfully:

"Peter, do you suppose we'll have to see our brother-in-law often?"

"Not if you make me a good wife," Peter said.

And you can understand what a good wife Linka became when I tell you that never again all her life long did she see the Devil.

Katcha and the Devil

THERE WAS ONCE A WOMAN named Katcha who lived in a village where she owned her own cottage and garden. She had money besides but little good it did her because she was such an ill-tempered vixen that nobody, not even the poorest laborer, would marry her. Nobody would even work for her, no matter what she paid, for she couldn't open her mouth without scolding, and whenever she scolded she raised her shrill voice until you could hear it a mile away. The older she grew the worse she became until by the time she was forty she was as sour as vinegar.

Now as it always happens in a village, every Sunday afternoon there was a dance either at the burgomaster's, or at the tavern. As soon as the bagpipes sounded, the boys all crowded into the room and the girls gathered outside and looked in the windows. Katcha was always the first at the window. The music would strike up and the boys would beckon the girls to come in and dance, but no one ever beckoned Katcha. Even when she paid the piper no one ever asked her to dance. Yet she came Sunday after Sunday just the same.

One Sunday afternoon as she was hurrying to the tavern she thought to herself: "Here I am getting old and yet I've never once danced with a boy! Plague take it, today I'd dance with the devil if he asked me!"

She was in a fine rage by the time she reached the tavern, where she sat down near the stove and looked around to see what girls the boys had invited to dance.

Suddenly a stranger in hunter's green came in. He sat down at a table near Katcha and ordered drink. When the serving maid brought the beer, he reached over to Katcha and asked her to drink with him. At first she was much taken back at this attention, then she pursed her lips coyly and pretended to refuse, but finally she accepted.

When they had finished drinking, he pulled a ducat from his pocket, tossed it to the piper, and called out:

"Clear the floor, boys! This is for Katcha and me alone!"

The boys snickered and the girls giggled hiding behind each other and stuffing their aprons into their mouths so that Katcha wouldn't hear them laughing. But Katcha wasn't noticing them at all. Katcha was dancing with a fine young man! If the whole world had been laughing at her, Katcha wouldn't have cared.

The stranger danced with Katcha all afternoon and all evening. Not once did he dance with any one else. He bought her marzipan and sweet drinks and, when the hour came to go home, he escorted her through the village.

"Ah," sighed Katcha when they reached her cottage and it was time to part, "I wish I could dance with you forever!"

"Very well," said the stranger. "Come with me."

"Where do you live?"

"Put your arm around my neck and I'll tell you."

Katcha put both arms about his neck and instantly the man changed into a devil and flew straight down to hell.

At the gates of hell he stopped and knocked.

His comrades came and opened the gates and when they saw that he was exhausted, they tried to take Katcha off his neck. But Katcha held on tight and nothing they could do or say would make her budge.

The devil finally had to appear before the Prince of Darkness himself with Katcha still glued to his neck.

"What's that thing you've got around your neck?" the Prince asked.

So the devil told how as he was walking about on earth he had heard Katcha say she would dance with the devil himself if he asked her. "So I asked her to dance with me," the devil said. "Afterwards just to frighten her a little I brought her down to hell. And now she won't let go of me!"

"Serve you right, you dunce!" the Prince said. "How often have I told you to use common sense when you go wandering around on earth! You might have known Katcha would never let go of a man once she had him!"

"I beg your Majesty to make her let go!" the poor devil implored.

"I will not!" said the Prince. "You'll have to carry her back to earth yourself and get rid of her as best you can. Perhaps this will be a lesson to you."

So the devil, very tired and very cross, shambled back to earth with Katcha still clinging to his neck. He tried every way to get her off. He promised her wooded hills and rich meadows if she but let him go. He cajoled her, he cursed her, but all to no avail. Katcha still held on.

Breathless and discouraged he came at last to a meadow where a shepherd, wrapped in a great shaggy sheepskin coat, was tending his flocks. The devil transformed himself into an ordinary looking man so that the shepherd didn't recognize him.

"Hi, there," the shepherd said, "what's that you're carrying?"

"Don't ask me," the devil said with a sigh. "I'm so worn out I'm nearly dead. I was walking yonder not thinking of anything at all when along comes a woman and jumps on my back and won't let go. I'm trying to carry her to the nearest village to get rid of her there, but I don't believe I'm able. My legs are giving out."

The shepherd, who was a good-natured chap, said: "I tell you what: I'll help you. I can't leave my sheep long, but I'll carry her halfway."

"Oh," said the devil, "I'd be very grateful if you did!"

So the shepherd yelled at Katcha: "Hi, there, you! Catch hold of me!"

When Katcha saw that the shepherd was a handsome youth, she let go of the devil and leapt upon the shepherd's back, catching hold of the collar of his sheepskin coat.

Now the young shepherd soon found that the long shaggy coat and Katcha made a pretty heavy load for walking. In a few moments he was sick of his bargain and began casting about for some way of getting rid of Katcha.

Presently he came to a pond and he thought to himself that he'd like to throw her in. He wondered how he could do it. Perhaps he could manage it by throwing in his greatcoat with her. The coat was so loose that he thought he could slip out of it without Katcha's discovering what he was doing. Very cautiously he slipped out one arm. Katcha didn't move. He slipped out the other arm. Still Katcha didn't move. He unlooped the first button. Katcha noticed nothing. He unlooped the second button. Still Katcha noticed nothing. He unlooped the third button and kerplunk! he had pitched coat and Katcha and all into the middle of the pond!

When he got back to his sheep, the devil looked at him in amazement.

"Where's Katcha?" he gasped.

"Oh," the shepherd said, pointing over his shoulder with his thumb, "I decided to leave her up yonder in a pond."

"My dear friend," the devil cried, "I thank you! You have done me a great favor. If it hadn't been for you I might be carrying Katcha till doomsday. I'll never forget you and some time I'll reward you. As you don't know who it is you've helped, I must tell you I'm a devil."

With these words the devil vanished.

For a moment the shepherd was dazed. Then he laughed and said to himself: "Well, if they're all as stupid as he is, we ought to be able for them!"

The country where the shepherd lived was ruled over by a dissolute young duke who passed his days in riotous living and his nights in carousing. He gave over the affairs of state to two governors who were as bad as he. With extortionate taxes and unjust fines they robbed the people until the whole land was crying out against them.

Now one day for amusement the duke summoned an astrologer to court and ordered him to read in the planets the fate of himself and his two governors. When the astrologer had cast a horoscope for each of the three reprobates, he was greatly disturbed and tried to dissuade the duke from questioning him further.

"Such danger," he said, "threatens your life and the lives of your two governors that I fear to speak."

"Whatever it is," said the duke, "speak. But I warn you to speak the truth, for if what you say does not come to pass you will forfeit your life."

The astrologer bowed and said: "Hear then, oh Duke, what the planets foretell: Before the second quarter of the moon, on such and such a day, at such and such an hour, a devil will come and carry off the two governors. At the full of the moon on such and such a day, at such and such an hour, the same devil will come for your Highness and carry you off to hell."

The duke pretended to be unconcerned but in his heart he was deeply shaken. The voice of the astrologer sounded to him like the voice of judgment and for the first time conscience began to trouble him.

As for the governors, they couldn't eat a bite of food and were carried from the palace half dead with fright. They piled their ill-gotten wealth into wagons and rode away to their castles, where they barred all the doors and windows in order to keep the devil out.

The duke reformed. He gave up his evil ways and corrected the abuses of state in the hope of averting if possible his cruel fate.

The poor shepherd had no inkling of any of these things. He tended his flocks from day to day and never bothered his head about the happenings in the great world.

Suddenly one day the devil appeared before him and said: "I have come, my friend, to repay you for your kindness. When the moon is in its first quarter, I was to carry off the former governors of this land because they robbed the poor and gave the duke evil counsel. However, they're behaving themselves now so they're to be given another chance. But they don't know this. Now on such and such a day do you go to the first castle where a crowd of people will be assembled. When a cry goes up and the gates open and I come dragging out the governor, do you step up to me and say: 'What do you mean by this? Get out of here or there'll be trouble!' I'll pretend to be greatly frightened and make off. Then ask the governor to pay you two bags of gold, and if he haggles just threaten to call me back. After that go on to the castle of the second governor and do the same thing and demand the same pay. I warn you, though, be prudent with the money and use it only for good. When the moon is full, I'm to carry off the duke himself, for he was so wicked that he's to have no second chance. So don't try to save him, for if you do you'll pay for it with your own skin. Don't forget!"

The shepherd remembered carefully everything the devil told him. When the moon was in its first quarter he went to the first castle. A great crowd of people was gathered outside waiting to see the devil carry away the governor.

Suddenly there was a loud cry of despair, the gates of the castle opened, and there was the devil, as black as night, dragging out the governor. He, poor man, was half dead with fright.

The shepherd elbowed his way through the crowd, took the governor by the hand, and pushed the devil roughly aside.

"What do you mean by this?" he shouted. "Get out of here or there'll be trouble!"

Instantly the devil fled and the governor fell on his knees before the shepherd and kissed his hands and begged him to state what he wanted in reward. When the shepherd asked for two bags of gold, the governor ordered that they be given him without delay.

Then the shepherd went to the castle of the second governor and went through exactly the same performance.

It goes without saying that the duke soon heard of the shepherd, for he had been anxiously awaiting the fate of the two governors. At once he sent a wagon with four horses to fetch the shepherd to the palace and when the shepherd arrived he begged him piteously to rescue him likewise from the devil's clutches.

"Master," the shepherd answered, "I cannot promise you anything. I have to consider my own safety. You have been a great sinner, but if you really want to reform, if you really want to rule your people justly and kindly and wisely as becomes a true ruler, then indeed I will help you even if I have to suffer hellfire in your place."

The duke declared that with God's help he would mend his ways and the shepherd promised to come back on the fatal day.

With grief and dread the whole country awaited the coming of the full moon. In the first place the people had greeted the astrologer's prophecy with joy, but since the duke had reformed their feelings for him had changed.

Time sped fast as time does whether joy be coming or sorrow and all too soon the fatal day arrived.

Dressed in black and pale with fright, the duke sat expecting the arrival of the devil.

Suddenly the door flew open and the devil, black as night, stood before him. He paused a moment and then he said, politely:

"Your time has come, Lord Duke, and I am here to get you!"

Without a word the duke arose and followed the devil to the courtyard, which was filled with a great multitude of people.

At that moment the shepherd, all out of breath, came pushing his way through the crowd, and ran straight at the devil, shouting out:

"What do you mean by this? Get out of here or there'll be trouble!"

"What do you mean?" whispered the devil. "Don't you remember what I told you?"

"Hush!" the shepherd whispered back. "I don't care anything about the duke. This is to warn you! You know Katcha? She's alive and she's looking for you!"

The instant the devil heard the name of Katcha he turned and fled.

All the people cheered the shepherd, while the shepherd himself laughed in his sleeve to think that he had taken in the devil so easily.

As for the duke, he was so grateful to the shepherd that he made him his chief counselor and loved him as a brother. And well he might, for the shepherd was a sensible man and always gave him sound advice.

Knights, Princesses & Magic

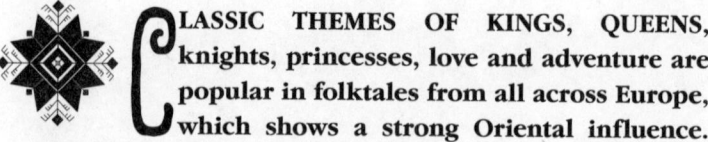

CLASSIC THEMES OF KINGS, QUEENS, knights, princesses, love and adventure are popular in folktales from all across Europe, which shows a strong Oriental influence. They are perhaps the stories that have endured the longest and have had the biggest impact.

The folktales in this section often include princes on adventures, or questionable princesses disappearing – as in 'The Enchanted Princesses' – and all have a greater or lesser magical theme running through them. Nemcova's elaborate tale, 'Prince Bayaya', is a mosaic of two or three simpler stories that come together beautifully and the famous tale 'The Three Golden Hairs' is included in part to contrast it with the German variant, which is generally agreed to be much simpler than the Slavic version.

The Knight Bambus

THE WAS A POOR GAMEKEEPER once, who had suffered from hard times all his life, so as he grew older, he wanted to get rich. He was only an under-forester. One day the forester said: "Near those old ruins, you know the ones I mean, a fox or a roe, or some creature of that sort, often crosses my path, and I can never manage to hit it, though I have shot at it a hundred times. If you happen to be going in that direction, look out for it."

When the gamekeeper heard this, the first thing he did was to go to the ruins. Just as he got there, a huge fox appeared with a rustling noise. The gamekeeper felt uneasy, but the fox disappeared at once, so he sat down, put five big charges in his gun, and waited. It wasn't long till the fox appeared again, and this time he was carrying a young fawn in his mouth. The gamekeeper shot at him – boom! The fox cried out, and ran off into the bushes. But the gamekeeper saw that the fawn had run away and hidden itself in a cave. He thought: "The fox cried out, so he has some of my shots in his fur coat. I'll get him some other time."

So he went into the ruins through the gate. Within, there was a courtyard all deserted, and with its wall fallen down. So the gamekeeper passed through the courtyard and came into a spacious cellar. There he saw three lamps burning, and looking round, he was filled with amazement. But all this was as nothing, for in the corner were three glittering heaps of golden coins and one heap of big gold pieces. The gamekeeper reflected: "If I had all that, I should give up gamekeeping and have a splendid time."

No sooner had he said this than a grey old man appeared and asked: "What are you looking for, gamekeeper?"

"Well, I shot at a fox and he ran in somewhere here, and so I'm wandering about looking for him."

"You won't get the fox you're looking for, for I am he."

"And why are you here in a fox's shape? What's the reason of that?"

"I am the Knight Bambus, and all these forests belong to this castle. I was a robber-knight, and so as a punishment I have to keep watch here now."

"And how long is it to last?"

"When three poor people come here, and each of them takes away two sackfuls of gold, I shall be delivered. I am bound to give all this gold away for nothing. Already I have outlived three generations of my kinsmen here."

Then he bade him fetch two leather sacks from the other room and collect the gold into them, filling them up to the brim. He must keep it all for himself and must not tell any one what he had seen. The gamekeeper promised that he wouldn't even tell his wife, Háticka, how he had got the money. So he filled the two sacks up to the brim, and the old man helped him to hoist them on to his shoulders and saw him out of the door. All the time he kept warning him to keep his mouth shut: "For what a woman knows all the world knows; that's gospel truth, sure enough."

So the gamekeeper left the castle, carrying those two sacks, and the man shook hands with him before he left. At the border of the forest, near a beech-tree, his wife, Háta, was standing looking for him. She ran up to him.

"Great Heavens, Florian! where have you been all this long time? I have been looking everywhere for you for three days."

Now Florian was delighted that his wife had come to meet him, so he blurted out: "Háticka, wife, Count Bambus has given me these two sacks of gold pieces. Have a look here – see what heaps of the stuff there are!" and he let one of the sacks fall on the ground. But behold! instead of gold there were only rustling leaves in it. Then he remembered that he was not to say anything about it. He frowned, and his wife burst into tears; and they had to spend the rest of their life, until they died, in poverty just as before.

The Enchanted Princesses

IN THE DAYS OF King Bambita, his two noble daughters oppressed the people, laying heavy taxes on them without the king's knowledge. The people cursed them, and the curses did their work. The princesses vanished. The king sent some of his servants to look for the princesses. But the servants came back empty-handed. None of them had been able to find the princesses.

Now, a captain and a lieutenant heard of the king's trouble. So the lieutenant went to the king, and "I see," says he, "that you are in trouble. I will go and look for the princesses."

"How much do you want for it?" asked the king.

"Twenty pounds."

The king agreed, and gave him the money. "If you find them," said he, "half of my kingdom is yours."

The lieutenant and the captain had plenty of money now, so they went to an inn and passed the time drinking. On the third day the captain said: "To-day I will go to the king. If he gave you twenty pounds, he is certain to give me more."

So he went to the king and said: "I see that your majesty is in trouble. I should like to go and look for the princesses."

"How much do you want for it?" said the king.

"Thirty pounds."

Well, the king gave him the money without any more ado, adding that, if he found the princesses, he would get half of his kingdom.

They fell to drinking again and had a splendid time.

There was a drummer near them, and he heard them saying that they were to look for the princesses. So he went to the king and said: "I hear that your majesty is prostrated by sore trouble. I, too, would like to look for the princesses."

"How much do you want for it?"

"Forty pounds, at least."

The king gave him the money without more ado. The two officers and the drummer left that inn for another, and so they went on spending their money recklessly in one drinking-house after another. The drummer went with the other two, but he was more careful than they were. He was not such a spendthrift as the two officers.

They asked him where he meant to go.

"Wherever you go, I will go too," he replied.

"Then why don't you join us and lead a gay life?"

"That I can't do until I know where to find the princesses."

They invited him to join them, but he refused to do it.

At last they bought some bread and other food, and they all set out together on their journey. They came to a dark forest, and for a fortnight they searched it through and through, but they could find nothing. They couldn't find their way out of the forest either, so they agreed that one of them should climb to the top of the highest tree to see which way they ought to go. The drummer, being the youngest, climbed up a pine-tree. He called out:

"I can see a cottage. Look, I will throw my hat towards it, and do you follow the hat."

Well, they went on until they reached the cottage.

"Go into the room," says the drummer.

"After you," said both the officers at once.

So the drummer stepped inside, and an old crone welcomed him.

"Welcome, Drummer Anthony," said she. "How did you get here?"

"I have come to deliver the princesses, and only for that."

"Well, you will find them, but those other two fellows will get them from you by a trick."

She gave him a rope three hundred fathoms long and told him to bind it round his body. She also gave him some wine and a sponge. Then she said: "Not far from here there is a well. When you come to it, you must say that you will let yourself down into the well, if the other fellows will drink the fountain dry."

When they got to the well, the captain and the lieutenant began to drink the fountain, but it was just as full as before.

"If we kept on drinking this fountain till doomsday," they said, "we could not drink it dry."

So the drummer took the sponge, and at once the water began to disappear, and soon the well was dry. They began to quarrel as to who should go down the well. The one on the right side said the other ought to go, but at last they agreed that the drummer, who was the lightest, should go.

So he went down, and, when he reached the bottom of the well, he found a stone there. He drew it aside, and then he saw the light of the other world. He lowered himself on the rope into the other world. There he saw a beautiful palace. He went towards it. When he reached it, he saw that the table was laid for two persons. He ate his meal and then went into the second room. There he laid himself down to sleep, and when he awoke in the morning, he found the Princess Anne in the third room.

"Welcome," she said; "what has brought you here?"

He told her that he had come to deliver her.

She said: "I don't know whether you will succeed in that. Here is a sword; see if you can brandish it."

The drummer took hold of the sword, but he could not even lift it, it was so heavy.

Then the princess gave him a ring. "Take this," she said, "and whenever you think of me, you will become strong. I have to hold the dragon in my lap for a whole hour. As soon as he comes, he will smell a man. But you must cut him in two, for then I shall be delivered. Just at nine o'clock he comes."

Just at nine o'clock the palace began to tremble and the dragon came in. But the drummer encountered him and struck him in two with the sword.

After that the princess took him into another room. "Now you have delivered me," she said. "But my sister is in worse trouble still. She has to hold a dragon in her lap for two hours, and that dragon is even stronger than this one."

Then they went into the fourth room, where was the Princess Antonia. She, too, greeted him, and told him that he would be able to deliver her if he could brandish the sword beside her. He tried, but he could not even move it. Then she gave him a ring and told him that, whenever he thought of her, he would have the strength of two hundred men. She said, too, that if he succeeded in setting her free she would marry him.

Soon eleven o'clock came. The hall began to tremble and the dragon appeared. But, as he was coming in, Anthony was ready for him near the door, and he managed to cut the dragon in two.

Now, when the two princesses had been set free, they gathered all the precious stones they could to take with them, and went to the opening that led into the world. But the drummer had quite forgotten the old crone's warning about the other two fellows, and he sent the princesses up before him. Each of the officers took a princess for himself, and the drummer was left behind at the bottom of the well. When his turn came, he was careful enough to tie a stone to the rope. His companions on the top pulled it up a little way and then suddenly let it drop, throwing down other stones into the well to kill the drummer. But he had remembered the crone's warning that his friends would try to trick him. So he jumped aside and remained there in the other world.

He went back to the palace and entered the seventh room. On the table were three boxes. He opened the first and found a whistle inside it. He blew the whistle, and in came some generals and asked what was his majesty's will. He said he had only whistled to find out if they were attending to their duty. Then he looked into the second box, and there he saw a bugle. He blew the bugle, and in came some officers, who said just what the generals had said. In the third box he found a drum. He beat the drum, and immediately he was surrounded by infantry and cavalry, a great multitude of soldiers. He asked whether any of them had ever been in Europe. Two men were found among them who had been shipwrecked.

"Where is the ship?" said the drummer.

"Here on the seacoast," they replied.

At that, Anthony decked himself out in a royal robe and started on his travels for Europe.

Meanwhile the two princesses had reached home. One was engaged to be married to the lieutenant, the other to the captain. But when the time for the wedding came, both the princesses, still thinking of Anthony, asked for a delay of one year, and their royal father granted their request.

Anthony arrived safely in that land. He met a traveller and said to him, "Look here, why should you not change clothes with me?"

He was glad to do so, and Anthony went on to the town in which the princesses lived and sought out a goldsmith. He asked the goldsmith for work.

"I haven't work enough for myself," said the goldsmith.

"Well," said the drummer, "I have had an order for two rings, although I was only walking the street."

"You are a lucky fellow," said the goldsmith, and his wife, when she heard of it, spoke in the drummer's favour, so he was taken on as assistant.

"Now," said he, "give me what I want and I will make the rings. But nobody must enter my room: I will take my meals in at the door."

On the third day one ring was finished, and this one was meant for the Princess Anne.

"You must take this ring to the Princess Anne, master," said he.

"So I will," said the goldsmith; "but what is your price for it?"

"A thousand pounds," said he.

"If that's so, I won't go. They would put me in jail."

"Be easy," said Anthony, "nothing will happen to you."

So the goldsmith went to the palace, and sent in a message that his assistant had made a ring for the Princess Anne. She sent a message that she had not ordered a ring, but she would look at it. As soon as she saw it, she asked: "How much do you want for this?" He replied that he was almost afraid to say that it was worth a thousand pounds.

"Oh! it is worth much more than that," she said, and she paid the sum at once.

The goldsmith returned home and told his wife what he had got for the ring. She wondered what sort of person their new assistant was. The master brought the money to him, but the assistant would not accept it.

"You can keep the money for yourself," he said, "and I have just finished the ring for the Princess Antonia. You will have to go to the palace again with this."

This time the master-goldsmith was ready enough to go. "How much am I to ask for this ring?" he said.

"Ask two thousand pounds."

So he was brought to the princess, and he told her that his apprentice had made a ring for her. She answered that she had not ordered a ring. "However, show it to me."

As soon as she glanced at it, she said: "How much do you want for this?"

"Two thousand pounds."

"Oh! it's worth much more than that," she said.

So she paid down the money and told the master-goldsmith to fetch his assistant to her. As soon as the master came home, he told his wife everything. She was still more astonished.

"O Lord!" she said, "I cannot understand it at all."

The master told Anthony that the princess bade him come and see her.

"She can come to me," was his reply.

When the princess heard that, she lost no time, but took some royal garments for him, and drove to Anthony's house in the royal coach. She went straight to him and said, "I am come to bring you home with me, Anthony."

She bade him put on the royal robe she had brought with her for him, and they drove together to the palace, and their marriage was celebrated not long after.

The two officers thought the king would banish them or inflict some punishment upon them, but he pardoned them and gave them sufficient money to live at the court. Anthony himself did not care for royalty. He and his wife arranged that they would return to the place where he had first found the princesses. So they departed for that land, but a storm drove them on shore near to the place where he had met the old crone. She gave him welcome.

"So you are back again," she said.

They explained to her that what they wished was to go back to that palace beneath the fountain.

"Well," she said, "I will show you the way to the other world, and I will let you down the well."

They came to the opening, and Anthony was about to enter the well, but the old hag begged him to wait with her and let the princess go on before.

So the princess was let down to the bottom of the well, and then the crone said: "I won't let you follow her unless you first cut off my head."

"This is a strange way to repay the good you have done me," said Anthony.

"Well, unless you promise this you will never see your princess again."

So he had to promise, and with that she waved her wand and a road appeared, which led them straight to the princess. Then Anthony struck off the crone's head, and they found themselves amid crowds of farmers who were ploughing and soldiers standing at attention, and one and all welcoming their new lords. For this land was an enchanted land, and the old crone was a witch.

Vitazko

ONCE THERE WAS A MOTHER and, being a mother, she had a son. She suckled him for twice seven years. After that she took him into a forest and told him to pull up a fir-tree, roots and all. But the lad could not pull up the fir-tree.

"You are not strong enough yet," said the mother. So she suckled him for another seven years. When she had suckled him for thrice seven years, she took him to the forest again and told him to pull up a beech-tree, roots and all. He seized hold of the beech and pulled it up.

"Now you are strong enough. So you are Victor (Vitazko). Now you can provide for me."

"Yes, I will. Only tell me what I can do for you."

"You must get me a good house first, and then you can take me there," said the mother, and she went home.

Vitazko took the beech-tree which he had pulled up, and, carrying it in his hand like a club, he started in search of a house for his mother. Following the wind, he walked by old roads and paths until he came to a castle. This castle was inhabited by griffins.

When Vitazko reached the castle, the griffins would not let him in. But he did not wait long for their permission: he smashed the gate and went into the castle and killed the griffins; their bodies he flung over the wall, and then he went for a walk through the castle. He was pleased with everything he saw. The rooms were nice, nine in number, but the tenth was closed. When he had gone through the nine he went into the tenth, and there he saw a griffin chained to the wall by three iron bands.

"What are you doing here?" asked Vitazko.

"I am sitting here, as you see. My brothers have chained me here. Untie my bonds and I will give you a splendid reward."

"You must be a wicked old rascal if your own brothers tied you there. I won't unfasten your bonds either," said Vitazko.

So he slammed the door, and went off to fetch his mother to the castle. When he had brought her there, he showed her everything, but he did not open the tenth room, and he forbade her to enter that room, for otherwise there would be trouble. As soon as Vitazko left the house, the mother could not rest, and she kept on walking near the door of that tenth room, till at last she went in, and, of course, she found the griffin there.

"What are you doing here, and who are you?"

"I am a griffin. My own brothers chained me here. They would have unfastened my bonds again, but your son has killed them all. Untie my bonds and I will reward you, and, if you like, I will marry you," said the griffin.

"And what would Vitazko say?" answered the mother.

"What could he say? We will put him out of the world, and you will be your own mistress."

The mother hesitated long enough, but at last she consented, and then she asked the griffin how she could untie his bonds.

"Go into the cellar and fetch me a cup of wine from the last cask."

The mother went into the cellar and brought him a glass of wine from the last cask. As soon as he had drained the first cup, crash! the first chain fell down. The mother brought him another cup and – well! the second chain snapped. So he begged her to bring him a third cup, and when she brought him the third cup the third chain broke too and the griffin was free again.

"But what am I to tell my son when he comes back?" said the mother anxiously.

"Oh! you must feign illness, and when he asks you what will save you, say that nothing can save you but a suckling of the earth sow. When he goes to get it, the sow will tear him in pieces."

Well (but not particularly well!), when Vitazko returned from the chase, bringing a buck for his mother, she groaned and complained: "Alas! my dear son, your toil has been in vain. It is no use your bringing me this good food; I cannot eat it, for I am deadly sick."

"Alas! mother, you must not die. Only tell me what would cure you, and I will bring it for you, even though it were from hell," cried the good Vitazko, for he loved his mother well.

"I can only be cured if I get the suckling of the earth sow."

Vitazko did not wait; he took his beech-tree and set off in quest of the earth sow. He wandered through the country, poor soul! for he did not know where to go, till at last he came to a tower, and there he found Holy Sunday.

"Where are you going?" asked Holy Sunday.

"I am going to the earth sow to get one of her sucklings. My mother is ill, but this will cure her."

"My dear boy, it will be a hard task for you to get that piglet. However, I will help you. Only you must follow my advice exactly."

Vitazko promised that he would follow it exactly. So first she gave him a long, sharp spit, and then she said:

"Go to the stable and take my horse. He will bring you to the place where the earth sow lies buried in the earth. When you have come there you must prick one of her pigs. The pig will squeak, and the sow, hearing it, will start up and run round the earth in a moment. But she won't see you or anybody else, and so she will tell the pigs that if they squeak again she will tear them to pieces. Then she will lie down to sleep, and then you must spit the pig and run quickly away. The pig will be afraid to squeak, the sow won't stir, and my horse will carry you away."

Vitazko promised to carry out her directions exactly. He took the spit, mounted the magic horse, and it brought him swiftly to the place – far, very far it was – where the earth sow lay buried in the earth. Vitazko pricked one of the pigs, and it squeaked terribly. The sow started wildly up and ran round the earth in one moment. But the magic horse did not move, so the sow did not see him or anybody else, and she said angrily to the pigs: "If one of you squeaks, I will tear you all to pieces at once."

Having said this, she buried herself again.

At once Vitazko spitted the pig. It kept quiet and didn't squeak at all, and the magic horse began to fly, and it wasn't long till they were home again.

"Well, Vitazko, how did it go?" asked Holy Sunday.

"Well, it went just as you said, and here is the pig."

"Very well. Take it to your mother."

Vitazko gave her back the spit; he led the magic horse back to its stall, thanked Holy Sunday, and, hanging the pig from the beech-tree, made haste to go home to his mother.

The mother and the griffin were feasting; they did not expect Vitazko, and here he was. They ran away and discussed what they should do with him.

"When he has given you the pig, you must still pretend to be ill," said the griffin; "and when he asks you what will save you, tell him that only the Water of Life and the Water of Death can cure you. If he goes in quest of that, he is bound to perish."

Vitazko came running to the castle full of joy. He gave the pig to his mother, but she still went on groaning and complaining that she was going to die, and that the pig would not cure her.

"Alas! mother, don't die, but tell me what will cure you, so that I may bring it for you at once," said Vitazko anxiously.

"Ah! my dear son, I can only be cured by the Water of Life and the Water of Death, and where would you get that?" sighed the mother.

Vitazko did not waste time thinking about it. He grasped his beech, and off he went to Holy Sunday.

"Where are you going, Vitazko?" asked Holy Sunday.

"I am coming to you to ask where I could find the Water of Life and the Water of Death, for my mother is still ill, and only those will cure her."

"It will be a hard task for you to get them, but I will help you as well as I can. Here are two jugs; mount my magic horse, and he will bring you to two banks. Beneath those two banks spring forth the Water of Life and the Water of Death. The right bank opens at noon, and from beneath it gushes the Water of Life. The left bank opens at midnight, and beneath it is the

Water of Death. As soon as the bank opens, run up to it and fill your jug with water, and so you must do in the other case too. When you have the water, come back. Follow my instructions carefully."

Saying this, she gave him two jugs. He took them and mounted the magic horse, and in a moment they were gone like the wind. The two banks were in a far distant land, and thither the magic horse brought Vitazko. At noon he raised the right bank and the Water of Life gushed forth, then, crash! the bank fell down again, and it was a wonder that it did not take Vitazko's heels off. Quickly Vitazko mounted the magic horse and made haste for the left bank. There they waited till midnight. When the bank lifted, beneath it was the Water of Death. He hurried to it and filled the jug, and, crash! down fell the bank again; and it was a marvel it didn't take Vitazko's hand off. Quickly he mounted the magic horse, the horse flew off, and soon they were home again.

"Well, Vitazko, how have you fared?" asked Holy Sunday.

"Oh! everything went all right, Holy Sunday; and here is the water," said Vitazko, giving her the water.

Holy Sunday kept the water, and gave him two jugs full of spring water and told him to take them to his mother. Vitazko thanked her and went home.

The mother and the griffin were carousing as before, for they did not expect that he would ever return – and there he was just outside. They were terribly frightened, and considered how they could get rid of him.

"You must pretend to be sick still, and tell him you won't recover unless you get the Pelican bird, and he will perish on the quest," said the griffin.

Vitazko brought the water joyfully, but the mother was still groaning and complaining; even that was no good, she was sure she was going to die.

"Ah! don't die, sweet mother. Tell me what will cure you, and I shall be glad to get it all for you," said the good lad.

"There is no help for me unless I can see the Pelican bird. Where could you get it for me?" groaned the mother.

Vitazko took his beech again, and it was no trouble to him to go to Holy Sunday once more.

"Where are you going?" asked Holy Sunday.

"Well, I am coming to you to ask for advice. Mother is still sick; the water did not cure her either, and she says she must see the Pelican bird. And where is the Pelican bird?"

"My dear child, it would be very hard for you to get the Pelican bird. But I will help you all I can. The Pelican bird is a gigantic bird. His neck is very long, and, whenever he shakes his wings, he raises such a wind that the trees begin to shake. Here is a gun; mount my magic horse, and he will bring you to the place where the Pelican bird lives. But be careful. Point the gun against the wind from whatever quarter it blows, and when the hammer falls, ram the gun with the ramrod and come quickly back. You must not look into the gun."

Vitazko took the gun and mounted the magic horse, and the horse spread his wings, and they were flying through the air a long way until they came to a vast desert, where dwelt the Pelican bird. There the magic horse stopped. Now Vitazko perceived that the wind was blowing strongly on his left cheek, so he pointed the gun in that direction, and, clap! the hammer fell. Vitazko rammed the gun quickly with the ramrod and flung it over his shoulder, and the horse started flying, and very soon they were home again.

"Well, how did things go?"

"I don't know whether they went well or ill, but I did what you commanded," answered Vitazko, handing down the gun to Holy Sunday.

"All right. You did quite right. Here he is!" she said. And then she took out the Pelican bird. Then she gave Vitazko another gun to shoot an eagle with. He went out into the forest, and returned before long with an eagle. She gave him this eagle for his mother, in place of the Pelican bird.

The griffin and the mother were making merry again, hoping that Vitazko would never come back, but he was already near. They were terrified, and began to consider what new task they were to set him.

"You must pretend to be sick still, and tell him nothing can do you any good but the golden apples from the garden of the Griffin. If he goes there the Griffin will tear him in pieces, for he is enraged because Vitazko has killed his brothers."

Joyfully Vitazko gave the bird to his mother, but she still kept on groaning; nothing was any good, only the golden apples from the garden of the Griffin could save her.

"You shall have them," said Vitazko, and without resting, he started again and came to Holy Sunday.

"Where are you going, Vitazko?"

"Well," he replied, "not even that did her any good. Mother is still sick, for only the golden apples from the garden of the Griffin will cure her."

"Well, you'll have to fight, my boy," said Holy Sunday; "but, even though you were stronger than you are, it would be a bad look-out for you. Still, I will help you all I can. Here is a ring for you; put it on your finger, and, when you are in need, think of me, turn the ring round on your finger, and you will have the strength of a hundred men. Now mount the magic horse; he will take you there."

Vitazko thanked her heartily, mounted the magic horse, and was carried by him a far journey, till they came to a garden hedged about by a high rampart. Had it not been for the magic horse Vitazko could never have got into the garden, but the horse flew like a bird over the rampart. Vitazko leapt down from the horse, and instantly began to look for a tree with golden apples. A beautiful girl met him and asked him what he was looking for. Vitazko said that he was looking for golden apples to cure his sick mother, and begged her to tell him where to look for them.

"The apple-tree is under my charge, and I must not give the apples to anybody, or the Griffin would tear me to pieces. I am a king's daughter, and the Griffin carried me off and brought me to this garden and put me in charge of the apples. Go back, good youth, go back, for the Griffin is very strong, and, if he sees you, he will kill you like a fly," said the girl.

But Vitazko was not to be turned back, and he hastened on into the garden. So the princess pulled off a priceless ring and handed it to Vitazko, saying: "Take this ring, and when you think of me and turn this ring round on your finger, you will have the strength of a hundred men, otherwise you could not gain the victory over the Griffin."

Vitazko took the ring and put it on his finger. He thanked her and went off to the centre of the garden. In the middle of the garden stood an apple-tree full of golden apples, and underneath it a horrible Griffin was lying.

"What do you want here, murderer of my brothers?" shouted the Griffin.

"I have come to get some apples from this tree," answered Vitazko undauntedly.

"You shall not have any of the apples unless you wrestle with me," exclaimed the Griffin angrily.

"I will if you like. Come on!" said Vitazko, and he turned the ring on his right hand and thought of Holy Sunday. He set his legs wide apart and they began to wrestle. In the first round the Griffin moved Vitazko a little, but Vitazko drove him into the ground above his ankles. Just at this moment they heard a swirl of wings above them, and a black raven shouted to them:

"Which am I to help, the Griffin or Vitazko?"

"Help me," said the Griffin.

"And what will you give me?"

"I will give you gold and silver as much as you like."

"Help me," cried Vitazko, "and I will give you all those horses grazing on yonder meadow."

"I will help you, then," said the raven. "But how am I to help you?"

"Cool me when I grow hot," said Vitazko. He felt hot indeed, for the Griffin was breathing out fire against him. So they went on wrestling. The Griffin seized Vitazko and drove him into the ground up to his ankles. Vitazko turned the ring, and again he thought of Holy Sunday. He put his arms round the Griffin's waist and drove him down into the ground above his knees. The black raven dipped his wings in a spring, and then he alighted on Vitazko's head and sprinkled cool drops over Vitazko's hot cheeks, and thus he cooled him. Then Vitazko turned the other ring and thought of the beautiful maiden, and they began wrestling again. So the Griffin drove Vitazko into the ground up to his ankles, but Vitazko took hold of him and drove him into the ground up to his shoulders, and quickly he seized his sword, the gift of Holy Sunday, and cut the Griffin's head off.

The princess came to him at once and plucked the golden apples for him. She thanked him too for delivering her, and said that she liked him well and she would marry him.

"I like you well too," confessed Vitazko, "and, if I could, I would go with you at once. But if you really love me, and if you will consent to wait a year for me, I will come to you then."

The princess pledged herself by shaking hands with him, and she said she would wait a year for him. And so they said good-bye to each other. Vitazko mounted his horse, cleared the rampart at a leap, killed the horses on the meadow for the black raven, and hastened home.

"Well, how have you fared?" asked Holy Sunday.

"Very well, but if it hadn't been for a ring which was given me by a princess I should have fared very badly," answered Vitazko, and he told her everything. She told him to go home with the golden apples and to take the magic horse with him too. Vitazko obeyed.

The griffin and the mother were carousing again. They were greatly startled when Vitazko came riding home; they had never expected that he would return alive even from the garden of the Griffin. The mother asked what she should do; but the griffin had no more shifts; he made off to the tenth room at once and hid himself there. When Vitazko had given the apples to his mother, she pretended that the mere sight of them had cured her, and, rising from the bed, she put the finest of food before Vitazko and then began to caress him as she used to do sometimes when he was a tiny baby. Vitazko was delighted to see his mother in good health again. The mother took a strong cotton cord and said jestingly: "Lie down, dear son; I will wind this cord round you as I used to wind it round your father, to see if you are as strong as he was, and if you can break it."

Vitazko smiled and laid himself down, and allowed his mother to wind the cord round him. When she had finished, he stretched his limbs and snapt the cord in pieces.

"You are strong," she said. "But wait! I will wind this thin silk cord round you to see if you can break it also."

So she did. Vitazko tried to stretch his limbs, but the more he stretched, the deeper the cord cut into him. So he was helpless, and had to lie like a baby in its swaddling-clothes. Now the griffin hastened to cut his head off; he hewed the body in pieces and hung the heart from the ceiling. The mother packed the body in a cloth, and put the bundle on the back of the magic horse, which was waiting in the courtyard, saying:

"You carried him alive, so you can carry him dead too, wherever you like."

The horse did not wait, but flew off, and soon they reached home.

Holy Sunday had been expecting him, for she knew what would probably happen to him. Without delay she rubbed the body with the Water of Death, then she put it together and poured the Water of Life over it. Vitazko yawned, and rose to his feet alive and well. "Well, I have had a long sleep," he said to himself.

"You would have been sleeping till doomsday if I hadn't awakened you. Well, how do you feel now?"

"Oh! I am all right! Only, it's funny: it's as though I had not got any heart."

"That is true; you haven't got a heart," answered Holy Sunday.

"Where can it be, then?"

"Where else should it be, but in the castle, hanging from the crossbeam?" said Holy Sunday, and she told him all that had happened to him.

But Vitazko could not be angry, neither could he weep, for he had no heart. So he had to go and get it. Holy Sunday gave him a fiddle and sent him to the castle. He was to play on the fiddle, and, as a reward, was to ask for the heart, and, when he got it, he must return at once to Holy Sunday – those were her orders.

Vitazko went to the castle, and when he saw that his mother was looking out of the window, he began playing beautifully. The mother was delighted with the music below, so she called the old fiddler (for Holy Sunday had put that shape upon him) into the castle and asked him to play. He played, and the mother danced with the griffin; they danced hard, and did not stop until they were tired. Then the mother gave the fiddler meat and drink, and she offered him gold, but he would not take it.

"What could I do with all that money? I am too old for it," he answered.

"Well, what am I to give you, then? It is for you to ask," said the mother.

"What are you to give me?" said he, looking round the room. "Oh! give me that heart, hanging there from the crossbeam!"

"If you like that, we can give it to you," said the griffin, and the mother took it down and gave it to Vitazko. He thanked them for it, and hastened from the castle to Holy Sunday.

"It is lucky that we have got it again," said Holy Sunday; and she took the heart in her hands, washed it first in the Water of Death and afterwards in the Water of Life, and then she put it in the bill of the Pelican bird. The bird stretched out his long neck and replaced the heart in Vitazko's breast. At once Vitazko felt it joyfully leaping. And for this service Holy Sunday gave the Pelican bird his freedom again.

And now she said to Vitazko: "You must go once more to the castle and deal out justice. Take the form of a pigeon and, when you think of me, you will regain your own shape."

No sooner had she said this than Vitazko was changed into a pigeon, and away he flew to the castle. The mother and the griffin were caressing each other when suddenly a pigeon alighted on the window-sill. As soon as the mother saw the pigeon she sent the griffin to shoot him, but before the griffin could get hold of his crossbow the pigeon flew down into the hall, took human form, seized the sword and cut the griffin's head off at a stroke.

"And what am I to do with thee, thou good-for-nothing mother?" he said, turning to his mother, who in terror fell at his feet begging for mercy. "Do not be afraid – I will not do you any harm. Let God judge between us." He took her hand and led her to the castle yard, unsheathed his sword, and said: "Behold, mother! I will throw this sword into the air. If I am guilty, it will strike me; if you are guilty, it is you it will strike. Let God decide."

The sword whirled through the air, it darted past Vitazko's head, and smote straight into his mother's heart.

Vitazko lamented over her and buried her. Then he returned to Holy Sunday and thanked her well for all her kindness. He girded on the sword, took his beech-tree in his hand, and went to his beautiful princess. He found her with her royal father, who had tried to make her marry various kings and princes, but she would marry none of them. She would wait a year, she said. The year was not yet over when one day Vitazko arrived in the royal palace to ask for the maiden's hand.

"This is my betrothed," exclaimed the princess joyfully, as soon as she saw him, and she went straight up to him.

A splendid feast was made ready, the father gave his kingdom into their hands, and that is the end of this story.

Sleepy John

ONCE THERE WAS a lad named John, and he used to go to sleep always and everywhere. One day he came to an inn where some farmers were feeding their horses. So he crept into the cart, lay down on the straw, and went to sleep. When the farmers had driven some distance, they noticed John asleep in the cart. They thought: "What are we to do with him? We have a beer cask here. We'll put him in it and leave him in the forest." So they shut him in the cask, and off they drove.

John went on sleeping in the cask for a long time. Suddenly he woke up and found himself in the cask, but he did not know how he had got into it, neither did he know where he was. There was something running to and fro near the cask, so he looked through the bunghole and saw a great number of wolves gathered under the rocks. They had flocked round, attracted by the human smell. One of the wolves pushed his tail through the hole, and Sleepy John began to think that the hour of his death was approaching. But he wound the wolf's tail round his hand. The wolf was terrified, and, dragging the cask after him, he ran after the rest of the wolves, who set off in all directions. Their terror grew greater and greater as the cask bumped after them. At last the cask struck against a rock and was smashed. John let go the wolf, who took himself off as fast as he could.

Now John found himself in a wild mountain region. He began walking about among the mountains and he met a hermit. The hermit said to him: "You may stay here with me. I shall die in three days. Bury me then, and I will pay you well for it."

So John stayed with him, and, when the third day came, the hermit, who was about to die, gave him a stick, saying: "In whatever direction you point this stick, you will find yourself there." Then he gave him a knapsack, saying: "Anything you want you will find in this knapsack." Then he gave him a cap, saying: "As soon as you put this cap on, nobody will be able to see you."

Then the hermit died, and John buried him.

John gathered his things together, pointed the stick, and said: "Let me be instantly in the town where the king lives." He found himself there on the instant, and he was told that the queen would every night wear out a dozen pairs of shoes, yet nobody was able to follow her track. The lords were all flocking to offer to follow the queen's traces, and John went too. He went into the palace and had himself announced to the king. When he came before the king, he said that he would like to trace the queen. The king asked him: "Who are you?"

He answered "Sleepy John."

The king said: "And how are you going to trace her, when you are sleeping all the time? If you fail to trace her you will lose your head."

John answered that he would try to trace her all the same.

When the evening was come the queen went to bed in one room and John went to bed in the next room, through which the queen had to pass. He did not go to sleep, but when the queen was going by he pretended to be in a deep slumber. So the queen lit a candle and scorched the soles of his feet to make sure that he was asleep. But John didn't stir, and so she was certain that he was asleep. Then she took her twelve pairs of new shoes and off she went.

John got up, put his cap on, and pointed with his stick and said: "Let me be where the queen is."

Now, when the queen came to a certain rock, the earth opened before her and two dragons came to meet her. They took her on their backs and carried her as far as the lead forest. Then John said: "Let me be where the queen is," and instantly he was in the lead forest. So he broke off a twig for a proof and put it in his knapsack. But when he broke off the twig it gave out a shrill sound as if a bell were ringing. The queen was frightened, but she rode on again. John pointed with his stick and said: "Let me be where the queen is," and instantly he was in the tin forest. He broke off a twig again and put it in his knapsack, and it rang again. The queen turned pale, but she rode on again. John pointed with his stick again and said: "Let me be where the queen is," and instantly he was in the silver forest. He broke off a twig again and put it into his knapsack. As he broke it, it gave out a ringing sound and the queen fainted. The dragons hastened on again till they came to a green meadow.

A crowd of devils came to meet them here, and they revived the queen. Then they had a feast. Sleepy John was there too. The cook was not at home that day, so John sat down in his place, and, as he had his cap on, nobody could see him. They put aside a part of the food for the cook, but John ate it all. They were all surprised to see all the food they put aside disappearing. They couldn't make out what was happening, but they didn't care very much. And when the banquet was at an end the devils began to dance with the queen, and they kept on dancing until the queen had worn out all her shoes. When her shoes were worn out, those two dragons took her on their backs again and brought her to the place where the earth had opened before her. John said: "Let me be where the queen is." By this time she was walking on the earth again, and he followed her. When they came near the palace he went ahead of the queen and went to bed; and, as the queen was going in, she saw him sleeping, and so she went to her own room and lay down and slept.

In the morning the lords gathered together and the king asked whether any of them had tracked the queen. But none of them could say "Yes."

So he summoned Sleepy John before him. John said:

"Gracious Lord King, I did indeed track her, and I know that she used up those twelve pairs of shoes upon the green meadows in Hell."

The queen stood forth at once, and John took from his knapsack the leaden twig and said: "The queen was carried by two dragons towards Hell, and she came to the leaden forest; there I broke off this twig and the queen was frightened."

The king said: "That's no good. You might have made the twig yourself."

So John produced the tin twig from his knapsack and said: "After that the queen drove through the tin forest, and there I broke off this twig. That time the queen grew pale."

The king said: "You might have made even this twig."

So John produced the silver twig and said: "Afterwards the queen drove through the silver forest, and when I broke off this twig she fainted, and so she was until the devils brought her to life again."

The queen, seeing that all was known, cried out: "Let the earth swallow me!" and she was swallowed by the earth.

Sleepy John got the half of the kingdom, and, when the king died, the other half too.

Kojata

ONCE THERE WAS A KING who had an only son. One day the king went to inspect his estates. He came to the first farm and found it all right. Before he had finished going the round of his estates, thirteen big farms in all, he forgot that his wife was about to have a child. On his way home he came to a forest, and such a thirst came upon him that he bade his driver stop and look for some water. The driver looked everywhere for water, but he couldn't find any. So the king himself went to look for it, and he found a well.

Now, just as he was going to drink, he kneeled down and he saw something in the well which had claws like a crab and red eyes. It seized him by the beard with one of its claws – he had a pretty long beard – and it refused to let him go unless he promised to give it the thing that he had at home unknown to himself. So he said to himself: "I know everything at home." But he forgot about his wife's condition. By this time his wife had been delivered of a prince, and so the king, without knowing it, had promised his son to the thing in the well. And on that it let him go.

When he got home he saw the new-born prince, and of course he was very sad. He remained so for twelve years. The prince asked him why he was so sad. And the king answered: "Because you are sold." The prince told him not to worry about it; he would be able to help himself.

The prince called for his horse and started out. He had been riding five days' journey from his home, when he came to a lake. There he tethered his horse. He saw thirteen ducks swimming on the lake, and there were thirteen shifts lying on the bank. So he carried off one of the shifts and hid himself. When they saw this, twelve of the ducks flew away, but the thirteenth was running hither and thither, looking for her shift. So when he saw her running hither and thither looking for her shift, he came out of his hiding-place. Now the father of those ducks was the being which had seized the king by the beard. He was a sorcerer, and his name was Kojata.

This girl was his youngest daughter. And she said to the prince:

"Now I will give you a good counsel. You will save me and I will save you. My father will set you a difficult task. I will perform it for you, but you must not let him know that I am helping you. Leave your horse here and hurry on to my father's. He will give you a lodging, and he will give you three days to consider over the task. You will be in your room alone, and in the evening I will come humming to your window, for I shall come to you in a bee's shape, because I can't come in any other way. And you must follow my advice. My father has thirteen daughters, and we all resemble one another exactly and we all wear the same sort of clothes. You will have to find out which is the youngest, but you will have no other means of recognizing me than by noticing a tiny fly under my left eye, so be very careful about it."

So it was. The sorcerer called him in and the thirteen daughters were standing in a row. The sorcerer asked him whether he could make out which was the youngest; if he could do so, his life would be spared. So he went the round of them three times, but it was as much as he could do to recognize her. But he pointed her out. She was the third from the end. So the sorcerer asked him who had been giving him advice. But the prince answered that it was none of his business.

The next day the sorcerer gave him another task: to build a palace of pure gold and silver without using hammer or trowel. The prince was very worried about it. But in the evening the youngest daughter came flying to him again, and she gave him a wand. At a single stroke of the wand the palace rose up ready-built, and it was more perfect than the old one. In the morning he was strolling about the palace looking round him. When King Kojata saw him, he came up to him and stopped: "Who has given you this counsel?" he asked. The prince answered that it was the person who had given him advice the time before.

So the sorcerer set him the third task, and this time the daughter was not able to advise him. She came to him in the evening and said: "I have no other advice than for both of us to flee at once, otherwise you will be lost and I too."

Now, in the evening she turned herself into a horse, and he mounted her and rode as far as the lake. There he found his own horse, and they both mounted it and rode off at full speed. Soon she heard a great noise behind her, so she turned herself into a church and the prince became a monk. The sorcerer's apprentices were riding in pursuit of them. When they got as far as the church they turned and went back to Kojata. When they came to him they said that they had not overtaken anybody; they had only seen a church and a monk in it. And he said: "Those were they!"

Next day he sent them again to pursue the runaways. Though they were riding faster than the day before, again they heard a trampling behind them. So she turned herself into a great river and him into an old broken bridge. Their pursuers came as far as the river and the bridge, and then they turned back and reported to their king, Kojata, that they had seen nothing but a river and a bridge. He said at once: "Well, those were they!"

On the third day the runaways started again and made for the border as fast as they could, and soon they were in their own land. When they reached the third church, the sorcerer had no more power over them. He began to tear his hair and knock his head against the ground and to curse his daughter for tricking him.

So the young king came home, bringing a lovely young princess with him. His father was very pleased at that!

Shepherd Hynek

TO CUT A LONG STORY SHORT, there was a prince and he had three sons. The first two followed in their father's footsteps, but the third did not. He said he would like to be a forester. The father was angry and turned him out of the house. What was

he to do with the fellow, when he was so obstinate and would be a forester?

"Well, be whatever you like," said the prince, and he gave him a shepherd's dress and Hynek went out into the world.

He had been walking through a forest for three days. He was hungry and cold, and everything seemed to be against him. He was tired too, and at last he fell asleep under a tree. As he was sleeping, a black man came to him. He would not leave him to sleep, but waked him up. Hynek was frightened. But he told him there was no need to be afraid. He was a good man, though his skin was black. So Hynek stayed with him for seven years and learnt the seven languages, zither playing, and all that sort of thing.

Now the seven years were over. In that land there was a king who had an only daughter. And there was a fierce dragon which was ravaging the whole of that kingdom, and everybody was forced to give him one sheep and one human being to appease him. So the lot fell upon the princess too. The black man told Hynek that something ought to be done to deliver the people and to save the princess from being devoured by that dragon.

"Go to the next homestead," he said, "and ask to be taken on as a shepherd, and in the morning you will have to drive the sheep into this forest."

So they took leave of one another. Hynek was engaged as shepherd, and in the morning he drove the sheep into the forest, where the black man was waiting for him. When he came with the sheep, the black man gave him a wand and a ring, and said:

"When you turn this ring, you will be brought to a castle where a giant dwells, and you will have to tackle the giant. This wand will help you to do it. Then you must take his robe, his horse, and his sword. Then you will be brought to the town, and it will be about the time that the princess will be brought out."

So Hynek took his leave and found everything just as he had said. As he came near to the castle, the giant was looking out and said:

"You earthworm, what are you looking for?"

"Oh! I should like to have a try for that big head of yours."

The giant fell into a rage. He was holding a great club in his hand, and he flung it at Hynek, but Hynek dodged aside and the club sank deep into the ground, it had been flung with such force. So Hynek went right up to him, and, crack! he struck him with the wand. So the giant tumbled over. Hynek took his sword and struck his head off. Then he took an iron key out of the giant's pocket. He opened the lock, took the robe and the horse, and dressed himself as became a knight. Then he turned the ring, and in a moment he found himself on the road along which they were bringing the princess to be devoured by the dragon. When he saw the procession, he asked:

"What's going on here, and why are the people in such grief?"

"Because the princess is to be devoured by a dragon to-day."

Hynek said: "For the sake of her beauty, show me his den where he dwells."

So he rode up to the rock and called out loudly: "Now, dragon, come on; your meal is ready here, waiting for you."

But the dragon answered: "I don't want it to-day; come to-morrow, at eleven."

So Hynek returned. He rode towards them and said that the dragon would not leave his den to-day. So they all went back to the town with the knight, and the king would not let him go away on any account. But Hynek began to make excuses. He had to deliver a letter for the field marshal and he could not remain there. Then he turned the ring on his finger, and instantly he was in the castle again. He left the clothes and the horse there, putting the clothes tidily together. Then he put on his shepherd's dress, turned the ring, and at once he was near the forest, where the black man had been tending his sheep meanwhile. He greeted him kindly:

"You have done everything well. Always act like that."

So he drove the sheep home and played the zither again. Everybody ran up to the door to listen to the magic playing of the shepherd. But he said nothing to anybody.

The next day he drove the sheep to the forest still earlier. The black man was there waiting for him, and said: "Follow my advice and you will be happy."

He said that he would do so. The black man was to mind the sheep again. He gave Hynek the wand and the ring, and Hynek came to another castle.

The giant was looking out as he came up; he was standing in the doorway. He asked the lad grimly what he was looking for.

"Oh! it's nothing. I only want to try for that big head of yours."

The giant was holding a hammer and he hurled it at him. No eye could see where it fell. Hynek leapt towards him, and, crack! he struck him with the wand, and the giant fell over and Hynek cut his head off too. He took a silver key out of the giant's pocket and went straight to the castle. There he chose a robe, girded on a sword, took a horse, and turned the ring again. Once more he was on the road where the princess was being brought to be devoured. He asked them in a different language why they were wailing so.

"Well, our princess is to be devoured by the dragon to-day. He would not leave his den yesterday."

"Show me his den: I will sacrifice myself for the sake of her beauty."

They showed him the rock, and he rode straight up to it and called out: "Now, dragon, come on; your meal is ready here."

"I don't want it to-day, wait till eleven to-morrow."

The king was still less willing to let him go this time, but he found some excuse, turned his horse, and went back with everything to the castle.

Then he returned to the forest and the black man. The black man said: "Drive your sheep home now, but come earlier to-morrow, for a heavy task awaits you."

Hynek could not rest that night: he was so afraid that he would be too late. As soon as dawn came he let out the flock and drove it to the forest. When he got there, the black man said to him: "There's only to-day now. It will be the last time. But it will be a heavy task for you to tackle the third giant and the dragon." Then he gave him the wand and the ring, and said that the key to-day would be of gold. He must choose the robe and take a black horse, and he must take with him the sword with which he had killed the giant and the dragon.

He turned the ring and was brought to the third castle. Here was a giant again, much huger than the other two. He ran at Hynek, but, crack! Hynek struck him with the wand. Then he took his sword and killed him. Then he opened the castle with a golden key; he went to the stable, then he put on a green robe and brought out a black horse. There was a sword hanging there, and he girded it on. Then he turned the ring, and in a moment he was on the road along which they were bringing the princess to be devoured by the dragon.

He asked them in yet another language why they were so sorrowful. He was ready to sacrifice himself for the sake of her beauty. So they showed him the den in which the dragon dwelt, and he called out: "Well, come on, dragon; your meal is ready and waiting for you here."

Now the rock began to shake; all the stones came rolling down, and the dragon flew out of the rock, his seven heads burning with flame, and he made straight for Hynek. Hynek began cutting at the seven heads until he was weary that he could not do any more. Then the horse began to crush the dragon, until after a while Hynek, being rested, took his sword, and at once he cut all the seven heads off.

He was so scorched by the fire that he could not run away, and he fainted on the spot. The people had seen what was happening, so they rode up and carried him away, lest he should perish of the dragon's poison. They brought him and laid him in the princess's lap. She gave him her ring and a golden neckchain, and so he recovered his senses and found himself lying in the princess's lap. He was afraid that he had stayed too long, for he was supposed to be with the marshal by this time. They were all trying to hold him back from going, but he found an excuse and promised he would come back within three days. So at last they just had to let him go.

He returned to the castle, where he put everything back in its place again, except the sword, which he took with him and gave to the black man. The black man said to him: "You have succeeded now, and it will be well with both of us."

So Hynek drove his sheep home rejoicing. He was playing the zither, and all the people gathered outside to listen to his rare and sweet music. He asked what had happened to the princess: had the dragon devoured her?

"Oh no! A knight delivered her, and the king is going to give her in marriage to him."

"Alas! silly shepherd that I am, why did I not tackle him myself with my shepherd's staff!"

But they all laughed at him: "You mind your sheep, that's what befits you."

In the royal castle the wedding-feast was ready. The sixth day had come and they were still waiting for him. But the bridegroom did not come and the princess was sad. On the sixth day he asked the marshal if he could go to the castle to play his zither to the princess; he would like to cheer her, since she was so sad.

"You may go, and, if you succeed, you shall make some extra money."

So Hynek went and played, and the music was so sweet that the lords could listen to nothing but his beautiful playing. He played for three hours, and then he must go home. They asked him what reward he would like.

"Nothing but to drink a cup of wine with the princess."

He had ready the ring which the princess had given him when he was in her lap. His request was granted, and the rest of the musicians who were there were angry with him for claiming so insignificant a reward. When they had filled the cup for him, he drank the wine and dropped the ring into the cup.

Now, the cupbearer who was filling the cup looked into it and saw the glittering ring. So he hastened to the princess with it. She recognized it as her own, so she ordered them to bring that shepherd before her.

"Well," he said, "surely they won't beat me!"

They brought him before the princess, and she made him tell her how he had got that ring and how he had been clothed.

So he said: "All those three days I was with you."

Hynek did not go back to the marshal, though he complained of the loss of his shepherd. He was clad in royal robes now, and they had a splendid wedding in the castle. But the princess did not know what his parentage was, although she could see that he was not a low-born man.

So after a year he said he would like to visit his parents, and he told her to prepare for the journey. She was to send a letter to Prince So-and-So that the young queen was going to visit him. He would go on ahead.

So he put his shepherd's dress on once more and purposely tore it in several places, and, when his princess arrived and everybody was welcoming her, he went straight into the great hall. Now, when the old

Prince saw that it was his son all tattered and torn, he bade them put him under lock and key. But he had no difficulty in escaping, and while they were feasting, he came into the hall again and sat down next to the princess. The father was furious that his son should behave so shamefully. But the princess reassured him. It was all right, she said. She did not mind at all; he might sit where he pleased.

After dinner she called for a bath. They prepared it for her. But Hynek was quicker, and slipped into the bathroom before her. She shut the door and he put on his royal robes, and then they went before his father. The Prince was frightened, since he had thought so ill of his son, and he fell on his knees. But Hynek lifted him up and himself kneeled before him and asked his forgiveness.

Then came in the black man. He gave Hynek the sword and bade him cut his head off. Hynek would not repay his kindness in this way.

"Then we shall both be unhappy."

So when he saw what he was to do, he cut the head off and, when he had done that, an English prince appeared in his stead. He was only eighteen years old. All his followers woke up too. Hynek accompanied him to England, and then took leave of him.

How are they all now?

I don't know.

The Shepherd's Nosegay

THERE WAS ONCE A KING who had a beautiful daughter. When it was time for her to get a husband, the king set a day and invited all the neighboring princes to come and see her.

One of these princes decided that he would like to have a look at the princess before the others. So he dressed himself in a shepherd's costume: a broad-brimmed hat, a blue smock, a green vest, tight breeches to the knees, thick woolen stockings, and sandals. Thus disguised he set out for the kingdom where the princess lived. All he took with him were four loaves of bread to eat on the way.

He hadn't gone far before he met a beggar who begged him, in God's name, for a piece of bread. The prince at once gave him one of the four loaves. A little farther on a second beggar held out his hand and begged for a piece of bread. To him the prince gave the second loaf. To a third beggar he gave the third loaf, and to a fourth beggar the last loaf.

The fourth beggar said to him:

"Prince in shepherd's guise, your charity will not go unrewarded. Here are four gifts for you, one for each of the loaves of bread that you have given away this day. Take this whip which has the power of killing any one it strikes however gentle the blow. Take this beggar's wallet. It has in it some bread and cheese, but not common bread and cheese for, no matter how much of it you eat, there will always be some left. Take this shepherd's ax. If ever you have to leave your sheep alone, plant it in the earth and the sheep, instead of straying, will graze around it. Last, here is a shepherd's pipe. When you blow upon it your sheep will dance and play. Farewell and good luck go with you."

The prince thanked the beggar for his gifts and then trudged on to the kingdom where the beautiful princess lived. He presented himself at the palace as a shepherd in quest of work and he told them his name was Yan. The king liked his appearance and so the next day he was put in charge of a flock of sheep which he drove up the mountain side to pasture.

He planted his shepherd's ax in the midst of a meadow and, leaving his sheep to graze about it, he went off into the forest hunting adventures. There he came upon a castle where a giant was busy cooking his dinner in a big saucepan.

"Good-day to you," Yan said politely.

The giant, who was a rude, unmannerly fellow, bellowed out:

"It won't take me long to finish you, you young whippersnapper!"

He raised a great iron club to strike Yan but Yan, quick as thought, flicked the giant with his whip and the huge fellow toppled over dead.

The next day he returned to the castle and found another giant in possession.

"Ho, ho!" he roared on sight of Yan. "What, you young whippersnapper, back again! You killed my brother yesterday and now I'll kill you!"

He raised his great iron club to strike Yan, but Yan skipped nimbly aside. Then he flicked the giant with his whip and the huge fellow toppled over dead.

When Yan returned to the castle the third day there were no more giants about. So he wandered from room to room to see what treasures were there.

In one room he found a big chest. He struck it smartly and immediately two burly men jumped out and, bowing low before him, said:

"What does the master of the castle desire?"

"Show me everything there is to be seen," Yan ordered.

So the two servants of the chest showed him everything – jewels and treasures and gold. Then they led him out into the gardens where the most wonderful flowers in the world were blooming. Yan plucked some of these and made them into a nosegay.

That afternoon, as he drove home his sheep, he played on his magic pipe and the sheep, pairing off two by two, began to dance and frisk about him. All the people in the village ran out to see the strange sight and laughed and clapped their hands for joy.

The princess ran to the palace window and when she saw the sheep dancing two by two she, too, laughed and clapped her hands. Then the wind whiffed her a smell of the wonderful nosegay that Yan was carrying and she said to her serving maid:

"Run down to the shepherd and tell him the princess desires his nosegay."

The serving maid delivered the message to Yan, but he shook his head and said:

"Tell your mistress that whoever wants this nosegay must come herself and say: 'Yanitchko, give me that nosegay.'"

When the princess heard this, she laughed and said:

"What an odd shepherd! I see I must go myself."

So the princess herself came out to Yan and said:

"Yanitchko, give me that nosegay."

But Yan smiled and shook his head.

"Whoever wants this nosegay must say: 'Yanitchko, please give me that nosegay.'"

The Princess was a merry girl, so she laughed and said:

"Yanitchko, please give me that nosegay."

Yan gave it to her at once and she thanked him sweetly.

The next day Yan went again to the castle garden and plucked another nosegay. Then in the afternoon he drove his sheep through the village as before, playing his pipe. The princess was standing at the palace window waiting to see him. When the wind brought her a whiff of the fresh nosegay that was even more fragrant than the first one, she ran out to Yan and said:

"Yanitchko, please give me that nosegay."

But Yan smiled and shook his head.

"Whoever wants this nosegay must say: 'My dear Yanitchko, I beg you most politely please to give me that nosegay.'"

"My dear Yanitchko," the princess repeated demurely, "I beg you most politely please to give me that nosegay."

So Yan gave her the second nosegay. The princess put it in her window and the fragrance filled the village until people from far and near came to see it.

After that every day Yan gathered a nosegay for the princess and every day the princess stood at the palace window waiting to see the handsome shepherd. And always when she asked for the nosegay, she said: "Please."

In this way a month went by and the day arrived when the neighboring princes were to come to meet the princess. They were to come in fine array, the people said, and the princess had ready a kerchief and a ring for the one who would please her most.

Yan planted the ax in the meadow and, leaving the sheep to graze about it, went to the castle where he ordered the servants of the chest to dress him as befitted his rank. They put a white suit upon him and gave him a white horse with trappings of silver.

So he rode to the palace and took his place with the other princes but behind them so that the princess had to crane her neck to see him.

One by one the various princes rode by the princess but to none of them did the princess give her kerchief and ring. Yan was the last to salute her, and instantly she handed him her favors.

Then before the king or the other suitors could speak to him, Yan put spurs to his horse and rode off.

That evening as usual when he was driving home his sheep, the princess ran out to him and said:

"Yan, it was you!"

But Yan laughed and put her off.

"How can a poor shepherd be a prince?" he asked.

The princess was not convinced and she said in another month, when the princes were to come again, she would find out.

So for another month Yan tended sheep and plucked nosegays for the merry little princess and the princess waited for him at the palace window every afternoon and when she saw him she always spoke to him politely and said: "Please."

When the day for the second meeting of the princes came, the servants of the chest arrayed Yan in a suit of red and gave him a sorrel horse with trappings of gold. Yan again rode to the palace and took his place with the other princes but behind them so that the princess had to crane her neck to see him.

Again the suitors rode by the princess one by one, but at each of them she shook her head impatiently and kept her kerchief and ring until Yan saluted her.

Instantly the ceremony was over, Yan put spurs to his horse and rode off and, although the king sent after him to bring him back, Yan was able to escape.

That evening when he was driving home his sheep the princess ran out to him and said:

"Yanitchko, it was you! I know it was!"

But again Yan laughed and put her off and asked her how she could think such a thing of a poor shepherd.

Again the princess was not convinced and she said in another month, when the princes were to come for the third and last time, she would make sure.

So for another month Yan tended his sheep and plucked nosegays for the merry little princess and the princess waited for him at the palace window every afternoon and, when she saw him, she always said politely: "Please."

For the third meeting of the princes the servants of the chest arrayed Yan in a gorgeous suit of black and gave him a black horse with golden trappings studded in diamonds. He rode to the palace and took his place behind the other suitors. Things went as before and again the princess saved her kerchief and ring for him.

This time when he tried to ride off the other suitors surrounded him and, before he escaped, one of them wounded him on the foot.

He galloped back to the castle in the forest, dressed once again in his shepherd's clothes, and returned to the meadow where his sheep were grazing.

There he sat down and bound up his wounded foot in the kerchief which the princess had given him. Then, when he had eaten some bread and cheese from his magic wallet, he stretched himself out in the sun and fell asleep.

Meanwhile the princess, who was sorely vexed that her mysterious suitor had again escaped, slipped out of the palace and ran up the mountain path to see for herself whether the shepherd were really with his sheep. She found Yan asleep and, when she saw her kerchief bound about his foot, she knew that he was the prince.

She woke him up and cried:

"You are he! You know you are!"

Yan looked at her and laughed and he asked:

"How can I be a prince?"

"But I know you are!" the princess said. "Oh, Yanitchko, dear Yanitchko, I beg you please to tell me!"

So then Yan, because he always did anything the princess asked him when she said: "Please," told her his true name and his rank.

The princess, overjoyed to hear that her dear shepherd was really a prince, carried him off to her father, the king.

"This is the man I shall marry," she said, "this and none other."

So Yan and the merry little princess were married and lived very happily. And the people of the country when they speak of the princess always say:

"That's a princess for you! Why, even if she is a princess, she always says 'Please' to her own husband!"

Clever Manka

THERE WAS ONCE a rich farmer who was as grasping and unscrupulous as he was rich. He was always driving a hard bargain and always getting the better of his poor neighbors. **One of these neighbors was a humble shepherd who in return for service was to receive from the farmer a heifer. When the time of payment came the farmer refused to give the shepherd the heifer and the shepherd was forced to lay the matter before the burgomaster.**

The burgomaster, who was a young man and as yet not very experienced, listened to both sides and when he had deliberated he said:

"Instead of deciding this case, I will put a riddle to you both and the man who makes the best answer shall have the heifer. Are you agreed?"

The farmer and the shepherd accepted this proposal and the burgomaster said:

"Well then, here is my riddle: What is the swiftest thing in the world? What is the sweetest thing? What is the richest? Think out your answers and bring them to me at this same hour tomorrow."

The farmer went home in a temper.

"What kind of a burgomaster is this young fellow!" he growled. "If he had let me keep the heifer I'd have sent him a bushel of pears. But now I'm in a fair way of losing the heifer for I can't think of any answer to his foolish riddle."

"What is the matter, husband?" his wife asked.

"It's that new burgomaster. The old one would have given me the heifer without any argument, but this young man thinks to decide the case by asking us riddles."

When he told his wife what the riddle was, she cheered him greatly by telling him that she knew the answers at once.

"Why, husband," said she, "our gray mare must be the swiftest thing in the world. You know yourself nothing ever passes us on the road. As for the sweetest, did you ever taste honey any sweeter than ours? And I'm sure there's nothing richer than our chest of golden ducats that we've been laying by these forty years."

The farmer was delighted.

"You're right, wife, you're right! That heifer remains ours!"

The shepherd when he got home was downcast and sad. He had a daughter, a clever girl named Manka, who met him at the door of his cottage and asked:

"What is it, father? What did the burgomaster say?"

The shepherd sighed.

"I'm afraid I've lost the heifer. The burgomaster set us a riddle and I know I shall never guess it."

"Perhaps I can help you," Manka said. "What is it?"

So the shepherd gave her the riddle and the next day as he was setting out for the burgomaster's, Manka told him what answers to make.

When he reached the burgomaster's house, the farmer was already there rubbing his hands and beaming with self-importance.

The burgomaster again propounded the riddle and then asked the farmer his answers.

The farmer cleared his throat and with a pompous air began:

"The swiftest thing in the world? Why, my dear sir, that's my gray mare, of course, for no other horse ever passes us on the road. The sweetest? Honey from my beehives, to be sure. The richest? What can be richer than my chest of golden ducats!"

And the farmer squared his shoulders and smiled triumphantly.

"H'm," said the young burgomaster, dryly. Then he asked:

"What answers does the shepherd make?"

The shepherd bowed politely and said:

"The swiftest thing in the world is thought for thought can run any distance in the twinkling of an eye. The sweetest thing of all is sleep for when a man is tired and sad what can be sweeter? The richest thing is the earth for out of the earth come all the riches of the world."

"Good!" the burgomaster cried. "Good! The heifer goes to the shepherd!"

Later the burgomaster said to the shepherd:

"Tell me, now, who gave you those answers? I'm sure they never came out of your own head."

At first the shepherd tried not to tell, but when the burgomaster pressed him he confessed that they came from his daughter, Manka. The burgomaster, who thought he would like to make another test of Manka's cleverness, sent for ten eggs. He gave them to the shepherd and said:

"Take these eggs to Manka and tell her to have them hatched out by tomorrow and to bring me the chicks."

When the shepherd reached home and gave Manka the burgomaster's message, Manka laughed and said: "Take a handful of millet and go right back to the burgomaster. Say to him: 'My daughter sends you this millet. She says that if you plant it, grow it, and have it harvested by tomorrow, she'll bring you the ten chicks and you can feed them the ripe grain.'"

When the burgomaster heard this, he laughed heartily.

"That's a clever girl of yours," he told the shepherd. "If she's as comely as she is clever, I think I'd like to marry her. Tell her to come to see me, but she must come neither by day nor by night, neither riding nor walking, neither dressed nor undressed."

When Manka received this message she waited until the next dawn when night was gone and day not yet arrived. Then she wrapped herself in a fishnet and, throwing one leg over a goat's back and keeping one foot on the ground, she went to the burgomaster's house.

Now I ask you: did she go dressed? No, she wasn't dressed. A fishnet isn't clothing. Did she go undressed? Of course not, for wasn't she covered with a fishnet? Did she walk to the burgomaster's? No, she didn't walk for she went with one leg thrown over a goat. Then did she ride? Of course she didn't ride for wasn't she walking on one foot?

When she reached the burgomaster's house she called out:

"Here I am, Mr. Burgomaster, and I've come neither by day nor by night, neither riding nor walking, neither dressed nor undressed."

The young burgomaster was so delighted with Manka's cleverness and so pleased with her comely looks that he proposed to her at once and in a short time married her.

"But understand, my dear Manka," he said, "you are not to use that cleverness of yours at my expense. I won't have you interfering in any of my cases. In fact if ever you give advice to any one who comes to me for judgment, I'll turn you out of my house at once and send you home to your father."

All went well for a time. Manka busied herself in her house-keeping and was careful not to interfere in any of the burgomaster's cases.

Then one day two farmers came to the burgomaster to have a dispute settled. One of the farmers owned a mare which had foaled in the marketplace. The colt had run under the wagon of the other farmer and thereupon the owner of the wagon claimed the colt as his property.

The burgomaster, who was thinking of something else while the case was being presented, said carelessly:

"The man who found the colt under his wagon is, of course, the owner of the colt."

As the owner of the mare was leaving the burgomaster's house, he met Manka and stopped to tell her about the case. Manka was ashamed of her husband for making so foolish a decision and she said to the farmer:

"Come back this afternoon with a fishing net and stretch it across the dusty road. When the burgomaster sees you he will come out and ask you what you are doing. Say to him that you're catching fish. When he asks you how you can expect to catch fish in a dusty road, tell him it's just as easy for you to catch fish in a dusty road as it is for a wagon to foal. Then he'll see the injustice of his decision and have the colt returned to you. But remember one thing: you mustn't let him find out that it was I who told you to do this."

That afternoon when the burgomaster chanced to look out the window he saw a man stretching a fishnet across the dusty road. He went out to him and asked:

"What are you doing?"

"Fishing."

"Fishing in a dusty road? Are you daft?"

"Well," the man said, "it's just as easy for me to catch fish in a dusty road as it is for a wagon to foal."

Then the burgomaster recognized the man as the owner of the mare and he had to confess that what he said was true.

"Of course the colt belongs to your mare and must be returned to you. But tell me," he said, "who put you up to this? You didn't think of it yourself."

The farmer tried not to tell but the burgomaster questioned him until he found out that Manka was at the bottom of it. This made him very angry. He went into the house and called his wife.

"Manka," he said, "do you forget what I told you would happen if you went interfering in any of my cases? Home you go this very day. I don't care to hear any excuses. The matter is settled. You may take with you the one thing you like best in my house for I won't have people saying that I treated you shabbily."

Manka made no outcry.

"Very well, my dear husband, I shall do as you say: I shall go home to my father's cottage and take with me the one thing I like best in your house. But don't make me go until after supper. We have been very happy together and I should like to eat one last meal with you. Let us have no more words but be kind to each other as we've always been and then part as friends."

The burgomaster agreed to this and Manka prepared a fine supper of all the dishes of which her husband was particularly fond. The burgomaster opened his choicest wine and pledged Manka's health. Then he set to, and the supper was so good that he ate and ate and ate. And the more he ate, the more he drank until at last he grew drowsy and fell sound asleep in his chair. Then without awakening him Manka had him carried out to the wagon that was waiting to take her home to her father.

The next morning when the burgomaster opened his eyes, he found himself lying in the shepherd's cottage.

"What does this mean?" he roared out.

"Nothing, dear husband, nothing!" Manka said. "You know you told me I might take with me the one thing I liked best in your house, so of course I took you! That's all."

For a moment the burgomaster rubbed his eyes in amazement. Then he laughed loud and heartily to think how Manka had outwitted him.

"Manka," he said, "you're too clever for me. Come on, my dear, let's go home."

So they climbed back into the wagon and drove home.

The burgomaster never again scolded his wife but thereafter whenever a very difficult case came up he always said:

"I think we had better consult my wife. You know she's a very clever woman."

Batcha and the Dragon

ONCE UPON A TIME there was a shepherd who was called Batcha. During the summer he pastured his flocks high up on the mountain where he had a little hut and a sheepfold.

One day in autumn while he was lying on the ground, idly blowing his pipes, he chanced to look down the mountain slope. There he saw a most amazing sight. A great army of snakes, hundreds and hundreds in number, was slowly crawling to a rocky cliff not far from where he was lying.

When they reached the cliff, every serpent bit off a leaf from a plant that was growing there. They then touched the cliff with the leaves and the rock opened. One by one they crawled inside. When the last one had disappeared, the rock closed.

Batcha blinked his eyes in bewilderment.

"What can this mean?" he asked himself. "Where are they gone? I think I'll have to climb up there myself and see what that plant is. I wonder will the rock open for me?"

He whistled to Dunay, his dog, and left him in charge of the sheep. Then he made his way over to the cliff and examined the mysterious plant. It was something he had never seen before.

He picked a leaf and touched the cliff in the same place where the serpents had touched it. Instantly the rock opened.

Batcha stepped inside. He found himself in a huge cavern the walls of which glittered with gold and silver and precious stones. A golden table stood in the center and upon it a monster serpent, a very king of serpents, lay coiled up fast asleep. The other serpents, hundreds and hundreds of them, lay on the ground around the table. They also were fast asleep. As Batcha walked about, not one of them stirred.

Batcha sauntered here and there examining the walls and the golden table and the sleeping serpents. When he had seen everything he thought to himself:

"It's very strange and interesting and all that, but now it's time for me to get back to my sheep."

It's easy to say: "Now I'm going," but when Batcha tried to go he found he couldn't, for the rock had closed. So there he was locked in with the serpents.

He was a philosophical fellow and so, after puzzling a moment, he shrugged his shoulders and said:

"Well, if I can't get out I suppose I'll have to stay here for the night."

With that he drew his cape about him, lay down, and was soon fast asleep.

He was awakened by a rustling murmur. Thinking that he was in his own hut, he sat up and rubbed his eyes. Then he saw the glittering walls of the cavern and remembered his adventure.

The old king serpent still lay on the golden table but no longer asleep. A movement like a slow wave was rippling his great coils. All the other serpents on the ground were facing the golden table and with darting tongues were hissing:

"Is it time? Is it time?"

The old king serpent slowly lifted his head and with a deep murmurous hiss said:

"Yes, it is time."

He stretched out his long body, slipped off the golden table, and glided away to the wall of the cavern. All the smaller serpents wriggled after him.

Batcha followed them, thinking to himself:

"I'll go out the way they go."

The old king serpent touched the wall with his tongue and the rock opened. Then he glided aside and the serpents crawled out, one by one. When the last one was out, Batcha tried to follow, but the rock swung shut in his face, again locking him in.

The old king serpent hissed at him in a deep breathy voice:

"Hah, you miserable man creature, you can't get out! You're here and here you stay!"

"But I can't stay here," Batcha said. "What can I do in here? I can't sleep forever! You must let me out! I have sheep at pasture and a scolding wife at home in the valley. She'll have a thing or two to say if I'm late in getting back!"

Batcha pleaded and argued until at last the old serpent said:

"Very well, I'll let you out, but not until you have made me a triple oath that you won't tell any one how you came in."

Batcha agreed to this. Three times he swore a mighty oath not to tell any one how he had entered the cavern.

"I warn you," the old serpent said, as he opened the wall, "if you break this oath a terrible fate will overtake you!"

Without another word Batcha hurried through the opening.

Once outside he looked about him in surprise. Everything seemed changed. It was autumn when he had followed the serpents into the cavern. Now it was spring!

"What has happened?" he cried in fright. "Oh, what an unfortunate fellow I am! Have I slept through the winter? Where are my sheep? And my wife – what will she say?"

With trembling knees he made his way to his hut. His wife was busy inside. He could see her through the open door. He didn't know what to say to her at first, so he slipped into the sheepfold and hid himself while he tried to think out some likely story.

While he was crouching there, he saw a finely dressed gentleman come to the door of the hut and ask his wife where her husband was.

The woman burst into tears and explained to the stranger that one day in the previous autumn her husband had taken out his sheep as usual and had never come back.

"Dunay, the dog," she said, "drove home the sheep and from that day to this nothing has ever been heard of my poor husband. I suppose a wolf devoured him, or the witches caught him and tore him to pieces and scattered him over the mountain. And here I am left, a poor forsaken widow! Oh dear, oh dear, oh dear!"

Her grief was so great that Batcha leaped out of the sheepfold to comfort her.

"There, there, dear wife, don't cry! Here I am, alive and well! No wolf ate me, no witches caught me. I've been asleep in the sheepfold – that's all. I must have slept all winter long!"

At sight and sound of her husband, the woman stopped crying. Her grief changed to surprise, then to fury.

"You wretch!" she cried. "You lazy, good-for-nothing loafer! A nice kind of shepherd you are to desert your sheep and yourself to idle away the winter sleeping like a serpent! That's a fine story, isn't it, and I suppose you think me fool enough to believe it! Oh, you – you sheep's tick, where have you been and what have you been doing?"

She flew at Batcha with both hands and there's no telling what she would have done to him if the stranger hadn't interfered.

"There, there," he said, "no use getting excited! Of course he hasn't been sleeping here in the sheepfold all winter. The question is, where has he been? Here is some money for you. Take it and go along home to your cottage in the valley. Leave Batcha to me and I promise you I'll get the truth out of him."

The woman abused her husband some more and then, pocketing the money, went off.

As soon as she was gone, the stranger changed into a horrible looking creature with a third eye in the middle of his forehead.

"Good heavens!" Batcha gasped in fright. "He's the wizard of the mountain! Now what's going to happen to me!"

Batcha had often heard terrifying stories of the wizard, how he could himself take any form he wished and how he could turn a man into a ram.

"Aha!" the wizard laughed. "I see you know me! Now then, no more lies! Tell me: where have you been all winter long?"

At first Batcha remembered his triple oath to the old king serpent and he feared to break it. But when the wizard thundered out the same question a second time and a third time, and grew bigger and more horrible looking each time he spoke, Batcha forgot his oath and confessed everything.

"Now come with me," the wizard said. "Show me the cliff. Show me the magic plant."

What could Batcha do but obey? He led the wizard to the cliff and picked a leaf of the magic plant.

"Open the rock," the wizard commanded.

Batcha laid the leaf against the cliff and instantly the rock opened.

"Go inside!" the wizard ordered.

But Batcha's trembling legs refused to move.

The wizard took out a book and began mumbling an incantation. Suddenly the earth trembled, the sky thundered, and with a great hissing whistling sound a monster dragon flew out of the cavern. It was the old king serpent whose seven years were up and who was now become a flying dragon. From his huge mouth he breathed out fire and smoke. With his long tail he swished right and left among the forest trees and these snapped and broke like little twigs.

The wizard, still mumbling from his book, handed Batcha a bridle.

"Throw this around his neck!" he commanded.

Batcha took the bridle but was too terrified to act. The wizard spoke again and Batcha made one uncertain step in the dragon's direction. He lifted his arm to throw the bridle over the dragon's head, when the dragon suddenly turned on him, swooped under him, and before Batcha knew what was happening he found himself on the dragon's back and he felt himself being lifted up, up, up, above the tops of the forest trees, above the very mountains themselves.

For a moment the sky was so dark that only the fire, spurting from the dragon's eyes and mouth, lighted them on their way.

The dragon lashed this way and that in fury, he belched forth great floods of boiling water, he hissed, he roared, until Batcha, clinging to his back, was half dead with fright.

Then gradually his anger cooled. He ceased belching forth boiling water, he stopped breathing fire, his hisses grew less terrifying.

"Thank God!" Batcha gasped. "Perhaps now he'll sink to earth and let me go."

But the dragon was not yet finished with punishing Batcha for breaking his oath. He rose still higher until the mountains of the earth looked like tiny ant-hills, still up until even these had disappeared. On, on they went, whizzing through the stars of heaven.

At last the dragon stopped flying and hung motionless in the firmament. To Batcha this was even more terrifying than moving.

"What shall I do? What shall I do?" he wept in agony. "If I jump down to earth I'll kill myself and I can't fly on up to heaven! Oh, dragon, have mercy on me! Fly back to earth and let me go and I swear before God that never again until death will I offend you!"

Batcha's pleading would have moved a stone to pity but the dragon, with an angry shake of his tail, only hardened his heart.

Suddenly Batcha heard the sweet voice of the skylark that was mounting to heaven.

"Skylark!" he called. "Dear skylark, bird that God loves, help me, for I am in great trouble! Fly up to heaven and tell God Almighty that Batcha, the shepherd, is hung in midair on a dragon's back. Tell Him that Batcha praises Him forever and begs Him to deliver him."

The skylark carried this message to heaven and God Almighty, pitying the poor shepherd, took some birch leaves and wrote on them in letters of gold. He put them in the skylark's bill and told the skylark to drop them on the dragon's head.

So the skylark returned from heaven and, hovering over Batcha, dropped the birch leaves on the dragon's head.

The dragon instantly sank to earth, so fast that Batcha lost consciousness.

When he came to himself he was sitting before his own hut. He looked about him. The dragon's cliff had disappeared. Otherwise everything was the same.

It was late afternoon and Dunay, the dog, was driving home the sheep. There was a woman coming up the mountain path.

Batcha heaved a great sigh.

"Thank God I'm back!" he said to himself. "How fine it is to hear Dunay's bark! And here comes my wife, God bless her! She'll scold me, I know, but even if she does, how glad I am to see her!"

The Three Golden Hairs

THERE WAS ONCE a king who took great delight in hunting. One day he followed a stag a great distance into the forest. He went on and on until he lost his way. Night fell and the king by happy chance came upon a clearing where a charcoal-burner had a cottage. The king asked the charcoal-burner to lead him out of the forest and offered to pay him handsomely.

"I'd be glad to go with you," the charcoal-burner said, "but my wife is expecting the birth of a child and I cannot leave her. It is too late for you to start out alone. Won't you spend the night here? Lie down on some hay in the garret and tomorrow I'll be your guide."

When they reached the cliff, every serpent bit off a leaf from a plant that was growing there. They then touched the cliff with the leaves and the rock opened. One by one they crawled inside. When the last one had disappeared, the rock closed.

The king had to accept this arrangement. He climbed into the garret and lay down on the floor. Soon afterwards a son was born to the charcoal-burner.

At midnight the king noticed a strange light in the room below him. He peeped through a chink in the boards and saw the charcoal-burner asleep, his wife lying in a dead faint, and three old women, all in white, standing over the baby, each holding a lighted taper in her hand.

The first old woman said: "My gift to this boy is that he shall encounter great dangers."

The second said: "My gift to him is that he shall go safely through them all, and live long."

The third one said: "And I give him for wife the baby daughter born this night to the king who lies upstairs on the straw."

The three old women blew out their tapers and all was quiet. They were the Fates.

The king felt as though a sword had been thrust into his heart. He lay awake till morning trying to think out some plan by which he could thwart the will of the three old Fates.

When day broke the child began to cry and the charcoal-burner woke up. Then he saw that his wife had died during the night.

"Ah, my poor motherless child," he cried, "what shall I do with you now?"

"Give me the baby," the king said. "I'll see that he's looked after properly and I'll give you enough money to keep you the rest of your life."

The charcoal-burner was delighted with this offer and the king went away promising to send at once for the baby.

A few days later when he reached his palace he was met with the joyful news that a beautiful little baby daughter had been born to him. He asked the time of her birth, and of course it was on the very night when he saw the Fates. Instead of being pleased at the safe arrival of the baby princess, the king frowned.

Then he called one of his stewards and said to him: "Go into the forest in a direction that I shall tell you. You will find there a cottage where a charcoal-burner lives. Give him this money and get from him a little child. Take the child and on your way back drown it. Do as I say or I shall have you drowned."

The steward went, found the charcoal-burner, and took the child. He put it into a basket and carried it away. As he was crossing a broad river he dropped the basket into the water.

"Goodnight to you, little son-in-law that nobody wanted!" the king said when he heard what the steward had done.

He supposed of course that the baby was drowned. But it wasn't. Its little basket floated in the water like a cradle, and the baby slept as if the river were singing it a lullaby. It floated down with the current past a fisherman's cottage. The fisherman saw it, got into his boat, and went after it. When he found what the basket contained he was overjoyed. At once he carried the baby to his wife and said:

"You have always wanted a little son and here you have one. The river has given him to us."

The fisherman's wife was delighted and brought up the child as her own. They named him Plavachek, which means a little boy who has come floating on the water.

The river flowed on and the days went by and Plavachek grew from a baby to a boy and then into a handsome youth, the handsomest by far in the whole countryside.

One day the king happened to ride that way unattended. It was hot and he was thirsty. He beckoned to the fisherman to get him a drink of fresh water. Plavachek brought it to him. The king looked at the handsome youth in astonishment.

"You have a fine lad," he said to the fisherman. "Is he your own son?"

"He is, yet he isn't," the fisherman answered. "Just twenty years ago a little baby in a basket floated down the river. We took him in and he has been ours ever since."

A mist rose before the king's eyes and he went deathly pale, for he knew at once that Plavachek was the child that he had ordered drowned.

Soon he recovered himself and jumping from his horse he said: "I need a messenger to send to my palace and I have no one with me. Could this youth go for me?"

"Your majesty has but to command," the fisherman said, "and Plavachek will go."

The king sat down and wrote a letter to the queen. This is what he said:

"Have the young man who delivers this letter run through with a sword at once. He is a dangerous enemy. Let him be dispatched before I return. Such is my will."

He folded the letter, made it secure, and sealed it with his own signet.

Plavachek took the letter and started out with it at once. He had to go through a deep forest where he missed the path and lost his way. He struggled on through underbrush and thicket until it began to grow dark. Then he met an old woman who said to him:

"Where are you going, Plavachek?"

"I'm carrying this letter to the king's palace and I've lost my way. Can you put me on the right road, mother?"

"You can't get there today," the old woman said. "It's dark now. Spend the night with me. You won't be with a stranger, for I'm your old godmother."

Plavachek allowed himself to be persuaded and presently he saw before him a pretty little house that seemed at that moment to have sprung out of the ground.

During the night while Plavachek was asleep, the old woman took the letter out of his pocket and put in another that read as follows:

"Have the young man who delivers this letter married to our daughter at once. He is my destined son-in-law. Let the wedding take place before I return. Such is my will."

The next day Plavachek delivered the letter and as soon as the queen read it, she gave orders at once for the wedding. Both she and her daughter were much taken with the handsome youth and gazed at him with tender eyes. As for Plavachek he fell instantly in love with the princess and was delighted to marry her.

Some days after the wedding the king returned and when he heard what had happened he flew into a violent rage at the queen.

"But," protested the queen, "you yourself ordered me to have him married to our daughter before you came back. Here is your letter."

The king took the letter and examined it carefully. The handwriting, the seal, the paper – all were his own.

He called his son-in-law and questioned him.

Plavachek related how he had lost his way in the forest and spent the night with his godmother.

"What does your godmother look like?" the king asked.

Plavachek described her.

From the description the king recognized her as the same old woman who had promised the princess to the charcoal-burner's son twenty years before.

He looked at Plavachek thoughtfully and at last he said:

"What's done can't be undone. However, young man, you can't expect to be my son-in-law for nothing. If you want my daughter you must bring me for dowry three of the golden hairs of old Grandfather Knowitall."

He thought to himself that this would be an impossible task and so would be a good way to get rid of an undesirable son-in-law.

Plavachek took leave of his bride and started off. He didn't know which way to go. Who would know? Everybody talked about old Grandfather Knowitall, but nobody seemed to know where to find him. Yet Plavachek had a Fate for a godmother, so it wasn't likely that he would miss the right road.

He traveled long and far, going over wooded hills and desert plains and crossing deep rivers. He came at last to a black sea.

There he saw a boat and an old ferryman.

"God bless you, old ferryman!" he said.

"May God grant that prayer, young traveler! Where are you going?"

"I'm going to old Grandfather Knowitall to get three of his golden hairs."

"Oho! I have long been hunting for just such a messenger as you! For twenty years I have been ferrying people across this black sea and nobody has come to relieve me. If you promise to ask Grandfather Knowitall when my work will end, I'll ferry you over."

Plavachek promised and the boatman took him across.

Plavachek traveled on until he came to a great city that was in a state of decay. Before the city he met an old man who had a staff in his hand, but even with the staff he could scarcely crawl along.

"God bless you, old grandfather!" Plavachek said.

"May God grant that prayer, handsome youth! Where are you going?"

"I am going to old Grandfather Knowitall to get three of his golden hairs."

"Indeed! We have been waiting a long time for just such a messenger as you! I must lead you at once to the king."

So he took him to the king and the king said: "Ah, so you are going on an errand to Grandfather Knowitall! We have an apple-tree here that used to bear apples of youth. If any one ate one of those apples, no matter how aged he was, he'd become young again. But, alas, for twenty years now our tree has borne no fruit. If you promise to ask Grandfather Knowitall if there is any help for us, I will reward you handsomely."

Plavachek gave the king his promise and the king bid him godspeed.

Plavachek traveled on until he reached another great city that was half in ruins. Not far from the city a man was burying his father, and tears as big as peas were rolling down his cheek.

"God bless you, mournful grave-digger!" Plavachek said.

"May God grant that prayer, kind traveler! Where are you going?"

"I'm going to old Grandfather Knowitall to get three of his golden hairs."

"To Grandfather Knowitall! What a pity you didn't come sooner! Our king has long been waiting for just such a messenger as you! I must lead you to him."

So he took Plavachek to the king and the king said to him: "So you're going on an errand to Grandfather Knowitall. We have a well here that used to flow with the water of life. If any one drank of it, no matter how sick he was, he would get well. Nay, if he were already dead, this water, sprinkled upon him, would bring him back to life. But, alas, for twenty years now the well has gone dry. If you promise to ask Grandfather Knowitall if there is help for us, I will reward you handsomely."

Plavachek gave the king his promise and the king bid him godspeed.

After that Plavachek traveled long and far into a black forest. Deep in the forest he came upon a broad green meadow full of beautiful flowers and in its midst a golden palace glittering as though it were on fire. This was the palace of Grandfather Knowitall.

Plavachek entered and found nobody there but an old woman who sat spinning in a corner.

"Welcome, Plavachek," she said. "I am delighted to see you again."

He looked at the old woman and saw that she was his godmother with whom he had spent the night when he was carrying the letter to the palace.

"What has brought you here, Plavachek?" she asked.

"The king, godmother. He says I can't be his son-in-law for nothing. I have to give a dowry. So he has sent me to old Grandfather Knowitall to get three of his golden hairs."

The old woman smiled and said: "Do you know who Grandfather Knowitall is? Why, he's the bright Sun who goes everywhere and sees everything. I am his mother. In the morning he's a little lad, at noon he's a grown man, and in the evening an old grandfather. I will get you three of the golden hairs from his golden head, for I must not be a godmother for nothing! But, my lad, you mustn't remain where you are. My son is kind, but if he comes home hungry he might want to roast you and eat you for his supper. There's an empty tub over there and I'll just cover you with it."

Plavachek begged his godmother to get from Grandfather Knowitall the answers for the three questions he had promised to ask.

"I will," said the old woman, "and do you listen carefully to what he says."

Suddenly there was the rushing sound of a mighty wind outside and the Sun, an old grandfather with a golden head, flew in by the western window. He sniffed the air suspiciously.

"Phew! Phew!" he cried. "I smell human flesh! Have you any one here, mother?"

"Star of the day, whom could I have here without your seeing him? The truth is you've been flying all day long over God's world and your nose is filled with the smell of human flesh. That's why you still smell it when you come home in the evening."

The old man said nothing more and sat down to his supper.

After supper he laid his head on the old woman's lap and fell sound asleep. The old woman pulled out a golden hair and threw it on the floor. It twanged like the string of a violin.

"What is it, mother?" the old man said. "What is it?"

"Nothing, my boy, nothing. I was asleep and had a wonderful dream."

"What did you dream about, mother?"

"I dreamt about a city where they had a well of living water. If any one drank of it, no matter how sick he was, he would get well. Nay, if he were already dead, this water, sprinkled on him, would bring him back to life. For the last twenty years the well has gone dry. Is there anything to be done to make it flow again?"

"Yes. There's a frog sitting on the spring that feeds the well. Let them kill the frog and clean out the well and the water will flow as before."

When he fell asleep again the old woman pulled out another golden hair and threw it on the floor.

"What is it, mother?"

"Nothing, my boy, nothing. I was asleep again and I had a wonderful dream. I dreamt of a city where they had an apple-tree that bore apples of youth. If any one ate one of those apples, no matter how aged he was, he'd become young again. But for twenty years the tree has borne no fruit. Can anything be done about it?"

"Yes. In the roots of the tree there is a snake that takes its strength. Let them kill the snake and transplant the tree. Then it will bear fruit as before."

He fell asleep again and the old woman pulled out a third golden hair.

"Why won't you let me sleep, mother?" he complained, and started to sit up.

"Lie still, my boy, lie still. I didn't intend to wake you, but a heavy sleep fell upon me and I had another wonderful dream. I dreamt of a boatman on the black sea. For twenty years he has been ferrying that boat and no one has offered to relieve him. When will he be relieved?"

"Ah, but that boatman is the son of a stupid mother! Why doesn't he thrust the oar into the hand of some one else and jump ashore himself? Then the other man would have to be ferryman in his place. But now let me be quiet. I must get up early tomorrow morning and go and dry the tears which the king's daughter sheds every night for her husband, the charcoal-burner's son, whom the king has sent to get three of my golden hairs."

In the morning there was again the rushing sound of a mighty wind outside and a beautiful golden child – no longer an old man – awoke on his mother's lap. It was the glorious Sun. He bade his mother farewell and flew out by an eastern window.

The old woman turned over the tub and said to Plavachek: "Here are the three golden hairs for you. You also have Grandfather Knowitall's answers to your three questions. Now good-by. As you will need me no more, you will never see me again."

Plavachek thanked his godmother most gratefully and departed.

When he reached the first city the king asked him what news he brought.

"Good news!" Plavachek said. "Have the well cleaned out and kill the frog that sits on its spring. If you do this the water will flow again as it used to."

The king ordered this to be done at once and when he saw the water beginning to bubble up and flow again, he made Plavachek a present of twelve horses, white as swans, laden with as much gold and silver as they could carry.

When Plavachek came to the second city and the king of that city asked him what news he brought, he said:

"Good news! Have the apple tree dug up. At its roots you will find a snake. Kill the snake and replant the tree. Then it will bear fruit as it used to."

The king had this done at once and during the night the tree burst into bloom and bore great quantities of fruit. The king was delighted and made Plavachek a present of twelve horses, black as ravens, laden with as much riches as they could carry.

Plavachek traveled on and when he came to the black sea, the boatman asked him had he the answer to his question.

"Yes, I have," said Plavachek, "but you must ferry me over before I tell you."

The boatman wanted to hear the answer at once, but Plavachek was firm. So the old man ferried him across with his twelve white horses and his twelve black horses.

When Plavachek was safely landed, he said: "The next person who comes to be ferried over, thrust the oar into his hand and do you jump ashore. Then the other man will have to be boatman in your place."

Plavachek traveled home to the palace. The king could scarcely believe his eyes when he saw the three golden hairs of Grandfather Knowitall. The princess wept again, not for sorrow this time but for joy at her bridegroom's return.

"But, Plavachek," the king gasped, "where did you get these beautiful horses and all these riches?"

"I earned them," said Plavachek proudly. Then he related how he helped one king who had a tree of the apples of youth and another king who had a well of the water of life.

"Apples of youth! Water of life!" the king kept repeating softly to himself. "If I ate one of those apples I should become young again! If I were dead the water of life would restore me!"

He lost no time in starting out in quest of the apples of youth and the water of life. And do you know, he hasn't come back yet!

So Plavachek, the charcoal-burner's son, became the king's son-in-law as the old Fate foretold.

As for the king, well, I fear he's still ferrying that boat across the black sea!

The Three Citrons

ONCE UPON A TIME there was an aged king who had an only son. One day he called the prince to him and said: "My son, you see that my head is white. Soon I shall be closing my eyes and you are not yet settled in life. Marry, my son, marry at once so that I can bless you before I die."

The prince made no answer but he took the king's words to heart and pondered them. He would gladly have done as his father wished but there was no young girl upon whom his affections were set.

One day when he was sitting in the garden, wondering what to do, an old woman suddenly appeared before him.

"Go," she said, "to the top of the Glass Hill, pluck the Three Citrons, and you will get a wife in whom your heart will delight." With that she disappeared as mysteriously as she had come.

Her words went through the prince's soul like a bright dart. Instantly he determined, come what might, to find the Glass Hill and to pluck the Three Citrons. He told his father his intention and the old king fitted him out for the journey and gave him his blessing.

For a long time the prince wandered over wooded mountains and desert plains without seeing or even hearing anything of the Glass Hill and the Three Citrons. One day, worn out with his long journey, he threw himself down in the shade of a wide-spreading linden tree. As his father's sword, which he wore at his side, clanked on the ground, twelve ravens began cawing from the top of the tree. Frightened by the clanking of the sword, they raised their wings and flew off.

The prince jumped to his feet. "Those are the first living creatures I have seen for many a day. I'll go in the direction they have taken," he said to himself, "and perhaps I'll have better luck."

So he traveled on and after three days and three nights a high castle came in view.

"Thank God!" he exclaimed, pushing joyfully ahead. "I shall soon have human companionship once more."

The castle was built entirely of lead. The twelve ravens circled above it and in front of it stood an old woman leaning on a long leaden staff. She was a Yezibaba. Now you must know that a Yezibaba is an ugly old witch with a hooked nose, a bristly face, and long scrawny hands. She's a bad old thing usually, but sometimes, if you take her fancy, she's kind.

This time when she looked the prince over she shook her head at him in a friendly way.

"Yi, yi, my boy, how did you get here? Why, not even a little bird or a tiny butterfly comes here, much less a human being! You'd better escape if life is dear to you, or my son, when he comes home, will eat you!"

"No, no, old mother, don't make me go," begged the prince. "I have come to you for advice to know whether you can tell me anything about the Glass Hill and the Three Citrons."

"No, I have never heard a word about the Glass Hill," Yezibaba said. "But wait until my son comes. He may be able to tell you something. Yes, yes, I'll manage to save you somehow. Go hide under the besom and stay there until I call you."

The mountains rumbled and the castle trembled and Yezibaba whispered to the prince that her son was coming.

"Phew! Phew! I smell human meat! I'll eat it!" shouted Yezibaba's son while he was still in the doorway. He struck the ground with his leaden club and the whole castle shook.

"No, no, my son, don't talk that way. It's true there is a pretty youth here, but he's come to ask you about something."

"Well, if he wants to ask me something, let him come out and ask."

"Yes, my son, he will, but only when you promise me that you will do nothing to him."

"Well, I won't do anything to him. Now let him come out."

The prince hidden under the besom was shaking like an aspen leaf, for when he peeped through the twigs he saw an ogre so huge that he himself would reach up only to his knees. Happily the ogre had guaranteed his life before Yezibaba ordered him out.

"Well, well, well, you little June bug!" shouted the ogre. "What are you afraid of? Where have you been? What do you want?"

"What do I want?" repeated the prince. "I have been wandering in these mountains a long time and I can't find what I'm seeking. So I've come to you to ask whether you can tell me something about the Glass Hill and the Three Citrons."

Yezibaba's son wrinkled his forehead. He thought for a moment and then, lowering his voice a little, he said: "I've never heard of any Glass Hill around here. But I tell you what you do: go on to my brother in arms who lives in the Silver Castle and ask him. Maybe he'll be able to tell you. But I can't let you go away hungry. That would never do! Hi, mother, bring out the dumplings!"

Old Yezibaba placed a large dish on the table and her giant son sat down.

"Well, come on! Eat!" he shouted to the prince.

When the prince took the first dumpling and bit into it, he almost broke two of his teeth, for the dumpling was made of lead.

"Well," shouted Yezibaba's son, "why don't you eat? Doesn't the dumpling taste good?"

"Oh, yes, very good," said the prince, politely, "but just now I'm not hungry."

"Well, if you're not hungry now you will be later. Put a few in your pocket and eat them on your journey."

So, whether he wanted them or not, the prince had to put some leaden dumplings into his pocket. Then he took his leave of Yezibaba and her son and traveled on.

He went on and on for three days and three nights. The farther he went, the more inhospitable became the country. Before him stretched a waste of mountains, behind him a waste of mountains with no living creature in sight.

Wearied with his long journey, he threw himself on the ground. His silver sword clanked sharply and at its sound twenty-four ravens circled above him, cawed in fright, and flew away.

"A good sign!" cried the prince. "I'll follow the ravens again!"

So on he went as fast as his legs could carry him until he came in sight of a tall castle. It was still far away, but even at that distance it shone and flashed, for it was built of pure silver.

In front of the castle stood an old woman, bent with age, and leaning on a long silver staff. This was the second Yezibaba.

"Yi, yi, my boy!" she cried. "How did you get here? Why, not even a little bird or a tiny butterfly comes here, much less a human being. You'd better escape if life is dear to you, or my son, when he comes home, will eat you!"

"No, no, old mother, he won't eat me. I bring greetings from his brother of the Leaden Castle."

"Well, if you bring greetings from the Leaden Castle you are safe enough. Come in, my boy, and tell me your business."

"My business? For a long time, old mother, I've been looking for the Glass Hill and the Three Citrons, but I can't find them. So I've come to ask you whether you could tell me something about them."

"No, my boy, I don't know anything about the Glass Hill. But wait until my son comes. Perhaps he can help you. In the meantime hide yourself under the bed and don't come out until I call you."

The mountains rumbled and the castle trembled and the prince knew that Yezibaba's son was coming home.

"Phew! Phew! I smell human meat! I'll eat it!" bellowed the mighty fellow. He stood in the doorway and banged the ground with his silver club until the whole castle shook.

"No, no, my son," said Yezibaba, "don't talk that way! A pretty little chap has come bringing you greetings from your brother of the Leaden Castle."

"Well, if he's been at the Leaden Castle and came to no harm, he'll have nothing to fear from me either. Where is he?"

The prince slipped out from under the bed and stood before the ogre. Looking up at him was like looking at the top of the tallest pine tree.

"Well, little June bug, so you've been at my brother's, eh?"

"Yes," said the prince. "See, I still have the dumplings he gave me for the journey."

"I believe you. Well, what do you want?"

"What do I want? I came to ask you whether you could tell me something about the Glass Hill and the Three Citrons."

"H'm, it seems to me I used to hear something about them, but I forget. I tell you what you do: go to my brother of the Golden Castle and ask him. But wait! I can't let you go away hungry. Hi, mother, bring out the dumplings!"

Yezibaba brought the dumplings on a large silver dish and put them on the table.

"Eat!" shouted her son.

The prince saw they were silver dumplings, so he said he wasn't hungry just then, but he'd like to take some with him for the journey.

"Take as many as you want," shouted the ogre. "And give my greetings to my brother and my aunt."

So the prince took some silver dumplings, made suitable thanks, and departed.

He journeyed on from the Silver Castle three days and three nights, through dense forests and over rough mountains, not knowing where he was nor which way to turn. At last all worn out he threw himself down in the shade of a beech tree to rest. As the sword clanked on the ground, its silver voice rang out and a flock of thirty-six ravens circled over his head.

"Caw! Caw!" they croaked. Then, frightened by the sound of the sword, they flew away.

"Praise God!" cried the prince. "The Golden Castle can't be far!"

He jumped up and started eagerly off in the direction the ravens had taken. As he left a valley and climbed a little hill he saw before him a beautiful wide meadow in the midst of which stood the Golden Castle shining like the sun. Before the gate of the castle stood a bent old Yezibaba leaning on a golden staff.

"Yi, yi, my boy," she cried to the prince, "how did you get here? Why, not even a little bird or a tiny butterfly comes here, much less a human being! You'd better escape if life is dear to you, or my son, when he comes home, will eat you!"

"No, no, old mother, he won't eat me, for I bring him greetings from his brother of the Silver Castle!"

"Well, if you bring greetings from the Silver Castle you are safe enough. Come in, my boy, and tell me your business."

"My business, old mother? For a long time I've been wandering over these wild mountains in search of the Glass Hill and the Three Citrons. At the Silver Castle they sent me to you because they thought you might know something about them."

"The Glass Hill? No, I don't know where it is. But wait until my son comes. He will advise you where to go and what to do. Hide under the table and stay there till I call you."

The mountains rumbled and the castle trembled and Yezibaba's son came home.

"Phew! Phew! I smell human meat! I'll eat it!" he roared. He stood in the doorway and pounded the ground with his golden club until the whole castle shook.

"No, no, my son," said Yezibaba, "don't talk that way! A pretty little fellow has come bringing you greetings from your brother of the Silver Castle. If you won't harm him, I'll call him out."

"Well, if my brother didn't do anything to him, I won't either."

So the prince crawled out from under the table and stood before the giant. It was like standing beneath a high tower. He showed the ogre the silver dumplings as proof that he had been at the Silver Castle.

"Well, well, well, my little June bug," shouted the monstrous fellow, "tell me what it is you want! I'll advise you if I can! Don't be afraid!"

So the prince told him the purpose of his journey and asked him how to get to the Glass Hill and pluck the Three Citrons.

"Do you see that blackish lump over yonder?" the ogre said, pointing with his golden club. "That is the Glass Hill. On that hill stands a tree. From that tree hang the Three Citrons which send out fragrance for seven miles around. You will climb the Glass Hill, kneel beneath the tree, and reach up your hands. If the citrons are destined for you they will fall into your hands of their own accord. If they are not destined for you, you will not be able to pluck them no matter what you do. As you return, if you are hungry or thirsty, cut open one of the citrons and you will have food and drink in plenty. Go now with God's blessing. But wait! I can't let you go away hungry! Hi, mother, bring out the dumplings!"

Yezibaba set a large golden dish on the table.

"Eat!" her son shouted. "Or, if you are not hungry just now, put some in your pocket and eat them on the way."

The prince said that he was not hungry but that he would be glad to take some of the golden dumplings with him and eat them later. Then he thanked the ogre most courteously for his hospitality and advice and took his leave.

He trudged quickly on from hill to dale, from dale to hill again, and never stopped until he reached the Glass Hill itself. Then he stood still as if turned into stone. The hill was high and steep and smooth with not so much as a scratch on its surface. Over its top spread out the branches of the magic tree upon which hung the Three Citrons. Their fragrance was so powerful that the prince almost fainted.

"Let it be as God wills!" he thought to himself. "But however the adventure is to come out, now that I'm here I must at least make the attempt."

So he began to claw his way up the smooth glass, but he hadn't gone many yards before his foot slipped and down he went so hard that he didn't know where he was or what had happened to him until he found himself sitting on the ground.

In his vexation he began to throw away the dumplings, thinking that perhaps their weight had dragged him down. He took one and threw it straight at the hill. Imagine his surprise to see it fix itself firmly in the glass. He threw a second and a third and there he had three steps on which he was able to stand with safety!

The prince was overjoyed. He threw dumpling after dumpling and each one of them became a step. First he threw the leaden ones, then the silver ones, and last of all the golden ones. On the steps made in this way he climbed higher and higher until he had reached the very summit of the hill. Then he knelt under the magic tree, lifted up his hands, and into them the Three Citrons dropped of their own accord!

Instantly the tree disappeared, the Glass Hill sank until it was lost, and when the prince came to himself there was neither tree nor hill to be seen, but only a wide plain.

Delighted with the outcome of his adventure, the prince turned homewards. At first he was too happy even to eat or drink. By the third day his stomach began to protest and he discovered that he was so hungry that he would have fallen ravenously upon a leaden dumpling if he had

had one in his pocket. But his pocket, alas, was empty, and the country all about was as bare as the palm of his hand.

Then he remembered what the ogre of the Golden Castle had told him and he took out one of the Three Citrons. He cut it open, and what do you suppose happened? Out jumped a beautiful maiden fresh from the hand of God, who bowed low before him and exclaimed:

"Have you food ready for me? Have you drink ready for me? Have you pretty clothes ready for me?"

"Alas, beautiful creature," the prince sighed, "I have not. I have nothing for you to eat or to drink or to put on."

The lovely maiden clapped her hands three times, bowed before him, and disappeared.

"Ah," said the prince, "now I know what kind of citrons you are! I'll think twice before opening one of you again!"

Of the one he had opened he ate and drank his fill, and so refreshed, went on. He traveled three days and three nights and by that time he began to feel three times hungrier than before.

"God help me!" thought he. "I must eat something! There are still two citrons and if I cut open one there would still be one left."

So he took out the second citron, cut it in two, and lo, a maiden twice as beautiful as the first stood before him. She bowed low and said:

"Have you food ready for me? Have you drink ready for me? Have you pretty clothes ready for me?"

"No, lovely creature, I haven't! I haven't!"

The maiden clapped her hands thrice, bowed before him, and disappeared.

Now there was only one citron left. The prince took it in his hand, looked at it, and said: "I won't cut you open until I'm safe at home in my father's house."

He took up his journey again and on the third day he came to his native town and his father's castle. He had been gone a long time and how he ever got back he didn't know himself.

Tears of joy rained down the old king's cheeks.

"Welcome home, my son, welcome a hundred times!" he cried, falling on the prince's neck.

The prince related the adventures of his journey and they at home told him how anxiously they had awaited his return.

On the next day a great feast was prepared. All the nobles in the land were invited. The tables were spread with food and drink the most expensive in the world and many rich dresses embroidered in gold and studded with pearls were laid out.

The guests assembled, seated themselves at the tables, and waited. Music played and when all was ready, the prince took the last citron and cut it in two. Out jumped a beautiful creature, three times lovelier than the others.

"Have you food ready for me?" she cried. "Have you drink ready for me? Have you pretty clothes ready for me?"

"I have indeed, dear heart!" the prince answered. "I have everything ready for you!"

He led her to the gorgeous clothes and she dressed herself in them and every one present marveled at her great beauty.

Soon the betrothal took place and after the betrothal a magnificent wedding.

So now the old king's wish was fulfilled. He blessed his son, gave over the kingdom to him, and not long afterwards he died.

The first thing that faced the young king after his father's death was a war which a neighboring king stirred up against him. So the young king had to bid farewell to the bride whom he had won so dearly and lead his men to battle. In order that nothing happen to the queen in his absence, he built a golden throne for her in the garden beside the lake. This throne was as high as a tower and no one could ascend it except those to whom the queen let down a silken cord.

Not far from the king's castle lived the old woman who, in the first place, had told him about the Three Citrons. She knew well enough how the young king had won his bride and she was deeply incensed that he had not invited her to the wedding and in fact had not even thanked her for her good advice.

Now this old woman had a gipsy for servant whom she used to send to the lake for water. One day when this gipsy was filling her pitcher, she saw in the lake a beautiful reflection. She supposed it was a reflection of herself.

"Is it right," she cried out, "that so lovely a creature as I should carry water for that old witch?"

In a fury she threw the pitcher on the ground and broke it into a hundred pieces. Then she looked up and discovered that it wasn't her own reflection she had seen in the water but that of the beautiful queen.

Ashamed of herself, she picked up the broken pitcher and went home. The old woman, who knew beforehand what had happened, went out to meet her with a new pitcher.

"It's no matter about the pitcher," the old woman said. "Go back to the lake and beg the lovely lady to let down the silken cord and pull you up. Tell her you will comb her hair. When she pulls you up, comb her hair until she falls asleep. Then stick this pin into her head. After that you can dress yourself up in her clothes and sit there like a queen."

It was easy enough to persuade the gipsy. She took the pitcher and the pin and returned to the lake.

As she drew water she gazed at the lovely queen.

"Oh, how beautiful you are!" she whined, leering up at the queen with an evil eye. "How beautiful you are! Aye, but you'd be a hundred times more beautiful if you but let me comb out your lovely hair! Indeed, I would so twine those golden tresses that your lord would be delighted!"

With words like these she beguiled and coaxed the queen until she let down the silken cord and drew the gipsy up. Once on the throne, the wicked gipsy combed out the golden tresses and plaited them and arranged them until the queen fell sound asleep. Then the gipsy took the pin and stuck it into the queen's head. Instantly a beautiful white dove flew off the golden throne and not a trace was left of the lovely queen except her rich clothing. The gipsy dressed herself in this, sat in the queen's place, and gazed down into the lake. But in the lake no lovely reflection showed itself, for even in the queen's clothes the gipsy remained a gipsy.

The young king waged a successful war against his enemies and made peace. Scarcely had he got home when he hurried to the garden to see whether anything had happened to his heart's delight. Who can express in words his astonishment and horror when instead of his beautiful wife he saw the evil gipsy!

"Ah, my dearest one, how you have changed!" he murmured and tears flowed down his cheeks.

"Yes, my dear, I have changed, I know I have," the gipsy answered. "It was grief for you that has broken me."

She tried to fall on his neck but the king turned quickly away and left her.

From that time forth he had no peace but day and night he mourned the lost beauty of his wife and nothing consoled him.

Grieving in this way and thinking always the same sad thoughts, he was walking one day in the garden when suddenly a beautiful white dove flew down from a high tree and alighted on his hand. She looked up at him with eyes as mournful as his own.

"Ah, my poor dove," the king said, "why are you so sad? Has your mate also changed?"

As he spoke he stroked the dove gently on the back and on the head. On the head he felt a little lump. He blew aside the feathers and discovered the head of a pin. He pulled out the pin and instantly the sad dove changed into his own beautiful wife.

She told him what had happened to her, how the gipsy had deceived her and stuck the pin into her head. The king had the gipsy and the old witch caught at once and burnt at the stake.

From that time on nothing happened to mar the king's happiness, neither the plots of his enemies nor the spite of evil people. He lived in love and peace with his beautiful wife and he ruled his kingdom wisely. In fact he's ruling it still if he hasn't died.

Prince Bayaya

WHILE THE KING of a distant country was off at the wars, his wife, the queen, gave birth to twin sons. There was great rejoicing throughout the court and immediately messengers were despatched to the king to carry him news of the happy event.

Both boys were well and vigorous and shot up like little trees. The one who was about a moment the older was the hardier of the two. Even as a toddling child he was forever playing in the courtyard and struggling to climb on the back of a horse that had been given him because it was just his own age.

His brother, on the other hand, liked better to play indoors on the soft carpets. He was always tagging after his mother and never went outdoors except when he followed the queen into the garden. For this reason the younger prince became the mother's favorite.

The boys were seven years old before the king returned from the wars. He looked at his sons with pride and joy and he said to the queen:

"But which is the older and which is the younger?"

The queen, thinking that the king was asking in order to know which was the heir to the throne, slipped in her favorite as the older. The king, of course, did not question his wife's word and so, thereafter, he always spoke of the younger one as his heir.

When the boys had grown into handsome youths, the older one wearied of life at home and of hearing his brother always spoken of as the future king. He longed to go out into the world and seek adventures of his own. One day as he was pouring out his heart to the little horse that had been his companion from infancy, much to his amazement the horse spoke to him with a human voice and said:

"Since you are not happy at home, go out into the world. But do not go without your father's permission. I advise you to take no one with you and to mount no horse but me. This will bring you good luck."

The prince asked the horse how it happened that he could talk like a human being.

"Don't ask me about that," the horse said, "for I can't tell you. But I wish to be your friend and counselor and I will be as long as you obey me."

The prince promised to do as the horse advised. He went at once to his father to beg his leave to ride out into the world. At first his father was unwilling to let him go but his mother gave her permission at once. By dint of coaxing he finally won his father's consent. Of course the king wanted the prince to set forth in a manner befitting his rank with a great company of men and horses. But the prince insisted that he wished to go unattended.

"Why, my dear father, do I need any such retinue as you suggest? Let me have some money for the journey and let me ride off alone on my own little horse. This will give me more freedom and less trouble."

Again he had to argue with his father for some time, but at last he succeeded in arranging everything to his liking.

The day of parting came. The little horse stood saddled at the castle gate. The prince bade farewell to his parents and his brother. They all wept on his neck and at the last moment the queen's heart misgave her for the deceit she had practised and she made the prince solemnly promise that he would return home within a year or at least send them word of his whereabouts.

So the prince mounted his little horse and off they trotted. The horse went at a surprising pace for an animal that was seventeen years old, but of course you have guessed before this that he was no ordinary horse. The years had not touched him at all. His coat was as smooth as satin and his legs were straight and sound. No matter how far he traveled he was always as fresh as a fawn.

He carried the prince a great distance until they came in sight of the towers of a beautiful city. Then the horse left the beaten track and crossed a field to a big rock.

When they reached the rock, the horse kicked it with his hoof three times and the rock opened. They rode inside and the prince found himself in a comfortable stable.

"Now you will leave me here," the horse said, "and go on alone to the nearby town. You must pretend you are dumb and be careful never to betray yourself. Present yourself at court and have the king take you into his service. When you need anything, no matter what it is, come to the rock, knock three times, and the rock will open to you."

The prince thought to himself: "My horse certainly knows what he's about, so of course I'll do exactly as he says."

He disguised himself by bandaging one eye and making his face look pale and sallow. Then he presented himself at court and the king, pitying his youth and his affliction of dumbness, took him into his service.

The prince was capable and quick at affairs and it wasn't long before the king gave over to him the management of the household. His advice was asked in matters of importance and all day long he hurried about the castle going from one thing to another. If the king needed a scribe, there wasn't a cleverer one anywhere than the prince. Everybody liked him and everybody was soon calling him Bayaya, because those were the only sounds he made.

The king had three daughters, each more beautiful than the other. The oldest was called Zdobena, the second Budinka, and the youngest Slavena.

The prince loved to be with the three girls and as he was supposed to be dumb and in his disguise was very ugly, the king made no objection to his spending his days with them. How could the king possibly think that there was any danger of Bayaya's stealing the heart of one of the princesses? They liked him, all three of them, and were always taking him with them wherever they went. He wove garlands for them, spun golden thread, picked them flowers, and drew them designs of birds and flowers for their embroidery. He liked them all, but he liked the youngest one best. Everything he did for her was done a little better than for the others. The garlands he wove her were richer, the designs he drew for her were more beautiful. The two older sisters noticed this and laughed, and when they were alone they teased Slavena. Slavena, who had a sweet and amiable disposition, accepted their joking without retort.

Bayaya had been at the court some time when one morning he found the king sitting sad and gloomy over his breakfast. So by signs he asked him what was the matter.

The king looked at him and sighed. "Is it possible, my dear boy," he said, "that you don't know what's the matter? Don't you know the calamity that threatens us? Don't you know the bitter three days that are at hand for me?"

Bayaya, alarmed by the seriousness of the king's manner, shook his head.

"Then I'll tell you," said the king, "although you can be of no help. Years ago three dragons came flying through the air and alighted on a great rock near here. The first was nine-headed, the second eighteen-headed, and the third twenty-seven-headed. At once they laid waste the country, devouring the cattle and killing the people. Soon the city was in a state of siege. To keep them away we placed all the food we had outside the gates and in a short time we ourselves were starving. In desperation I had an old wise woman called to court and asked her was there any way to drive these monsters from the land. Alas for me, there was a way and that way was to promise the awful creatures my three beautiful daughters when they reached womanhood. At that time my daughters were only small children and I thought to myself many things might happen in the years before they grew up. So, to relieve my stricken land, I promised the dragons my daughters. The poor queen died at once of grief, but my daughters grew up knowing nothing of their fate. As soon as I made the monstrous bargain, the dragons flew away and until yesterday were never again heard of. Last night, a shepherd, beside himself with terror, brought me the news that the dragons are again settled in their old rock and are sending out fearful roars. Tomorrow I must sacrifice to them my oldest child, the day after tomorrow my second child, and the day after that my youngest. Then I shall be left a poor lonely old man with nothing."

The king strode up and down and tore his hair in grief.

In great distress Bayaya went to the princesses. He found them dressed in black and looking ghastly pale. They were sitting in a row and bewailing their fate most piteously. Bayaya tried to comfort them, telling them by signs that surely some one would appear to rescue them. But they paid no heed to him and kept on moaning and weeping.

Grief and confusion spread throughout the city, for every one loved the royal family. Every house as well as the palace was soon draped in black and the sound of mourning was heard on every side.

Bayaya hurried secretly out of the city and across the field to the rock where his magic horse was stabled. He knocked three times, the rock opened, and he entered.

He stroked the horse's shining mane and kissed his muzzle in greeting.

"My dear horse," he said, "I have come to you for advice. Help me and I shall be happy forever."

So he told the horse the story of the dragons.

"Oh, I know all about those dragons," the horse answered. "In fact, it was that you might rescue the princesses that I brought you here in the first place. Early tomorrow morning come back and I will tell you what to do."

Bayaya returned to the castle with such joy shining in his face that if any one had noticed him he would have been severely rebuked. He spent the day with the princesses trying to comfort and console them, but in spite of all he could do they felt only more terrified as the hours went by.

The next day at the first streak of dawn he was at the rock.

The horse greeted him and said: "Lift up the stone under my trough and take out what you find there."

Bayaya obeyed. He lifted the stone and under the stone he found a large chest. Inside the chest he found three beautiful suits of clothing, with caps and plumes to match, a sword, and a horse's bridle. The first suit was red embroidered in silver and studded with diamonds, the second was pure white embroidered in gold, and the third was light blue richly embroidered with silver and studded with diamonds and pearls.

For all three suits there was but one mighty sword. Its blade was beautifully inlaid and its scabbard shone with precious stones. The horse's bridle was also richly jeweled.

"All three suits are for you," the horse said. "For the first day, put on the red one."

So Bayaya dressed himself in the red suit, buckled on his sword, and threw the bridle over the horse's head.

"Have no fear," the horse said as they left the rock. "Cut bravely into the monster, trusting to your sword. And remember, do not dismount."

At the castle heartbroken farewells were being taken. Zdobena parted from her father and her sisters, stepped into a carriage, and accompanied by a great multitude of her weeping subjects was slowly driven out of town to the Dragon Rock. As they neared the fatal spot the princess alighted. She took a few steps forward, then sank to the earth in a faint.

At that moment the people saw galloping toward them a knight with a red and white plume. In a voice of authority he ordered them to stand back and leave him to deal alone with the dragon. They were glad enough to lead the princess away and they all went to a hill near by from which they could watch the combat at a safe distance.

Now there was a deep rumbling noise, the earth shook, and the Dragon Rock opened. A nine-headed monster crawled out. He spat fire and poison from all his nine mouths and cast about his nine heads, this way and that, looking for his promised prey. When he saw the knight he let out a horrible roar.

Bayaya rode straight at him and with one blow of his sword cut off three of his heads. The dragon writhed and enveloped Bayaya in flames and poisonous fumes. But the prince, undaunted, struck at him again and again until he had cut off all nine heads. The life that still remained in the loathsome body, the horse finished with his hoofs.

When the dragon had perished the prince turned and galloped back the way he had come.

Zdobena looked after him, wishing she might follow him to thank him for her deliverance. But she remembered her poor father sunk in grief at the castle and she felt it was her duty to hurry back to him as quickly as she could.

It would be impossible to describe in words the king's joy when Zdobena appeared before him safe and uninjured. Her sisters embraced her and wondered for the first time whether a deliverer would rise up for them as well.

Bayaya capered happily about and assured them by signs that he was certain they, too, would be saved. Although the prospect of the morrow still terrified them, yet hope had come to them and once or twice Bayaya succeeded in making them laugh.

The next day Budinka was led out. As on the day before, the unknown knight appeared, this time wearing a white plume. He attacked the eighteen-headed dragon and, after valiant conflict, despatched him. Then before any one could reach him, he turned and rode away.

The princess returned to the castle, grieving that she had not been able to speak to the knight and express her gratitude.

"You, my sisters," Slavena said, "were backward not to speak to him before he rode off. Tomorrow if he delivers me I shall kneel before him and not get up until he consents to return with me to the castle."

Just then Bayaya began laughing and chuckling and Slavena asked him sharply what was the matter. He capered about and made her understand that he, too, wanted to see the knight.

On the third day Slavena was taken out to the Dragon Rock. This time the king also went. The heart of the poor girl quaked with terror when she thought that if the unknown knight failed to appear she would be handed over to the horrible monster.

A joyous shout from the people told her that the knight was coming. Then she saw him, a gallant figure in blue with a blue and white plume floating in the wind. As he had killed the first dragon, and the second dragon, so he killed the third although the struggle was longer and the little horse had much to do to stand up against the poisonous fumes.

Instantly the dragon was slain, Slavena and the king rushed up to the knight and begged him to return with them to the castle. He scarcely knew how to refuse, especially when Slavena, kneeling before him, grasped the edge of his tunic and looked up at him so bewitchingly that his heart melted and he was ready to do anything she asked.

But the little horse took matters into his own hands, reared up suddenly, and galloped off before the knight had time to dismount.

So Slavena, too, was unable to bring the knight back to the castle. The king and all the court were greatly disappointed but their disappointment was swallowed up in their joy that the princesses had been so miraculously saved.

Shortly after this another disaster threatened the king. A neighboring king of great power declared war against him. The king sent far and wide and summoned together all the nobles of the land. They came, and the king when he had laid before them his cause promised them the hands of his three beautiful daughters in return for their support. This was indeed an inducement and every young noble present swore his allegiance and hurried home to gather his forces.

Troops poured in from all sides and soon the king was ready to set forth.

He handed over the affairs of the castle to Bayaya and also intrusted to him the safety of the three princesses. Bayaya did his duty faithfully, looking after the castle and planning diversions for the princesses to keep them happy and cheerful.

Then one day he complained of feeling sick, but instead of consulting the court physician, he said he would go himself to the fields and hunt some herbs. The princesses laughed at his whim but let him go.

He hurried to the rock where his horse was stabled, knocked three times, and entered.

"You have come in good time," the horse said. "The king's forces are weakening and tomorrow will decide the battle. Put on the white suit, take your sword, and let us be off."

Bayaya kissed his brave little horse and put on his white suit.

That night the king was awake planning the morrow's battle and sending swift messengers to his daughters instructing them what to do in case the day went against him.

The next morning as the battle joined an unknown knight suddenly appeared among the king's forces. He was all in white. He rode a little horse and he wielded a mighty sword.

He struck right and left among the enemy and he caused such havoc that the king's forces were instantly heartened. Gathering around the white knight they fought so valiantly that soon the enemy broke and scattered and the king won a mighty victory.

The knight himself was slightly wounded on the foot. When the king saw this he jumped down from his horse, tore off a piece of his own cape, and bound up the wound. He begged the knight to dismount and come with him to a tent. But the knight, thanking him, refused, spurred his horse, and was gone.

The king nearly wept with disappointment that the unknown knight to whom he was under one more obligation had again ridden off without so much as leaving his name.

With great rejoicing the king's forces marched home carrying vast stores of booty.

"Well, steward," said the king to Bayaya, "how have the affairs of the household gone in my absence?"

Bayaya nodded that everything had gone well, but the princesses laughed at him and Slavena said:

"I must enter complaint against your steward, for he was disobedient. He said he was sick but he would not consult the court physician. He said he wanted to go himself and get some herbs. He went and he was gone two whole days and when he came back he was sicker than before."

The king looked at Bayaya to see if he was still sick. Bayaya shook his head and capered about to show the king that he was all right.

When the princesses heard that the unknown knight had again appeared and saved the day they were unwilling to become at once the brides of any of the nobles, for they thought the knight might perhaps come demanding one of them.

Again the king was in a quandary. All the various nobles had helped him valiantly and the question now arose to what three of them would the princesses be awarded. After much thought the king hit upon a plan which he hoped would decide the matter to the satisfaction of them all. He called a meeting of the nobles and said:

"My dear comrades in arms, you remember that I promised the hands of my daughters to those of you who would support me in battle. All of you gave me valiant support. Each of you deserves the hand of one of my daughters. But, alas, I have only three daughters. To decide therefore which three of you my daughters shall marry I make this suggestion: let all of you stand in the garden in a row and let each of my daughters throw down a golden apple from a balcony. Then each princess must wed the man to whom her apple rolls. My lords, do you all agree to this?"

The nobles all agreed and the king sent for his daughters. The princesses, still thinking of the unknown knight, were not enthusiastic over this arrangement, but not to shame their father they, too, agreed.

So each of the girls, dressed in her loveliest, took a golden apple in her hand and went up to a balcony.

Below in the garden the nobles stood in a row. Bayaya, as though he were a spectator, took his place at the end of the line.

First Zdobena threw down her apple. It rolled straight to the feet of Bayaya but he turned quickly aside and it rolled on to a handsome youth who snatched it up with joy and stepped from the line.

Then Budinka threw her apple. It, too, rolled to Bayaya but he cleverly kicked it on so that it seemed to roll straight to the feet of a valiant lord who picked it up and then looked with happy eyes at his lovely bride.

Last Slavena threw her apple. This time Bayaya did not step aside but when the apple rolled to him he stooped and picked it up. Then he ran to the balcony, knelt before the princess, and kissed her hand.

Slavena snatched away her hand and ran to her chamber, where she wept bitterly to think she would have to marry Bayaya instead of the unknown knight.

The king was much disappointed and the nobles murmured. But what was done was done, and could not be undone.

That night there was a great feast but Slavena remained in her chamber refusing to appear among the guests.

It was moonlight and from the rock in the field the little horse carried his master for the last time. When they reached the castle Bayaya dismounted. Then he kissed his faithful friend farewell, and the little horse vanished.

Slavena still sat in her chamber, sad and unhappy. When a maidservant opened the door and said that Bayaya wished to speak to her, the princess hid her face in the pillows.

Presently some one took her by the hand and when she raised her head she saw standing before her the beautiful knight of her dreams.

"Are you angry with your bridegroom that you hide from him?" he asked.

"Why do you ask me that?" Slavena whispered. "You are not my bridegroom. Bayaya is my bridegroom."

"I am Bayaya. I am the dumb youth who wove you garlands. I am the knight who saved you and your sisters from death and who helped your father in battle. See, here is the piece of your father's cape with which he bound up my wounded foot."

That this was so was joy indeed to Slavena. She led the white knight into the banquet hall and presented him to the king as her bridegroom. When all had been explained, the king rejoiced, the guests marveled, and Zdobena and Budinka looked sideways at each other with little gasps of envy.

After the wedding Bayaya rode away with Slavena to visit his parents. When he reached his native town the first news he got was of the death of his brother. He hurried to the castle to comfort his parents. They were overjoyed at his return, for they had long ago given him up for dead.

After a time Bayaya succeeded to the kingdom. He lived long and prospered and he enjoyed unclouded happiness with his wife.